BRIGHTER
THAN
THE
MOON

Also by David Valdes

Spin Me Right Round

BRIGHTER
THAN
THE
MOON

David Valdes

BLOOMSBURY
NEW YORK   LONDON   OXFORD   NEW DELHI   SYDNEY

BLOOMSBURY YA
Bloomsbury Publishing Inc., part of Bloomsbury Publishing Plc
1385 Broadway, New York, NY 10018

BLOOMSBURY and the Diana logo are trademarks of Bloomsbury Publishing Plc

First published in the United States of America in January 2023 by Bloomsbury YA

Bloomsbury books may be purchased for business or promotional use. For information on
bulk purchases please contact Macmillan Corporate and Premium Sales Department at
specialmarkets@macmillan.com

Library of Congress Cataloging-in-Publication Data
Names: Valdes Greenwood, David, author.
Title: Brighter than the moon / by David Valdes.
Description: New York : Bloomsbury Children's Books, 2023.
Summary: When online friends Jonas and Shani meet for the first time, they, along with
Shani's best friend, Ash, find they are all keeping secrets, and coming clean
will require them to figure out who they really are, which is not easy
when one's identity goes beyond labels.
Identifiers: LCCN 2022022025 (print) | LCCN 2022022026 (e-book) |
ISBN 978-1-5476-0716-7 (hardcover) · ISBN 978-1-5476-0870-6 (e-book)
Subjects: CYAC: Online dating—Fiction. | Identity—Fiction. | Secrets—Fiction. |
Gay people—Fiction. | LCGFT: Romance fiction. | Novels.
Classification: LCC PZ7.1.V333 Br 2023 (print) | LCC PZ7.1.V333 (e-book) |DDC [Fic]—dc23
LC record available at https://lccn.loc.gov/2022022025
LC e-book record available at https://lccn.loc.gov/2022022026

Book design by John Candell
Typeset by Westchester Publishing Services
Printed and bound in the U.S.A.
2 4 6 8 10 9 7 5 3 1

To find out more about our authors and books visit www.bloomsbury.com
and sign up for our newsletters.

To the queer kids,
who make the world better by being who they are
&
to my kid,
the brightest light in my sky

BRIGHTER
THAN
THE
MOON

PART ONE | SEEING IS DECEIVING

ONE
JONAS

He makes little speeches in his head. All the time, really. At 3 a.m., he'll be lying awake, staring at the slash of light thrown inside the room from the streetlamp, thinking about how to explain himself or replaying an argument he lost because he got tongue-tied. Often, he does it in the shower, the water hot enough to redden his tan back, as he stands there stock still, rehearsing a conversation he may never have. Tonight, six days before Christmas, he sits on the ancient futon, forgetting what he was watching on Netflix as he works out what he wishes he could say to Shani.

We haven't met and still you know me better than anyone else.

You aren't like anyone I've ever talked to.

Wanna be my–

It's that last part that hangs him up. Be my what: *online girlfriend?*

He's been practicing this speech a lot and it always goes wrong just at the end. TV and movies offer no example of how to say you

want to date someone you only know online. And where else would he learn? Foma was fifty-nine and had stopped dating before he arrived on the scene, and what he remembers of Valerie, his birth mom, pretty much serves as the opposite of dating advice: none of her men ever lasted more than a few weeks, maybe a month or two at most. The fact that she stayed in Jonas's life for seven years was kind of a feat.

He's never dated anyone. Shani makes him want to change this. But first he has to get the words out, which shouldn't be so hard at seventeen.

Rising from the sofa, he paces to the window and dials his boss, Flasker, who is only seven or eight years older but seems like a wise elder of dating.

"Gentler Giants!"

"You really think someone's calling this late to hire movers?"

It's a rhetorical question; Flasker thinks every call is an opportunity to earn a little cash with the not-entirely-legit moving company he started. "Branding, my friend. It's what separates you and me."

That and a girlfriend and a life plan... He doesn't say any of this out loud. He can hear an *Apex Legends* livestream in the background. Knowing he's interrupted Flasker's favorite nightly ritual, he hesitates.

"You gonna cough it up or what?" Flasker's pretty chill, so there's no real edge to the question. "Why are you calling?"

"I want to ask Shani out." Jonas's heart races a little just saying the words.

"Finally. It's been, what, six months? I was starting to think you made her up."

He's not above making things up, but Shani is real. "Yeah, six months today."

Flasker's curious. "So why are you on the phone with me instead of out with her?"

"I don't know what to say."

"Dude, you talk every night."

"Yeah, but this is different. I want her to be my girlfriend . . . but, um, we've never actually met." There, it's out.

He doesn't have to see it to know Flasker is rolling his eyes. "Okay. That's just weird."

"It's not *that* weird—" It is, actually, and he knows it, but somehow it feels worse to be called out. "*Lots* of people meet online."

"Yeah." Flasker laughs. "*Meet.* Not *stay.* Unless she's in like Hawaii or Uzbekistan or something. But didn't you say—"

"I mean, she lives in Arlmont."

"That's one town over—"

"But, like six miles, and neither of us drive, so . . ."

"Okay. Uber . . . buses . . ."

There's no way Jonas can afford to Uber anywhere, but he can't pretend he doesn't know how the buses run. It wouldn't be easy to get to her place from his, but it's not impossible, either.

Flasker knows he's onto something. "Fess up. Why don't you want to meet her?"

"I do!" Jonas gulps. "I just—"

"Wait," Flasker interrupts. "Are you catfishing this girl?"

"No!"

He blurts out a different kind of truth. "I'm just nervous about, you know, what if she sees me and I'm not everything she hoped?"

Flasker laughs. "Everyone who's ever dated online feels that way."

"Even you? I mean, you make it look easy."

"I wouldn't go that far." But it's true. Flasker is a chick magnet: good with his hands and dressed in jeans and flannel all the time, he has this rugged white dude thing going on. Like a lot of trans guys, Flasker's age is hard to read, so college girls *and* their moms flirt with him.

Flasker digs a little deeper. "What's the real problem here? Think she'll say no?"

Jonas drifts to the secondhand Formica table where he eats and does homework. There are things he should have said to Shani sooner and wishes he had; when he finally gets the words out, she might see him differently. Right now, he's still this same artist boy she met online who texts every day and calls every night.

Jonas has one talent: illustration. He's fast with a pen, but with his iPad, he's next level. Avatars, portraits, graphics, his own manga—there's nothing he can't make. He even set up an Instagram page so kids could hire him. Some of the requests have been strange, but he always say yes; he needs the experience and the cash. A cartoon Kylie Jenner dressed like Marvel's Black Widow? No problem. Olaf the Snowman's face on the body of a centaur? Sure. He draws whatever, because it's a free country that's not free at all; you can be who you want to be, but everything still costs money.

That's how he met Shani: she hired him to make an avatar of her favorite anime character to use on Discord. He usually charged twenty bucks, but she talked him into a barter, saying she'd promote his Insta on her YouTube if he did her avatar for ten. Like Flasker, she's always thinking.

He didn't know anything about her YouTube channel, and when he checked it out, it was a window into another world. Every episode starts with tips on Black hair care, which is way more involved than he ever knew. As she shows her techniques, she works in a lot of inspirational messages from her icons Beyoncé, SZA, and Lizzo, and calls out racism in Arlmont, Boston, and anywhere else she sees it. She's so impressive, so effortlessly confident. He can't imagine feeling that way.

"You still there, bud? I got things to do..." Flasker's voice jolts him.

"Yeah, man. Sorry. So..."

"Just say, *Do you wanna be my girlfriend?*"

"Just like that? No warm-up or nothing?"

"That's how I asked Melory. Exact words."

"So... you're saying, don't make a big thing of it..."

Jonas looks at the iPad on the table, open to a slideshow of famous memes repurposed as in-jokes from his conversations with Shani. He's organized them into an online flip-book to play for her, ending with a cartoon of himself asking her out, but maybe it's too much?

He just wants to be able to keep up with her. Shani is the kind of girl who has a vision board in her room—he's seen it behind her when they chat—and her visions go well beyond this month or

semester, stretching into the future. He can't even see the end of this conversation.

"What were you thinking, bud?"

Jonas fudges the details. "I don't know. Like a card or pictures or something." He can't bring himself to explain the rest of it, so he doesn't.

"Are you *proposing?*"

"No!" The online flip-book seems more corny by the minute. "You're right. Just keep it simple."

"I love you, J, but this didn't need a phone call."

"Sorry. Go back to *Apex.*"

"Don't forget we have a gig tomorrow."

Jonas *hates* moving people in the snow, but he's not in a position to say no. "Yeah. I'll see you there."

When he hangs up, the memes stare at him, almost mocking.

Outside, snow is coming down hard, not so much as flakes but as chunks. Globs of white hit the window and stick a minute, and it's near impossible to see as far as the sidewalk below. It's snowing so hard that even the plows are waiting it out.

Do you want to be my girlfriend?

Hey, I was wondering if you'd be my girlfriend.

I want you to be my girlfriend.

His eyes drift to the wall where he taped up his latest stab at a poster of Kurai Kage, one of the Tomo-e Girls from the anime series. A secret society of twenty-first-century female samurai possessed by the spirit of some ancient Japanese badass, Tomo-e Girls are best known for beheading their enemies, which makes them sound

kinda Tarantino, but the show is really all about insecurities and fears, and how their success depends on their relationships (so, the opposite of Tarantino). Kurai Kage is Black and Black girl leads are still sorta rare for anime, so it's Shani's favorite show.

Jonas is on his fifth attempt at the drawing. He can mimic anything, but there's something missing in this drawing—it's not flowing yet. Maybe it's because he's only a half-hearted anime fan. He's doing this for Shani as a surprise.

Speaking of . . . His phone lights up.

Ready?

He hesitates. What will he say?

Making dinner. Gimme 5.

Kind of a lie. When it comes to his feelings, he always tells the truth; for everything else, not so much. Which is pretty much the problem with asking Shani out. He's not entirely the guy she thinks he is.

Is the real him enough? If he knew the answer to that question, his heart wouldn't be drumming so fast in his chest as he works up his nerve to make the call.

TWO
SHANI

It has been a *day*.

She spent the bulk of it doing her co-op placement. Minuteman, the regional vo-tech school where she studies health sciences, sends juniors to work at Woodlawn Nursing Home twice a week. They get class credit for making beds, washing old people, checking vitals, and delivering sort-of-warm meals all day. (Some of that stuff is just straight-up nasty, but she always plasters on a smile when she serves it.)

As soon as she was done at Woodlawn, she headed straight for Yaki's, Arlmont's best pizza place. (Don't get her started on Olympus, which somehow manages to have a following despite being greasy *and* soggy.) She's guaranteed three shifts a week and sometimes gets in as many as five, which helps her save for college (goal number one) but still have money to go out with her girls once in a while.

Now she's home and has already crushed her homework. She

has two days before her next scheduled vlog, so she has a little time for group chat with BB5 *and* her nightly talk with Jonas. Shani and her cousin Sheree are two of the five self-proclaimed Bad Bitches, their clique from Arlmont Middle School, when they bonded over being the only girls of color. Tati likes being part of a group but hates the name, which Yanique and Julie insisted on with a very sixth-grade belief that it was cool. Split among three high schools now, the BB5 aren't as close as they were, but Sheree keeps the group chat going and makes sure they have meet-ups. She knows they need each other.

Yanique is the first on Snap tonight.

My parents are being assholes about SATs.

Julie feeds the fire. Your parents are assholes about EVERYTHING.

Ha ha. They hired a tutor for Christmas week.

Shani doesn't text the first thought in her head. *Must be nice.*

Tati chimes in. You already got a 1300!

Yanique. RIGHT?

Sheree. Beat me and aint no one making me take it again.

Julie again. Hire Miss 1400.

What's her problem? Julie's been trippin' about Shani's SAT score since the results came back. Shani spent hours last summer watching the free Khan academy videos to get ready for her first try. *1200.* Maybe enough for Howard, but not a slam dunk. Definitely not enough for Stanford. She doubled down on her second try and got 1400. No ways she's telling Julie she's going to take the test a third time, even though it means once again paying fifty-plus bucks of hard-earned money.

Shani replies. Pay me as much as one of them white dudes and I'll do it.

She doesn't have time to tutor anyone, but she also knows that Yanique's parents—the summer-on-the-Vineyard types—won't settle for anything less than a tutor who got into Harvard.

Sheree. Tell your folks to chill. We're juniors.

"Chill" and "junior year" aren't two things that go together, at least for Shani. She sees the next eighteen months like a countdown clock; mostly, it's exciting, like she's waiting for the ball to drop on New Year's. But sometimes, it feels like a doomsday clock, as if her plans might blow up.

She's been planning her adult life pretty much since her mom died. She's seen how her dad, who never bothered with college, has struggled to provide for them over the years. She's going to get her degree, maybe two, in a medical field—something that makes money, even though what she loves is fashion and style. Her dad's Uber gigs aren't going to help much with this plan, which is why she not only has her Yaki's job, but volunteers for extra shifts at Woodlawn, and even why she keeps her YouTube channel going, though it takes up more time than she really has free. Admissions will see a carefully curated gallery of Shani: grades, hard work, humanitarianism, and Black girl magic. It ain't her fault Julie can't keep up.

Tati changes the topic. Broke up with Jay.

Sheree texts praise hands.

Shani. Period!

But Julie counters with an eyeroll emoji. Cap.

Shani. Ignore Julie.

The others all heart that last part and Julie texts a middle finger emoji.

After a few minutes of Tati texting Jay's sins (which the others already know, including Julie by firsthand experience), Yanique redirects the conversation to Shani.

What up with artist boy?

We talkin.

Julie is primed. That all?

Like I'd tell YOU if it wasn't.

Sheree texts a burn emoji and a skeleton.

Shani's famous in their group for not saying much about dating. No one's ever going to accuse her of being one of those girls who *has* to have a boyfriend. The average boy—short on words, eager for action, unconcerned with politics, but excited about sports the way she's excited about anime—holds pretty much no appeal. She's drawn to the quirky guy with a secret passion, the creative guy who doesn't go with the flow, and if they're a little rebellious, even better. Not a lot of boys like this at Minuteman. There might be more at the town's two other schools—Memorial, which is public, and St. Joe's, the private prep school—but that doesn't help her much.

With a light tap on the doorframe, her dad pokes his head into the room. "You eat?" he says, knowing that a few months of working at Yaki's has pretty much exhausted her capacity for pizza. He's just in from twelve hours driving his Uber, but she knows he'd cook for her if she said yes.

"I'm good," she says, giving his hand a squeeze. He lingers in the doorway for a minute like he wants to stay, but it's almost 9:30,

and she needs her dad out of the room before Jonas calls. It also means she needs to ditch this chat.

Ima dip.

Julie texts. Girl I was just playin.

Shani texts an eyeroll. I got plans.

Yanique sends a gif of the little girl from *Monsters, Inc.* waving goodbye, and Sheree likes it. Shani closes the chat.

She's pretty sure Jonas is going to (finally) ask her on a date. It's taken so long, she'd started to wonder if she played the part of Tough Girl *too* well. He's been kind of jangly the past couple of nights, mentioning three times that they've known each other six months. It's adorable—he's obviously working up his nerve, which is him all over.

Some boys strut about, cocks of the walk, but Jonas is more thoughtful. Maybe it's because he's a creative type or maybe cause he lives with his mom, but he's so different than the guys at her school. Comparing a would-be artist to aspiring plumbers and mechanics is a little unfair, but she can't help it, and Jonas always comes out ahead. It doesn't hurt that he's cute, with clear, dusky skin, curls that have a little shine, and shoulders for days.

More importantly, he's kind and curious, full of questions about her life and not just talking over her with stories of his. It's been like that from the start. Like anyone else who has caught her interest, they met on online. When they first started chatting, it was through Insta, where she'd found his art page, and it took him a few weeks to dare ask for her number. When he did, she'd given him a hard time.

TomoeGrrl16: You don't need my digits.

EtchaSketch: I wanna do more than DM.

TomoeGrrl16: !!!

EtchaSketch: (Face palm emoji) Not like that! I want to FaceTime!!!

TomoeGrrl16: I'm just playin.

EtchaSketch: So . . .

TomoeGrrl16: So keep askin and someday I'll say yes. (Winking emoji)

She's been burned in the past, so she always keeps her guard up, and she tried to do that with Jonas, but as soon she saw him, she was hooked—she just didn't let him know that. She made him ask a few more times before relenting, and they've been chatting every night since.

It's so easy to talk that they can go hours, sometimes falling asleep with their phones still on, glowing rectangles unseen by closed eyes. At this point, he probably knows more about her inner life than anyone but her best friend, Ash. She and Jonas complement each other: she's bold and he's chill; she's tough and he's gentle. How someone this cute and this sweet got this far without a girlfriend, she can't even guess.

Not meeting him in person yet hasn't been hard, really. Taking it slow doesn't cost her anything; past experience makes her distrustful of most guys. Aside from her dad, she really only trusts Ash, even though he can be a little selfish and a lot capricious. He'd admit both himself, which means she never has to doubt that he's anything but who he always has been.

Jonas is the first new guy in a while who seems worth trusting. If he wants to meet, she's game.

While she waits for their call, she cleans up the Studio, which

is really just her room. She started it calling it the Studio (and insisting her dad do the same) when she began filming her videos there. She has a decent ring light for nighttime and perfect natural light by day and has made a little set with a pillow-covered sofa positioned well out from the brick wall, because the depth of field makes the room look bigger that way. There's even a little tree from IKEA (one that's hard to kill, which is good, because she's no green thumb).

Outside the camera's field of vision, empty half-and-half iced tea lemonade bottles dot her desk and windowsill. On the floor, her book bag is vomiting notebooks, and colored pens are scattered all over the floor between her Yaki's polo and her scrubs. Crouching to pick them up, she sees Grave Bear, lone remaining stuffed animal from childhood, lying on his side beneath her bed.

She never lets it get full-on disgusting in the Studio—she's a Capricorn, after all—because it's a cosmic truth that you can't manifest in a messy room. Creative visualization is important to her. And it works: her vision board at New Year's included "decent boyfriend" and five months later, along came Jonas.

They have a huge amount of stuff in common: mixed kids raised by single parents and both into anime, Chinese food, hip hop, Christmas, pools over beaches, and sneakers they can't afford to buy. Match made in internet heaven—not that they're calling it a match. *Yet.*

Lately, she's been feeling ready to meet him, but with jobs and school, and the fact that technically they're still just friends, she isn't sweating it too much. Better a guy who takes it slow than one who goes right from *hey* to *nudes*? She could just ask him out, but she's

not chasing *anyone*. It's not about being old-fashioned; it's about pride. A boy worth her time will work for it.

She settles onto her sofa, phone in hand, making a little fortress of pillows around herself, Rapunzel in a memory foam tower. When her phone rings, her heart gets that feeling that belies her cool. What can she say? Boy's got her good. She's primed to say yes if he can calm down and ask her out.

But when she grabs the phone to answer, it's Ash. Grr. He *knows* this is when Jonas will call, but that doesn't stop him. Ash likes to play the part of uninvited bodyguard meets ruiner; he never thinks any boy is good enough for her and he tends to make mischief when she's really into someone. He says it's his way of being protective; she says he just likes drama.

Boy, I'm busy!

Girl, you know I don't care.

He tries calling again and she lets it go to voicemail. He texts once more and she leaves it on read, knowing this will drive him bananas. Not replying to a message is, like, low-key cruel because the sender can't 100 percent know for sure something else isn't going on, so they can't 100 percent be mad at you, which they really want to be.

Ash can wait. This is *her* time.

THREE
JONAS

9:28. He takes up his spot on the couch with what will pass for dinner: two Pop-Tarts, a food Foma always refused to buy. The last time he'd asked her, she made him read an article titled "15 Unhealthiest Foods." (How were Pop-Tarts number one? And did she, like, bookmark it just to get him?) Buying his own groceries now means freedom of choice and more Pop-Tarts, though a lot of the time it also means he's hungry sooner after eating than he should be.

He props up his iPad, which cost him two years of savings. (Every time he touches it now, he feels a little guilty, thinking how Foma and he both could use the money, but it's too late to do anything about that.)

Time to call.

Keep it simple. Keep it simple.

Will you be my girlfriend?

He always makes the call from the exact same place. He props his phone up on the shipping crate turned coffee table so that it

frames only the upper half of the futon and the wall behind, which he has covered with a cloth photo backdrop of a Hawaiian beach that he found at Boomerang, his favorite thrift shop. He really wants to paint a mural, but renters can't be choosers, so this beach scene has to do, and it does at least remind him of Foma's place.

On camera, the backdrop looks exactly like it did the first time Shani saw it. Her exact words then were *that is some serious white boy Margaritaville crap*. She doesn't really sugarcoat anything. She has no idea that he's moved; the backdrop keeps him from needing explain why he had to.

Quickly, he slips on the color-block hoodie she got him for his birthday back in October. Most of the time, the new apartment is cold—the windows barely seal—and he can't control the thermostat; it's a far cry from the old place, which was constantly hot and pretty much required staying half dressed. If Shani noticed that he used to show up onscreen in tank tops and is now always bundled up, she hasn't commented on it.

Though they've been talking for months, he only realized a week or two ago that he felt differently about her than anyone else. It started with this astrology app she'd downloaded and which she said was scarily accurate for her. When he told her he was a Libra, she ran his birth date and time through her app, and some of what came out was right on the money. They kept going: they checked the birthdays of people they knew. After that, they started guessing the signs of famous people—both guessed correctly that SZA was a Scorpio—and then moved on to people who weren't real at all: pretty much everyone in *Squid Game*, the cast of *Stranger*

Things, all the Avengers. By the time they started assigning astro-logical signs to anime series (Shani's idea), it was 3 a.m., and Jonas knew two things: they had to hang up, and it was the most he had ever talked to anyone of his life. He felt giddy.

Wearing the birthday hoodie tonight is intentional. Will she notice?

She does. "Nice fit."

"Thanks." He grins. "The person who gave it to me has great taste." But then he can't think what to say next. Their conversations always flow so easily and now he's tripping up over the unspoken. Just say it. Just say it.

He almost misses her question.

"How far'd you get?"

"I'm still doing the colors—"

"Nah, in *Tomo-e Girls*."

"Almost caught up. The part where the new guy kisses the police-man." He smiles at the memory; it was a pretty perfect scene.

Shani's voice takes on the warm pleasure that only good anime brings out. "I shipped them from the policeman's first scene. If he was into girls, he'd be my next boyfriend."

Jonas grins. "*Anime* boyfriend, you mean."

"Real boys can't keep up."

"Not even me?" he blurts, too soon, without thought.

"You're okay." She smirks in a way that means he's more than okay.

"I... uh... I think you're okay, too." A look in her eyes says his sudden awkwardness has surprised her, so he rushes on, half

pleading, half trying to keep it light. "I know I'm not a *demon slayer* or anything, but I really like you and I kinda thought you were into it . . ." So much for Flasker's suggestion to keep it simple.

Shani's smile (which she does not deploy lightly for most people) spreads wide across her face, pushing her cheeks up, her eyes narrowing even as they glow. "I *am* into it."

"So . . ." Jonas waits for her to say more, but nothing comes. "So is that a yes?"

"Was there a question?"

"Oh, uh–"

Damnit. He hasn't even asked. "Do you . . ." *Why is it so hard to say "wanna be my girlfriend"?*

Shani raises an eyebrow. "You trying to ask me out?"

It's both embarrassing and sheer relief that she said it for him. "Yeah, I was. I am." God, he sounds like an idiot.

"Okay."

His heart pounds–he feels like jumping up and down. "Really?"

"You heard me. Where we finnago?"

Damnit. She thinks he wants to go on a *date*. Of course she does. He's such a moron, he didn't even ask the right question.

She's waiting and he has no answer. Because he's not ready to meet her.

No, they *can't* meet.

Because if they meet, she'll *know.*

➤ **SHANI**

Boy! All hyped to ask her and doesn't even have a plan.

But he looks so nervous now, she can't help but let him off the hook. "You want me to pick?"

Jonas stammers, "I . . . I guess I meant . . . well–"

He's kind of red-faced for someone his color. What's he tripping about?

And then it hits her. "You were asking me *out* out?" He doesn't respond but she can see it in his eyes. "We haven't even gone on a date!"

He palms his forehead, like a living emoji. "I guess . . . I just–I kinda thought we'd already had a lot of dates online."

He can hardly look at the camera and she feels a little bad for making him sweat it. But it's weird, too. He went straight to girl-friend? People date online all the time, but not so much ones who live like six miles from each other.

She imagines saying yes–she wants to say yes–but something holds her back. It's not his fault; there's history he doesn't know. She could explain but she keeps her tone light. "How do I even know you're for real? Maybe you're like a baby-face twenty-two so this is illegal, or you're some AI deal, like a Japanese sex robot." Jonas blushes, just like he does anytime she brings up sex. She forces a smile. "I'm just playin'."

Is she, though? A seed of doubt has planted itself in her mind, little root hairs burrowing down into her excitement. "I know how to solve this problem."

"Me being a sex robot?"

"Time for a real date. Like, live." (Never in a million years would it have occurred to her that she'd have to define "real.")

"Oh—" For a moment it sounds like he's gonna complete that thought with *no*, but at the last second "oh" becomes "okay."

Okay? Boy doesn't sound very excited. Her warning bells are ringing. But she can't make everything about the past. "You free Sunday?"

His voice comes out strangled. "For what?"

"Brain surgery. What else?" She's trying to be funny but it doesn't feel funny. "Our *first date*."

"Um. I just—It's *Christmas Eve*—"

"Which is also my BIRTHDAY."

"I know! I've been working on your present." That's more like it. Until he adds, "But it's a big day in my house."

She can't actually picture what that means for him. He has never mentioned his dad, even in passing, and she's only seen his mom—a short Black woman with white snowcaps dotting tight curls—one time months ago, stepping into the frame before he shooed her away. Single parents can make a big deal of every little thing, so maybe it's true when he says, "I mean, we have these traditions and, like, it's our *favorite* day of the year."

"More than Christmas?"

"Christmas doesn't even come close!"

"Okay, then," she says. "I'll come on Christmas instead."

It takes him a second to react. The giveaway is not in his one-word answer—"Great!"—but the way he says it, like someone had to slap his back for him to croak out a reply.

Really?

➤ JONAS

It's a nightmare. She wants to meet *this weekend*. He's not close to ready but she's already making plans, suggesting, "The Ivy's doing holiday matinees."

Jonas feels a flicker of panic. "They are? Cool . . . but . . . you really want your dad to be alone on Christmas?"

"It's just a couple of hours."

"I'm just saying. If all I had was one kid and she went to see her boyfriend on *Christmas*—"

"So now you think you're my boyfriend?"

"I, uh—I thought . . . I did just ask . . ." Is it just panic or his voice ratcheting up higher?

"Ask me again when you see me." Her smile is sweet but her eyes are narrow, and the disconnect scares him a little.

"I can't wait to, but . . ." he gulps. "*Christmas?* I mean . . . you know."

➤ SHANI

She knows he's right—Christmas is a big ask—yet his reluctance makes her want to press him. He's either in the grip of a massive wedgie or he's terrified of her. And why would he be? Her emotional radar is going off, and it's completely fair. She's been catfished twice. *Twice.*

Freshman year, she wasn't meeting a lot of guys in Health Sciences (and the one she did meet had a fire truck obsession that bordered on a fetish), so she got on Kik. It was easy to get around

the age settings then. It seemed great until a cute boy she'd been chatting with started asking for money. The second guy turned out to be her dad's age. But that has nothing to do with Jonas. She never FaceTimed those guys. She didn't fall asleep with her head on the phone talking to them. They didn't draw her pictures or start watching the shows she liked. They weren't *him*.

Yet something's up. He just asked her to be his girlfriend while obviously not wanting to meet. There can only be one explanation: he must be lying to her. About what? She has no idea.

Maybe she oughta just go off, tell him that she sees right through him. But she bites her lip. What if she's imagining it? It's not his fault she's so paranoid. He might mean it—all of it.

She tries to play it cool. "I hear ya."

"Are you sure? Cause I feel bad—"

"We can wait. I'm not going anywhere." She tosses a smile like a rope to a drowning man. "It's gonna be brick anyway. They're saying polar vortex."

"You're the best." Jonas smiles his real smile, the one that tugs up just at one corner like he's about to tell a joke. She wants to believe he means it.

➤ JONAS

When Shani hangs up, Jonas sits back on the futon. The snow continues to pile up outside, flakes thick enough to throw shadows on the wall. He stares at the pattern. He'd seen quite clearly how her face changed, the dimming of the electricity that she always

projects. She's weirded out, maybe even mad. How had he managed to screw this up so badly?

It was ridiculous to think they could stay online forever. Had he really believed that it was possible? Or was he just in denial?

Time to face the facts: Meeting Shani is inevitable. Maybe it'll go okay. Once she can look right into his eyes, the stuff he left out won't matter.

Maybe she'll understand.

Maybe she'll understand.

Maybe she'll understand.

He repeats this to himself until it almost sounds believable.

➤ SHANI

Shani paces around the Studio, trying to figure out what just happened. Jonas has always had a low-key, chill vibe—nothing flashy, no big emotions. So now he's all big cheesy smile and *you're the best*, and that, more than anything, tells her something's not right.

What do you do when you think someone's hiding something from you? And not just anyone, but the guy you look forward to talking to every single day? How do you know if he's telling you the truth?

She needs to call an expert, someone good at manipulation. A pro at digging dirt, unafraid to bruise a few feelings along the way. She needs the one person she knows who thinks the ends justify the means every single time.

She needs Ash.

FOUR
ASH

Ash *loves* a little drama. (And he doesn't mind making some.) So when he wakes up to Shani's text—Boy's acting all weird, maybe hiding something?—he's all over it. The word "maybe" doesn't put him off at all; his mind is already spinning out *To Catch a Predator-*style fantasies.

The more likely a plan is to blow up in the face of your average person, the more drawn to the idea he is. It's a challenge: What can he pull off that no one else would? Sometimes, *most* of the time, it works out for him—like when he convinced a bunch of taggers to cover the back wall of the old gymnasium at St. Joe's with spray-painted versions of *Lux et veritas*, the school motto, and won Spirit Week for his class instead of being expelled. (The tags are still there!) Sometimes, it does not—like when he started growing pot in the lobby garden of the new St. Joe's atrium. (As much as his parents annoy him, thank god they're both public figures and smooth talkers, or he'd have gotten in a lot more hot water that time.)

He texts Shani back:

Gimme 10.

He can't do anything till he gets his order at Curious Liquids. It's the kind of coffee shop where everybody's a little queer, even the "straight" kids. He hates going inside wearing his St. Joe's uniform, an ensemble with absolutely no point of view, because he knows the baristas are all likely to be dressed cool, skater-meets-goth or gender-fucked-vintage-pin-up. When he walks in today, Tee is on first shift, and they greet him the way they always do when he's in the uniform: "Prep School Killer!"

"You know that's insensitive, right?" Ash only vaguely knows where the nickname comes from, but murder's murder.

Tee shrugs off his feeble attempt to be woke and starts making his turmeric latte without waiting to be asked.

"Is my office open?" The back-corner booth, which boasts two outlets and a table covered in Edward Gorey sketches, is his favorite spot in the shop. If it's not a school morning like this, he can sit there forever skimming TikTok to come up with ideas for his own account, @AshMeAnything. He honestly feels cheated if someone else beats him to his seat.

"You're only the second person who has ordered in, so I think you're safe." Tee tucks a long strand of jet-black hair behind their ear. Unlike Darius, who gives Ash a gay discount (not official, but like, not *un*official), Tee always rings him up for the full amount. Once, when Tee was hanging out at his place, he asked them *why*. Tee said he hardly needed a handout; since they were both sprawled on the leather sectional sofa facing the 82-inch flat screen TV in his room at the time, Ash couldn't really argue.

"Come see me in a few," he says now. "I'm plotting!"

"On it. You know I like you when you're evil!"

Settled into his booth, he video calls Shani. She answers, her camera pointed at the ceiling of her room. This means she's multi-tasking, probably doing something with her hair. It kind of makes no sense to video call and then not be onscreen, but nobody makes phone calls anymore, so . . .

"Hit me."

"That guy I told you about?"

"The one you talk about every. Single. Day?"

Shani ignores that. "I think he's playin' me, but I don't know how."

Intrigue—he likes it. "Playing how?"

"He asked me if I want to be his girlfriend—"

"Have you even gone out?"

"Exactly! I tried to make a date and he's like, *Oh, great* and *I can't wait*—"

"But wouldn't commit?" Ash sips his latte. Shani *mm-hmms* affirmatively. *Interesting.* "You met online, right?" He doesn't let her answer. "Of course you did. And you've never seen where he lives?"

Her face comes into view onscreen long enough for him to see her shaking her head.

"Where does he *say* he is?"

"East of the Square somewhere."

"Maybe he's embarrassed." Shani makes a *hmmpf* noise at this theory. But Ash means it. Arlmont spans the gamut economically, from hilltop single-family houses in the west end with killer views of Boston to poorly maintained affordable housing clusters in the

east on the Mooreville line. The Square is the midpoint, a little downtown area with a mix of quaint houses divided into condos and apartments, anchored by a few old grand Victorians, one of which Ash's family tore down and replaced. After seeing his very large, very modern house (which looks more Silicon Valley tech guru than Massachusetts lefty), more than one of his classmates suddenly found excuses not to invite him over to their own places. Shani doesn't care what he thinks about her apartment, which is big enough for two people but smaller than the first floor of his house. The not caring is impressive. But not everyone is Shani.

"What's his place like?"

Offscreen again, Shani admits she doesn't know. "He's got some Hawaii thing on the wall."

"'The' wall? He's only got one?"

"Ha ha. He's always in the same spot."

A clue! "So maybe he doesn't want you to see the rest. How about his family?"

"Only seen his mom once, like, in passing."

"What's she like?"

"A little old. Darker than me. Gave me a church-lady vibe."

"All this time and you never said he was Black."

"You know I'm not dating a white boy." She says this un-self-consciously. It doesn't matter that her own dad is white; with dark skin and 4c hair like her mom's, Black is how everyone sees her and how Shani has moved through the world since she was born. When she and Ash met at rec when they were twelve, she was the only kid with extensions; he was the only other brown

kid in their class. He knows she's not down for some guy who doesn't know what that's like.

"And his dad?"

"Don't know. He never talks about him. Like, not once."

"So . . . mixed?"

"Could be."

Ash has an affinity for other mixed kids. He's half Indian, half Cuban, but no one ever guesses his identity right. He gets Mexican the most, but also Central American, Arab, and Native American (groups who share little apart from their non-Aryan looks). No one ever guesses Cuban because the only Cubans most Americans can picture are Fidel Castro and Scarface (who was played by an Italian in the movie).

"What else do you know about this guy?"

It's quiet a minute, with nothing to look at but ceiling, before Shani answers. "Not much. He's always broke but I know he's got a job. Some sketchy moving company."

The money has to go *somewhere* . . . "Oooh—it's drugs."

Shani is defensive instantly. "Boy's not on drugs. I've seen his eyes."

"Okay, how old is he?"

"Seventeen, like us."

"Like *me*," he teases. "It's not Sunday *yet!*" Shani reaches one hand into view on the screen to flip him off. Ash ignores it. "Send me that picture of him you like."

Ash would swipe right on that picture. Smooth skin the color of toasted pine nuts, loose coils of brown hair long enough to fall into

his face kind of randomly, and a gaze that looks—what's the best word?—*concerned*. Jonas's smile is lopsided, which could be a flaw but really works for him. His age? Well, that's not 100 percent clear.

Ash has lied about his age before, usually to seem older on dating apps, which "require" everyone to be over eighteen. Looking at the photo Shani sent, Ash is pretty sure Jonas isn't lying upward; he's at least seventeen. There's something a little world-weary in those big brown eyes.

"Maybe he's older. Nineteen?"

Shani scoffs. "Not like that makes me jailbait. Why lie about it?"

Tee appears at the booth and slides in. Ash shows them the picture and asks what they see. Tee chews their lip for a minute. "Closeted lead singer in a boy band." This is why Ash loves Tee. They zoom in to focus on Jonas's eyes and then down to his mouth. "Weirdly sexy and vanilla all at once, dying to sleep with his bandmates." With that description, they head back to the bar.

Ash looks at the photo through new eyes. Could that be right? The plain white T-shirt and lack of an intentional haircut both scream cis het dude, but Ash knows better than to trust the visuals. Ash's own daily uniform is a case in point: a navy St. Joe's blazer over khakis hardly communicates how queer he is.

Shani tells him he's mad gay for a trans guy and Tee says he's where the term "sissy" comes from, a comment he's only okay with coming from another queer person. Being gay is kind of his brand—as @AshMeAnything, he's one of the most popular #LGBTQ TikTok accounts, and he made two of the Top 50 videos under #Pride. But five days a week he looks like a representative from Young Republicans.

Jonas might not be what he appears either. "Maybe he's not really into girls?" Ash floats this like it was his idea.

Shani picks up her phone to answer onscreen. "Then why ask me out?" It's all over her face that this idea unsettles her. "Like anybody needs a beard in this town. I mean even your school has a GSA—and it's Catholic!"

Fair enough. "Agreed. He must be hiding *something*."

Shani's eyes are full of storm clouds. "I don't know for sure that he is. It could just be me, right? But my gut says something is off. You gotta help me find out what."

Tee passes by with a tray of mugs but leans into the camera view to say hi to Shani. "Why bother? Ditch boy band guy." They flash a smile. "*I'm* an open book, babe."

Ash rolls his eyes. Tee is gorgeous—wide-set eyes over strong cheekbones, pale Vietnamese skin, and glossy black hair—but they're pan and enbi, and Shani's old-school straight: she's a cis girl who has only ever dated guys. No matter how many times Ash tells them that, Tee flirts with her at every chance. Can't blame them for trying.

After Tee heads off, Shani gets back to the topic at hand. "Can you help me?"

"Depends. Can I do it *my* way?" Ash's wheels are already turning.

Shani hesitates—she's too type A for this but also feeling pangs of disloyalty to Jonas—but when she says yes *within reason*, he leaps on it.

"First, do you ever talk to him about me?"

"You? No."

"Good. Our friendship is over."

"What now?"

"*On social media.*" He can see the light dawning in her eyes. "On TikTok, Snapchat, Insta, whatever. I'm going to unfollow you as soon as I hang up. He can't know we're friends."

The expression on her face reads somewhere between eager conspirator and guilty rat. "Go on . . ."

An alert chimes on his phone. "Can't now. I have ten minutes to get to school. Gotta go."

The walk to St. Joes isn't long, but by the time Ash is stashing his backpack in his locker, he already has a plan worked out. He looks at the lopsided grin in the photo of Jonas and feels almost bad for the guy. When Ash is done, kid won't know what hit him.

FIVE
JONAS

Across town, Jonas knows he's blown it. All day at school, he's been beating himself up when he should be listening. Mrs. Ham, his English teacher, had to ask him three times to read a passage from *My Name Is Asher Lev*. She says she likes to call on him because his voice is deep and round, like an old-time radio announcer. Today, he stumbled over his words, anything but smooth.

He's been ducking Shani, as much as you can duck on text. He doesn't dare leave her on read, because it would be too obvious he's avoiding her, but he keeps his reply minimal: hearting a text and replying to two more with just emojis.

In gym class, Mr. Ham (yes, married to Mrs.) puts them through lay-up drills. Jonas doesn't play any team sports but lay-ups are usually fine. This afternoon, he bounces eight of ten shots off the rim, mocked by the bonk of rubber on metal instead of the expected swoosh.

His only saving grace is that he won't run into Shani in the halls here at Memorial. Memorial kids think the Minuteman kids are a

little weird for wanting to learn a trade; the Minuteman kids think the Memorial kids are idiots for *not* wanting to. And St. Joe's kids feel superior because their school has the word "prep" in the name.

High school is just one more division in a town with three middle schools and eight elementary schools. There's not a lot of social overlap between schools after the bell rings; kids in the hills stay in the hills, driving to each other's parties, while east side kids walk or take buses to hang with their friends. The Square is a nexus for overlap because it has the restaurants and the Ivy cinema, but unless you're hanging at Curious Liquids with the queers and arty kids, you still kind of stay in your pack. In a town of 60,000, you can easily spend seventeen years of life living a mile from someone you might like and never know they're there. (Or, in this case, six miles.)

Even though Jonas moved across the Mooreville line after school started, he still goes to Memorial, for now. The superintendent has been pretty kind about his situation but says he might have to switch schools for second semester. He doesn't have a lot of friends at school, so maybe it doesn't matter that much.

When final bell rings, he heads straight for the school lobby; no club to linger at, no one to hang out with. Elise Li, head of the pep squad, is on a ladder, tearing down a huge countdown calendar sheet with the number three on it, revealing a glittery green two announcing how many days before Christmas break. "Smile, Jonas!" she calls out when he passes by her perch, and he complies, because Elise is always so positive. But he's not feeling it.

Memorial High is three miles from the new apartment, which isn't the end of the world when it's warm out. But the temperatures

have been dropping since the snow stopped and the sidewalks are a lawless mess, only about half of them cleared out, which means taking the public bus. The bus routes are great if you live in Arlmont right along Madison, the main street that runs the length of the town, and crappy if you live anywhere else. In Mooreville, the stops are further apart, and his place on Prospect is almost a full mile off the route, so even on a bus day, he faces a twenty-minute walk. In this cold, he'll take whatever time inside the warmth of the bus he can get.

He pays with dollar bills from Gentler Giant tips. Every fare eats into what little spending money he has. It was easier for him at his old place, a skinny rowhouse nearer the center of Arlmont.

His favorite bus driver is on today. She reminds him of the actress Rosie Perez and always greets him in Spanish before switching to Spanglish. She seems to think he's Latinx and he lets her. She could be right, after all. She frowns as he steps into the bus. "No chaqueta?"

He was in such a fog when he left for school that he was out the door in only a hoodie and gloves, and he'd made it all the way to the bus stop before he'd processed that his big army surplus parka was still hanging on its peg in his little kitchen. At the old place, coats hung on the back of the front door, so you kind of had to see them to leave. He's paying now for spacing out this morning.

But he plays it off. "I'm from Boston—I can take anything."

"You can catch things, too!" she admonishes. "La gripe!"

With the last dollar bill fed into the pay slot, he pretends to sneeze and she slaps his arm, laughing. "Sientate!"

Elise . . . the bus driver . . . these are the kinds of relationships he likes best. Brief flurries of warmth, delivered in passing; nothing risky. He's never let anyone but Foma get close until Shani. And maybe he's screwed that up.

She said she was fine with waiting, but she didn't sound—or look—entirely fine. He could see it in her eyes when he ducked out of Christmas Eve. He hadn't been lying, not entirely; Christmas Eve really is his big day with Foma. But that wasn't why he'd put Shani off and he knows she could tell.

The bus rolls through the Square, Arlmont's pretty little downtown area, which glitters with fairy lights. The marquee for the Ivy, the town's second-run movie house, reads *Edward Scissorhands*, *Die Hard*, and *Scrooged*. He pictures himself opening the heavy glass door of the Ivy for Shani, heading inside to buy Butterfingers for him and a blue raspberry slushie for her, and settling into the vintage movie seats, side by side, their legs touching and fingers entwined. But the vision vanishes and the bus keeps its course up Madison, him in his seat alone.

When the bus enters Mooreville, he presses the button to call for a stop. He exits at the rear with a wave to the driver and starts the slog home. The route is still pretty new to him; he's only seen its few trees when they've been empty of leaves and the earth frozen cold. Is it ever pretty? The new snow at least helps hide how concrete and asphalt dominate this neighborhood. None of Arlmont's Japanese maples and flowering hedges.

By the time he reaches the apartment building, his cheeks burn from the cold. Is burning a good or bad sign? Is it even possible to

get frostbite that quickly? The heat of the lobby is a reward, except that the massively freckled redhead who lives down the hall from him is about to step into the elevator. He half hides behind the fake Christmas tree so that she won't see him and hold the door. She's always offering to show him around (as if he moved here from Alaska, not Arlmont) or asking him if he wants to get takeout, and it's too intense, like she's Merida and he's the bear. He avoids her so hard, he can't even remember her name.

Jonas hurriedly checks his mailbox, the battered gold metal door a throwback to a time from before he was born, when this was probably still a nice address. A couple of letters from the state, one from building management, and three credit offers. Nothing *real*.

There's only one elevator and he doesn't feel like waiting, so he bounds up the stairs, letting the climb help warm him up. He lives on the fifth floor, which the guys below him say is a lucky draw. He's not sure what that means exactly—his view is nothing special, taking in the lawn, the street, the auto body place across the street, the dollar store to one side, and the weird martial arts place on the other. Maybe he gets more light than they do?

He drops the mail on the cluttered dining table. This is where he does homework, makes his art, and eats when he gets around to it. On the table, stacks of files rise like mesas: a pile of untouched college applications; a bunch of folders labeled Prosper, Evelyn; random homework; forwarded mail.

He microwaves a cold coffee in his plastic Dunks mug to refuel himself before heading back out into the cold. While he waits, he

checks his email, which is usually as empty as his mailbox. Again, there's nothing from 23andMe, the only sender he cares about.

For his birthday in October, Foma got him 23andMe's ancestry kit. She knew how much it bothered him to not know where his people came from, but she admitted to him that she'd sat on the idea for a good long while before pulling the trigger. Who knows what all his DNA might tell him? But his reaction—he'd whooped and actually picked her up and spun her—seemed to allay her fear. He couldn't believe it was so easy to do something that could change his life: he just spat into the tube, which was kind of gross, and mailed it back that same day. Results should have come Monday but they didn't. If they had, maybe he would have said yes to Shani about Christmas Eve.

The ding of the microwave summons him and he empties the last of his sugar into the coffee. Dammit—it'll be almost a week before he gets his SNAP, so he'll be out for days. This is why he needs to make a grocery list (well, make one and not lose it).

Pulling a gator over his head, he tucks the bottom into the neck of his parka, adding a black wool slouch cap last, which leaves open only a four-inch-wide swath of face. He examines his reflection in the wall-mounted mirror. Valerie used to tell him they were gypsies, but she didn't actually mean the Roma people, who he learned about in fifth grade, years after she died. He thinks "gypsy" was really Valerie's (kinda racist) way of saying *dark, a little hard to pin down, restless*. Sometimes she claimed that her people were Spanish or Native American or that her family was from Sicily. After the King Tut exhibit at the Museum of Science, she said she was

descended from a female Pharaoh. Jonas has looked up every culture she'd ever claimed, but it's pointless: each time, he thinks he finds a little of himself in them.

He can see in the mirror the person Shani sees—or thinks she sees. If only he knew whether it was true.

. . .

On his second FaceTime with Shani, he had left his bedroom door open, and Foma had shuffled behind him.

"Your mom's way darker than you," Shani said.

He should have told her then that Foma—short for Foster Ma, as Evelyn coined herself—was not his birth mother. But it was still so early in knowing Shani and he hadn't wanted to drop the foster kid bomb on her. 90 percent of the people he ever told ended up feeling sympathetic or wary and he didn't like either response. He just wanted to be a regular guy with a nice mom. So why correct her?

Instead of clarifying, he switched the focus. "Yeah, guess my dad must've been light-skinned." The words were out before he considered what he was implying: *Yes, I'm Black, too.*

She caught the hedging. "You don't know?"

That was his moment: he should have admitted that he didn't know if he was mixed or just mixed up. Suddenly afraid Shani would be less interested in him if he wasn't Black at all, he doubled down. "He was gone before I was on the scene."

That part was true as far as he knew. Whoever gave him the spark of life really *could* have been light-skinned . . . or just white. Which might even have been true of Valerie, no matter how

she looked. But he didn't say that because Shani didn't know Valerie existed. Only their second phone call and he was two lies in.

When she started on the subject of her cousins who had hair more like his, it led to her talking about her YouTube channel, and he was happy to let the conversation drift away from the truth until they were far, far out to sea and he didn't even try to row back.

No one has ever had this effect on him—he waits for her texts and is sad if none come, he reads up on things she's into so he can talk to her about them, and he's been working on her Christmas present for weeks. It makes no sense that he let the early misunderstandings harden into fact, even as they grew closer. He's got to find a way to make it up to her.

Foma would know what to do. But it's not the right moment to ask. This is going to eat him up all day. At least work will be a distraction.

Gentler Giants is on the Arlmont/Mooreville line, less than a mile from his new place, which is pretty much the only upside of moving here. The crew is small, three guys that Flasker goes to college with plus Jonas and Sandy, a Suquamish girl from Seattle, who met Flasker the same way he did: at a BLM protest in Mooreville last summer. Jonas doubts that what they do is on the books: all the clients come from craigslist, the crew get paid in cash, and there's no Gentler Giants logo on their truck. But it's not like they operate under cover of darkness, so who cares?

There's no Flasker today; he's in the seaport at the tiny studio where he makes wood-and-metal sculptures. The crew will be just Sandy and Jonas, which either means it's a small job or everyone

else turned the gig down because it's freezing. If Jonas has to work with just one person, Sandy's the one. She's only five feet tall but her broad frame and serious lifting power make her a force; plus, she's not like the college guys who spend a lot of time discussing the Pats, which isn't his thing.

The gig turns out to be easy, at least physically, helping a pink-cheeked white woman in her eighties move from one senior living apartment to another in the same building. (At a glance, Jonas can't tell the difference between the units, but he gets paid either way.) Her furniture is heavy, all of it overstuffed, but there aren't many pieces, so the job won't take more than an hour or two. That sucks for income but will leave him time to talk to Foma later.

As they carry a faux-brass bedframe up the switchback stairwell between floors, Sandy talks about her girlfriend. "She's made all these Christmas Eve plans for us, like the lights tour Arlmont puts on, and, I don't know, making a gingerbread house, and I still don't have even a stocking stuffer for her."

"Everybody scrambles this time of year," Jonas says, not revealing that he's had Shani's Christmas presents, a series of drawings, finished for days. He made posters of the characters she calls her anime boyfriends, each drawn in the style of the specific show they come from. They're the most complicated, detailed pieces he's ever done, and he can't wait to show her. The only question is whether to give them to her at the same time as her birthday present—the eternal problem for people born at Christmas.

"What are you doing for the holidays?" Sandy's question is innocent, but it stings because this Christmas won't be like others.

"All the usual. Presents, food, naps," he mumbles, hoping she can't tell he's making this up.

"What about your girlfriend?"

"What—uh—"

"Shawnee or whatever—you always talk about her."

Thank god they've arrived at the second apartment and have to focus on getting through the doorway without scratching the frame. It gives him time to think about what to say. "She's not my girl-friend . . . Yet . . . I mean . . . *You know.*"

"What are you waiting for?"

He feels exposed. He looks at Sandy, who doesn't know Shani, and feels an impulse to confess the ways he's hidden things from the one person he wants to be close to.

"I, um, haven't really told her everything I need to."

Sandy laughs. "Yeah, you're a *guy*. Big surprise."

"No, I mean—"

"If you're not a big talker, then show her."

As they approach the first apartment, they can hear the old woman complaining to the daughter who hired them. "These two don't look very . . ." She fishes for an adjective that won't get her in trouble with her daughter. "*Careful.* Why didn't you hire, I don't know . . . someone *else*?"

When they enter, the daughter looks mortified but the woman turns instantly cheerful. "You're making good time!"

When they grab the next load, Sandy is talking about how fake old white people are, but Jonas is still thinking about her advice: *Show her.*

Maybe she's right. If Jonas meets Shani in person, it'll be clear he's wild about her. If they're together, it'll be easier for him to admit that he hasn't told her the whole truth about himself, and maybe it will be easier for her to understand. If she can *see* in his eyes how he feels, it will be okay.

Has hiding his real life from her been the wrong move all along? It feels so obvious now.

"You're right," he says to Sandy, as they *carefully* deposit a bureau in the new space.

She laughs. "I'm *always* right."

When the job is done, he feels lighter. Inspired, even. Where could he take Shani—maybe the Ivy or that lights tour? He could print out the posters and deliver them in person. Or—

What if it's not enough? His inner voice deflates the rising bubble of optimism. Like a beacon on a flight tower, hope flashes and dims and flashes again.

Show her. As if it was that easy.

SIX
SHANI

After making her plan with Ash, it feels different to be waiting for Jonas's call. She tries to tell herself that it's not a big deal: Ash will get to know Jonas, and if Jonas is everything he says he is, Shani can trust him and he'll be none the wiser. But if Ash discovers Jonas is pulling a fast one on her, then she deserves better and he deserves whatever comes next.

She organizes her dresser to keep her mind busy. She's been getting a ton of mail from Fashion Institute of Technology and it stings a little every time. She knows medicine is a more stable career path with a higher number of jobs, but she doesn't throw the FIT mailers away. She just slides them lower in the pile, letting the Stanford admissions catalog rest on top to remind her of a more lucrative future.

When Jonas calls in, she takes a deep breath. He can't know anything has changed. It's hard to keep her face neutral, though, when he appears onscreen. He seems to be shifting a lot in his seat. Is he

swallowing more, too? Boy is off. But his eyes! They still glow with warmth and she can't not notice. It's like he's as beautiful as ever and not beautiful at all.

She hopes the doubt doesn't register in her voice. "How's the new picture coming?"

"Great," he says. "Almost done."

"Can I see it?"

He bites his lip. "Wait till it's perfect."

Uh-huh.

He asks about her day and she can hear herself answering but it feels remote. It's almost like she's watching the conversation take place. Until he mentions Ash and she tunes back in.

"I got a new client."

"Cool, cool," she murmurs. She's not sure she's pulling it off. "Where'd you meet this guy?"

Does she detect hesitation? Maybe not. "He saw my Insta."

"What are you making for him?"

"Don't know. He didn't say yet. Just likes my work, I guess."

"Cool." She can't think of what else to say. She's so tired all at once that she just wants to sleep.

"You okay?" Those brown eyes (damn!) fill with concern. It could be real.

"Long day. You know?" She can't let him comfort her; this is *his* fault.

"Aww . . ." A smile steals across his face. "Maybe I can make it better."

"Ya think?"

"Yeah ... I realized it's ridiculous to wait. I want to see you sooner."

So not what she expected.

"Really?"

"I want to give you your birthday and Christmas presents in person. Let's do Christmas Eve after all."

This is too much. Presents *and* a change of heart? She doesn't trust it. She *shouldn't*: Has he forgotten the story he told her about how he and his mom have a big day planned?

"What about your mom?" There's no hiding her doubt when she sounds like that.

The smile seizes on Jonas's face and then dims. He looks like he's trying to recover. "Not a problem. I made it work." He looks a little nervous. "Unless ... unless you don't want to."

"I do!"

But she's not sure she does anymore. It's a pretty big leap from *I have to spend Christmas Eve with my mom* to *no problem*. Either he was lying before or he's lying now.

"Then it's a date," he says with obvious relief.

She decides to test his sincerity. "Where exactly do you live? I'll come to you. My dad won't mind dropping me off and then we can go somewhere you like."

"Oh, uh ... I mean, there's nothing really near me." He blinks, then looks away from the screen just long enough for it to be noticeable.

He *is* hiding something. Why else wouldn't he want her to know where he lives? Maybe he isn't even from Arlmont ... or

Massachusetts ... or? But then he wouldn't have suggested a date, right, so—

"We could do that lights tour thing ..." He bounces in his seat. "The one where you take the trolley from one over-the-top house to the next."

"During a polar vortex?"

"We won't have to fight to get tickets!"

If this had been a normal day and this was a normal conversation, she'd have told him she wasn't sitting on some freezing-ass trolley bench for their first date. But she plays along. "Okay. This better be worth it."

"It will be," he says, grin at full radiance. "I promise."

Like that *means anything.* She keeps her smile on till he's gone.

She texts Ash.

You hired him?

Yeah baby: cash is king.

And? Anything else?

Even I'M not that good—I'm a snoop not a psychic.

He asked me out. Like, live.

Ash texts a gif of *The Scream.* You didn't lead with that?

Christmas Eve.

That's not a lot of time to expose his darkest secrets.

Maybe he doesn't have any?

Do you believe that?

Does she? Shani's fingers float about the keypad, wanting to type YES but settling on NO.

I'm coming over.

It's almost 10! Won't your folks freak?

Like they're the boss of me? LOL

Shani hesitates. Anybody else would just call, but Ash has to make it a big production. Then again, her talk with Jonas has her really thrown off, and Ash's presence is a great stabilizer. As much as they tease each other and sometimes bicker, he's her anchor.

C'mon, he adds. Your dad loves me. (More than you maybe?)

Shani texts 100%, LOL. And then Okay okay.

Even if Jonas isn't who he says, she thinks, Ash is always Ash.

. . .

Now Ash is sprawled across her bed, lying on his back, phone above him like a satellite. He's taking notes on Jonas's profile for possible bait. "Tell me that last one again—*Skrim?*"

"*Skyrim.* Nobody plays a game called *Skrim.* Don't be referencing anything you don't understand or you'll get tripped up."

"Whatever—I can always say I'm a newbie. Tell me what music he likes."

Shani thinks for a moment. "Hip hop. Pop. A lot of stuff, I guess. I mean, we don't really talk about it more than *have you heard this song?*"

"Good note, Shanz. So helpful."

"Focus on anime."

"Speaking of things I don't understand . . ."

"It's TV—what's not to understand?"

"Sorry, I meant 'care about.' Unless it's *Spirited Away,* which is a masterpiece, I pass."

She thinks about it a minute. "Boy loves *Stranger Things*."

"That could be something. I saw the season with the Russians."

This blows Shani's mind. "Who starts a show on season three?"

"I heard the clothes were good. Even if whoever did the hair was committing a crime against humanity."

Shani's dad pokes his head into the Studio. "You kids hungry? I can make a midnight snack or reheat supper." Boston-born and raised, his accent is like early Matt Damon/Ben Affleck, so the word comes out *suppah*.

Ash sits up. "I could eat," he says eagerly. He loves anything free and he has no problem announcing what he'd like; he's the only rich person Shani knows, so she isn't sure if this is unique to him or how they all are. "Is there any of your carbonara?"

"You wish, kid," her dad says, which sounds like a no, but his happiness at the request makes it clear that the answer will be yes in about twenty minutes. Then he's out the door. Before Shani's mom died, he was the kind of guy who let his wife do most of the cooking, but lately, he's started bringing home the specialty magazines at the Stop & Shop checkout counter—*101 Easy Home Meals! Weeknight Dishes for Your Family!* When he discovered the Food Network, it was all over.

"Back to work," Ash says, adopting his best evil villain voice. "Gimme more."

"Hmmm . . . he loves all those old teen movies. *Clueless, Mean Girls, Heathers, 10 Things I Hate About You* . . ."

"Anything else?"

"His Marvel thing. Boy's obsessed."

"You *know* I love the Marvelverse. Why didn't you start with that?"

Now he sounds inspired. "Marvel movies are universal. I've had long conversations with the bro-iest of dudes about whether or not it made any sense that Infinity Stones used to be deadly to touch and then suddenly everyone's running around lugging them through portals. Anytime I'm stuck hanging out with somebody's straight boyfriend at a party I just ask what Hawke's actual super-power is and we're good to go."

"Well, if you don't find any dirt, Jonas will be *my* straight boyfriend . . ." As she says this, she realizes how much she wants it to be true. She fights to tamp down the feeling. In her experience, wanting just puts her at risk.

Ash's eyes widen as an idea forms. "For a while now, I've been working on these If-the-Avengers-were-gay bits, but I haven't uploaded any because I'm still having costumes made."

"You're crafty. Make 'em yourself!"

"Thank you, Frau Maria, I'm not going to wade into the biggest franchise in movie history in outfits made from curtains, or worse, from Amazon Halloween. I found a woman on Etsy who designs costumes for cosplayers and the first one arrives this week—"

"Black Widow?"

"Ha ha. *Thor.* A very, very gay Thor." He taps a few ideas into his phone. "I'll hire Jonas to create Marvel images to use as my back-drops, different for each character, which means we won't be one and done, and then I'll heart everything he posts on Insta, slide into his DMs, start chatting . . ."

"Reporting back whatever he says . . ."

"Obviously!"

Shani nods. "This could work."

"Girl, it's catnip."

Shani doesn't love it when he says *girl* like he's a Black woman talking to her friends, which he most certainly is not, but she stopped calling him on it a while ago because at a certain point, there's no keeping up.

A new thought crosses her mind. "Say this works, but then he sees us together somewhere. It's not impossible."

"You just have to be dead to me until we're done."

"For real—we need a story."

"Why would we? I'm supposed to be a client; how would I know who his friends are or aren't? *If* it happens—and I personally think it's unlikely—we just do the *wow, what a small world* thing and play it off. No bigs."

"Easy for you to say. You're a way better liar than me!"

"You better practice. If he's not hiding something from you and you end up together, you can't very well pretend I'm not your best friend."

Ugh. That piece had never occurred to her. She's grateful when her dad distracts them by arriving with carbonara in the glass pasta bowls he likes. He hands one to each of them and slides in next to Shani on her other side. The couch isn't meant for three, so it's a little tight, but she doesn't boot him off because she knows it means a lot to him. She put an end to hugs from adults, her dad included, after she learned about agency in sex ed class. He'd taken this ban

hard at first, but had mostly gotten used it. (He once told her, seriously, that the greatest constancy of parenthood is letting go.) Joining her now on the couch is like a stealthy side hug delivery system, which she knows and pretends she doesn't.

"What are you kids up to? Working on a clip together?" Her dad still doesn't quite get that YouTube and TikTok are two different things. He watches whenever Shani uploads a new video, and every time, he tells her she looks beautiful (which she discounts because it's not exactly an unbiased opinion), but he's only seen one of Ash's TikToks: Ash's take on the banana split challenge, where kids do a full split and try to pop back up without using their hands to push off the ground. Ash wore an all-white bodysuit in his and did the split into an actual banana split with chocolate syrup and the works. Shani thought that was a little corny, but the banana and the whipped cream made it funny and kind of nasty, which was why it got 200,000 views. Her dad naturally asked all the wrong questions: How did Ash get the bodysuit clean? Wasn't it *cold*? Shani hasn't bothered to shown him any of Ash's stuff since.

"We're catfishing this guy Shani likes."

Hearing Ash say it that way makes Shani cringe a little—she wouldn't call it that. She just needs to make sure Jonas is the real deal.

"Catfishing?" Her dad sounds concerned. "Like that Timmo guy?"

Ash looks at Shani, confused. "Timmo from ninth grade?"

"Well . . ." Here it comes; she never told Ash the whole story because it made her look weak.

Ash looks put out. "All I remember is how you went on and on about how much he loved anime. I mean, you texted each other so much, I'm surprised your screens didn't crack."

"He was cooler than everyone else! Including you."

"You *never* said he catfished you!"

She rises from the couch, leaving a void between her friend and her father. "It made me feel different, special, to have so much attention, right? Till he started asking me to loan him money. I didn't even have a bank account so I don't know where he thought it was coming from, and I said no. And then he asked if I could send Amazon gift cards, which is when I figured his ass out for a liar and told Dad. For all I know, the guy was a bored 'Nigerian prince.'"

"You let me think you just ghosted him or whatever. You omitted the part where you never even met."

"Like I'm putting myself on blast for being gullible?"

Her dad shakes his head. "You shoulda been ready the next time!"

Ash's eyes widen. "The *next* time?"

Shani paces across the room from them. "I don't tell you *all* my business!" She pauses by her vision board and takes a breath. "Same year. My Discord avatar was a photo of me in a Minuteman hoodie and this other kid on the boards saw the logo and texted; told me he went there, too. We were in different shops—he was plumbing—and didn't have the same advisory, so I never saw him at school, just texted a lot. But I knew what he looked like from his profile picture and one day I finally spotted him in the hallway. I went up to say hi, all nervous and shit, only to find out that the kid

was not who I'd chatted with; his *dad*, divorced and not even in the state, had been hijacking the pic to scam girls."

"This is why I don't like all these apps you're on!" her dad huffs. "It's too easy to take advantage!"

Ash crosses his arms across his chest. "Okay, so you made up an ending for this Timmo guy and didn't even mention the other to me. I'm *wounded*." He actually sounds like he means it. *Damn. I should have told him.*

But her pride wasn't the only reason. The first semester of ninth grade was weird. She and Ash were spending so much time together, everyone assumed they were a couple. Sometimes, it had felt like they were; if he wasn't gay and she wasn't straight, maybe they would have been. (Do all best friends go through this?) One reason she got hooked on Timmo was that it distracted from the tension in the air, and by the time it all blew up, things felt normal with Ash again, and she didn't want to ruin that by telling him she'd kept him in the dark. So for the rest of that year, her love life (especially when it flopped) wasn't a subject she talked with Ash about.

Going back to these places in her mind, she feels her anger rising. She's absolutely right to doubt Jonas. The fact that she loves that sweet smile of his is not enough to erase all memory of her bad experiences in the past.

Shani's dad has other issues. "I don't see how it's nice to do this to Jonah—"

"*Jonas.* God, Dad."

"I mean, *you* didn't like it, why do it to someone else?"

Really? "*He* started it. He's hiding something—"

"What?"

"If I knew, it wouldn't be hidden! But it's definitely *something*. That's what Ash is for."

Her dad, seeming perplexed, turns to Ash, who is used to a searching look from a baffled parent.

He tries to lower the heat. "I'm just helping her catch him in a lie, that's all." He smiles his most ingratiating smile at Shani's dad. "You and me, we're Team Shani, right?"

Shani fixes her dad with a look that might as well be a neon arrow pointing his way out of the Studio. She hands him her half-eaten carbonara and gives him the same tight smile she deployed on Jonas the night before. "Thanks for the snack."

He accepts her bowl and takes Ash's, too (which Ash is not ready to part with, not that anyone asked) and stands there a moment, wearing the expression of a man who waited hours in line for ice cream only to have the shop window close when he got to the front. "Okay . . . You kids wants brownies?"

"Good night, Loser." It's one of their little things, affection wrapped in a joke, and it's a peace offering now. He looks relieved as he carries the dishes away.

She stares at the door a moment and then looks at Ash. "I'm not an asshole, right—watching out for myself like this?"

"What's the harm? If we do it right, he never has to know about any of this."

Shani looks satisfied. "You were born to be a spy."

"Like Perry the Platypus or Mata Hari?"

"I don't know either of those people."

"A *good* guy or a *bad* guy?"

"Why not both?" She laughs.

"That," he says, joining her, "is why we're friends."

SEVEN
ASH

"Ashok!"

Ash's dad says his name a thousand times a day. Raj Patel says this personalizes conversation, a tactic which has made him very successful, but sometimes Ash wants to scream, "Girl, I know who you're talking to!" But that would lead to a heart-to-heart about how disrespect of others is a form of hostility that springs from the well of one's own self-doubt. There's a whole chapter on this in his dad's latest book. If he has to hear it out loud, Ash will combust.

"What?" He likes to keep his replies neutral, as he never knows which kind of amusement park ride their conversation will be—the kind that loops around and around, or one with some scary drops.

"I went on the Hammer and guess what I saw?"

Supposedly, St. Joe's named its academic portal after a tool because Jesus was a carpenter, but Ash thinks they called it the Hammer so parents can continually pound kids with it.

"Ms. Lim is a fascist. She takes off points if your work isn't in her

corny little wheelbarrow the moment the bell rings. I swear my journals were in that thing before end of class."

"Your journals are late, too?" Raj's brown eyes widen.

He kicks himself for not following his own rule of never saying anything to his parents he doesn't have to. If his dad's issue is not the journals, Ash has preemptively ratted himself out for something Raj isn't yet pissed about.

Raj taps at his Apple watch. Squints. "B- in American history, Ashok? You have never had less than a 94 percent in history. What topic could have been so challenging that your grade would drop by 10 percent?"

Honestly, Ash doesn't know. He can't remember studying for the last test, but he almost never does; usually, he can just read the material once and summon up the visual in his mind by scrolling over to wherever the info is on the page. But he also doesn't recall having any panicky holy-shit-am-I-being-punked moments, and if a lot of kids had tanked the test, there would messages about it in St Blo's, the private student group chat.

He's not lying when he says, "I'm pretty sure I did okay. Maybe it's an error?"

"You're a junior, Ashok. This is a time not for casual error, but serious growth." Raj looks like he might cry or hug Ash or both, which would be very on-brand for an inspirational speaker who helps people tap into the power of their potential.

"Not *my* error. The teacher's."

The bubble of Raj's gentleness is popped and his type A side assumes control. "It's always someone else's problem with you,

Ashok." Disapproval settles onto his face like one of those cheap charcoal scrub masks. It isn't pretty.

"Okay, Raj, I hear you." Ash has been calling his parents Raj and Gloria since sixth grade, not just because he knows they hate it, but because it equalizes them, forcing them to recognize his maturity. He speaks to them like an adult, often using their own ridiculous therapeutic language. The more reasonable he sounds, the less they can dismiss him, and the less they dismiss him, the more he gets what he wants. They're blissfully unaware how little control over him they actually have, despite all the huffing and puffing.

"I'll look into it. Don't make me late for school to lecture me about academics!"

He wishes he had chill parents who just wanted him to find his bliss or whatever. Instead, he got the kind who expect model behavior, good grades, strict adherence to their values (blue state hearts/red state wallets), and a career path that starts in college and ends up on par with their own levels of achievement. It's not lost on him that they're the classic immigrant parents out of a movie, except *neither of them is an immigrant.*

Gloria's parents left Cuba years before she was born, and she grew up in Maine, which seems pretty All-American to Ash, a sentiment he is only allowed to voice when she's up for re-election. Raj is actually a third-generation Californian whose family left India so long ago that Ghandi was still just a lawyer who couldn't get a job. Ash's aunties both think it's hilarious that Raj—birth name Roger because his mother loved James Bond movies—has made a career off his mystic Indian identity when he spent all his 1980s

channeling the Brat Pack. Is this an old person thing? You hit a certain age and *boom*, you magically rediscover you have a culture?

The parental bark is worse than its bite in this house. When push comes to shove, he's all they have, and he knows it. He endures the occasional scolding with a martyr's grace because the same love that spawns their concern also yields things like his shiny new Jaguar, annual beach vacations, and a wardrobe no one in this town can keep up with.

Thank god Curious Liquids is on the way to St. Joe's, because it gives him an escape from morning conversation with his parents most days. When he gets to Curious Liquids, there's a line. His dad's lecture has made him just late enough to not be first in the door. Across the room, he sees Garrett. Oh, god. Ash is prone to white-hot crushes on those boys who walk the line between arty and butch. Garrett, bike mechanic with copper hair and a torso that winds like a canyon, was everything last spring. Ash thought he was gay- or bi-questioning, but he turned out to be mostly straight but horny. It's mortifying now to think of the little presents and cute texts and sexy banter Ash deployed in his campaign to snare Garrett. (He tries *not* to think about the pics.) The reward for his efforts was one supremely awkward night and a hundred mornings like this, where he has to see his failure live in the flesh. *So this is how my day is gonna be.*

While he waits, he checks his Insta. He's happy to see a new message from Jonas. Jonas's first message had been short and Ash thought he'd sounded doubtful. But the wariness didn't last; once Jonas heard about the Marvel angle, he'd been as enthusiastic as a

puppy who'd seen a bag of tennis balls. He hasn't even needed to deploy any of the other reconnaissance he'd gathered from Shani to win Jonas over.

Actually, that wasn't 100 percent true. Shani had shared Jonas's rates for drawings, so Ash had intentionally offered twice that. Jonas hadn't acted surprised, just replied with a casual sounds good and let Ash overpay him. This was as Ash expected; in his experience, most people avoid the subject of money. And it's even truer at school. Kids whose families don't have as much as his family don't want to hear about it, and kids whose families do—well, he doesn't really know that many.

With rates set, their DMs had started flying back and forth as they discussed the project. The thread of conversation was so easy, Ash could almost forget they didn't know each other. But he might have overshot with his last message, just before 1 a.m.: Might be easier to FaceTime. Granted, it was kind of a big jump in a short time, but he'd hoped that the business angle bought him some latitude.

Jonas hadn't responded at first. The silence didn't necessarily mean anything. He could have just fallen asleep or gotten distracted. The problem for Ash is not knowing where he stands. It isn't like Ash cares that much about the Thor backdrops; he just hates being on read.

Ash opens the message, a little nervous. The answer is terse: Okay.

The brevity makes it obvious that the FaceTime request threw Jonas off. But since it's the answer Ashok wanted, *win*.

By the time he gets to the front of the line, his Ariana Grande alarm tone—*I see it, I like it, I want it, I got it*—lets him know that he has exactly ten minutes before American Lit. Tee starts his oat milk turmeric latte and he feels a little giddiness coming on. Plotting is his sweet spot; he'll spend the entire first period ignoring Father Brian's lecture on the rise of the British Empire and figuring out to how make himself Jonas's new bestie. Maybe the day won't be so bad after all.

➤ JONAS

The lobby of Sunrise House is painted lemon yellow, like someone is trying to fool visitors into thinking the name is meaningful. Every time Jonas steps into the quiet, carpeted visitors' area, he thinks the same thing: *They ought to call it what it is*—Sunset *House.*

When he comes in for his after-school visit, Parelle sees him and waves him over to the snack cart she is loading up for rounds. "Whatcha like today? Butterfingers, Hershey's, Reese's?" She always asks, he always says he's good, and then she presses a few candy bars into his hand anyways. Today, she gives him one of each and he slides them into his parka, embarrassed that she can tell he's broke, but also knowing he will eat them as soon as he's home.

Foma took to Parelle instantly. She's responsible for Sunrise House's cats and Foma has been wanting a cat since their calico, Yowza, died over a year ago. They hadn't hurried to replace Yowza, thinking they needed to get over the loss first, and now it's too late.

It's only been eight days. When they settled Foma in, Parelle helped Jonas set up a Christmas tree to make things homier, but Foma wrinkled her nose. "If it isn't a real tree, what do I want with it? It's the *smell* I like." She wasn't trying to be difficult; she was just too tired to censor at that point. It was her second move in three months; the first was to Maple Crest, a long-term rehab place, after her third fall in a year. She hated it and told Jonas every day that she was going to sneak out and go home, even though she knew better.

Foma's sister Marion had to rent out the apartment to raise cash to cover the expenses, even though it meant displacing Jonas. Apartments in Arlmont go for a lot more these days than when Foma moved in, way more than Jonas could afford with his part-time moving job. Marion made a deal with the Department of Children & Family Services to set him up in a one-room studio in Mooreville. It's subsidized, not free, but she promised to cover his part till he turns eighteen and ages out of the system entirely—which is pretty generous, since she's also paying Foma's medical bills. She never asked if he wanted to live with her, which was okay, because she's really mopey. She'd told him she trusted the Lord to work out his future.

It was Maple Crest that figured out Foma was dying. The falls and the cancer weren't actually related, just a cosmic shitstorm of bad luck and bad news meeting in a body approaching seventy. Sunrise is Maple Crest's hospice wing and it looks nearly indistinguishable from the rehab unit where she started out: both employ the same curtains, throws, and carpets in powdery hues of after-dinner

mints to distract from the grim adjustable beds and the nurses' whiteboards which remind you where you are. The biggest difference, aside from monitors with wires sneaking into the bed, is the absence of a roommate.

That doesn't mean Foma is always alone when he visits. Today, a hospice volunteer and a nurse he's not seen before are chatting with her. She looks tired—she always does now—but dives right in when she sees Jonas. "You could be a nurse like Miguel here!"

Foma is obsessed with the notion that he needs a degree other than art—despite having been a graphic artist for thirty years herself. Laid off at sixty-three, just before she could retire, she'd tried to set up her own small business; she'd been shocked at how slowly work trickled in, perhaps no surprise in the age of online editing tools, and in the last few years the trickle became a desert.

"I *could* be a nurse!" Jonas doesn't argue anymore. It's not like he can afford to go to college full-time anyway. He can't imagine himself doing anything related to science, one of his worst subjects, but as Miguel departs, Jonas notices that the nurse's kicks look new. A regular paycheck *would* be nice.

Jonas leans in to kiss Foma on her forehead, which feels clammy. "How are you today?"

The volunteer, whose name tag reads Dorice, answers for her. "I was just discussing that with Miguel here. Evelyn is having more pain." She looks at Foma. "You are, aren't you?"

Foma waves that off. "It's hospice, not HonkFest. I wasn't expecting brass bands."

Dorice frowns. "We can make you feel better."

Foma smiles weakly. "How much better? Go-home level? Dance-like-Michael level? What're you promising?" But her retorts stop when she seems to seize up for a moment with a pain she can't joke away. And then it passes.

Dorice catches Jonas's eye. "Maybe you can make her feel better!" She offers up the mint-colored side chair next to Foma so he can sit and leaves them alone.

Jonas rubs Foma's hands with his own, fingers drawing aimless patterns back and forth. Touch has always been their language. At bedtime, after she read him exactly three stories a night, she would trace a figure-eight on his back until he fell asleep. When they'd watch Marvel movies, nestled together on the sofa, she would play with his curls as he rested his head on her leg. Even once he was too big for all that, he still liked to be close, resting a knee against hers as they binged a TV show. It wasn't unusual for her to fall asleep on his shoulder.

But they're in new territory now. Foma could never abide ashy skin and since she's been in rehab, it's like all moisture has evaporated from her body. He hadn't ever imagined massaging her dry legs and bare feet daily, and part of him wonders why not just have the nurses do it, but she asked *him* to do it a few days ago, and now it feels like a sacred ritual. Jonas looks for the shea butter lotion Foma can no longer apply herself and squeezes a dollop into his hands to warm up.

He works quietly, thinking about Shani and wondering what to say or do next. Sandy's advice seemed so simple yesterday but seems less so now. Maybe he could print out Shani's poster and frame it

nice to bring with him. But if she doesn't like what he has to say after, will she forever associate the present with the outcome? God, he'd hate that—

"That's a human foot, you know." Foma tries to make a joke about the deepening intensity of his grip, but her pain edges in.

"Oh, god, Foma, sorry." Jonas lowers the first foot gently and raises the other, trying to be more careful.

"Maybe don't be a nurse after all." She manages a small laugh. "What's all this brooding about? Is it that girl?"

Jonas is caught between impulses: considering where they are, it seems the wrong time to ask for help untangling his love life; but in a month or two, he won't be able to seek her advice again. He's only had ten years when he could.

"I asked her out."

"And she said no, I take it?"

"No, she said yes."

Foma narrows her eyes. "So what's the problem?"

"I'm not sure it was a good idea." Should he tell her all of it? Only part? "We haven't exactly met yet."

A weak sigh escapes. "Why're you asking out a girl you haven't laid eyes on?"

"I have *seen* her! We talk every day. I just . . . We haven't . . ." Why does what seems normal to him sound so bizarre whenever he explains it to someone else? "I mean, I *know* her. I do."

"Then why don't you want to see her?"

"I never said that!"

"If you want it, you'll do it and stop fretting." The sentiment is

emphatic, but the words escape drowsily. Her eyelids lower like a steel gate coming down over a shop door at night.

He rests Foma's foot on the pale green sheet and covers it with a blanket. Sitting back, he closes his eyes a moment. And then says one true thing. "I'm afraid when she meets me, I won't be . . . enough."

Foma's eyes are all the way closed now, but she reaches out one hand to try and pat his arm. The distance is too great and she can't sit up, so her hand flutters in the air, a paper plane trying to catch a draft, before dropping onto the coverlet. This guts Jonas, who leans close and holds it.

He waits for the advice she is sure to offer: she will tell him he *is* enough, that he has to believe it, and until he does, Shani never will.

But there is only silence. Her breathing tells him the visit is over.

Flasker. Sandy. Foma—all their advice seems to take for granted that there's a straight line between wish and fact. Jonas's whole life has taught him that wishing guarantees only a place in your chest that hurts. But it feels like the universe is telling him to give it one more try.

He'll go through with meeting on Shani's birthday. If it goes smoothly, he wants to tell Foma all about it. If it doesn't, it may be the last time ever he can cry on her shoulder.

➤ **SHANI**

Facetiming with your boy ltr.

Shani is surprised that Ash's text stings so much. He's doing just

what she asked and it seems like he's succeeding—which may be the issue. They're FaceTiming already? It took Jonas a couple of weeks to ask *her*. She tries to remind herself that Jonas thinks Ash is a client, not a potential date, so it doesn't mean anything. But does she know that for sure? Really? Or is he actually into Ash? Did Jonas see Ash's profile pic (she can't argue: it's cute) and feel something right away?

She texts back You work fast LOL, though she's not feeling the LOL at all.

It's Thursday, which means she has a video to upload, but she's still editing it. Today's vlog features a review of Bounce 'n' Shine, a new curl crème a potential sponsor sent her. She hates to say no to a sponsor—her channel isn't yet big enough to be super choosy—but she has box braids in and there's no way she's taking them out for a product trial (especially for a brand owned by a white lady). She's done what she could to make a big fuss over the crème anyway, unboxing it on camera, praising its "summertime scent" (by which she means straight up Banana Boat) and how its "rich and creamy" texture (real talk: it's gooey) is sure to keep coils elongated despite humidity. This episode is going to be weak sauce and she knows it. But editing is giving her something to do other than think about Jonas.

When the video is uploaded, she checks her phone, as though she wouldn't have heard it buzz if Ash had texted intel. Her homework is all done—not surprising for her—and her own call with Jonas isn't for a couple of hours, which leaves her feeling restless. She grabs her one stuffed animal. "Talk to me, Grave Bear."

The funeral director who took care of her mom gave Shani the

bear to carry at the interment. She was ten, too old for teddy bears really, and she thought it was kind of weird, but she ended up carrying it all that day anyway.

It's not a cute bear. A single line slashes straight down from its fabric nose but never meets up with a smile, like whoever made it was too tired or too sad to finish it. Her dad guessed that the funeral guy got it cheap, probably in bulk, because no parent would ever buy their kid such a downer. But it looked like how she felt that day and she named it Grave Bear. Her dad hates it and she doesn't care; it's slept with her ever since.

Grave Bear offers the same silence it always offers, so she decides to declutter her desk. The IKEA desk is covered with hair product she needs to donate, including the curl crème that smells like a beach and feels like glue; sweeping it all into an old Shein bag makes her feel better. Globs of eyelash glue are giving the desktop acne, so she pries the dots up with tweezers. She can't manifest with this mess.

Once everything is neat, she sits on the end of her bed and looks at her Vision Board. She starts a new one each year and updates it every couple of months. This summer, she put up six YouTubers who each have 100,000 followers and tons of sponsors, plus pictures of a Fendi bag, Megan Thee Stallion's dress from the most recent BETs, a photo of a custom Yukon Denali XL, and a BLM poster. Dad says that's the only good thing on the board because the rest is materialistic, but she shrugs it off because he doesn't understand anything. She—*they*—need the money to pull off college, and if she's bringing that into being, why not manifest more?

She uses her restlessness to edit the board. She adds the latest flyer from Howard and a postcard from Stanford, a Sephora sticker, and a picture of Caleb McLaughlin after his glow up. She already has her Yaki's job, but who wouldn't rather sell perfume at the mall (even if the long walk and two bus rides would be a pain)? Caleb is just a reminder that Jonas isn't the only brother out there.

Her phone vibrates and she leaps for it. Sheree has started a BB5 video chat.

The timing of the call is perfect. Shani will ask them what to do about Jonas. But when she joins, Yanique is already talking about K-pop as she unwinds her braids, and though everyone is just about rolling their eyes, they play along. Shani only feigns interest for about sixty seconds before interrupting.

"What would ya'll do if you thought a guy was lying to you about something?"

Julie, her face as always too close to the camera, answers first. "When is a guy NOT lying to you?"

"Come on. I mean it."

"I mean it too. Boys are different! They hide shit all the time."

Yanique disagrees. "They don't lie that much—they just don't talk."

Sheree, shears in hand from working on an art class project, nods. "*Teen Vogue* says they're socialized to shut down their feelings." She waves the blades like a professor's pointer.

"Who's talking about feelings? I'm talking facts."

"Like, what kind of facts?" Julie asks.

Shani is stuck. Good question. "I'm not sure."

Yanique looks confused. "If you don't know what he's lying about, how do you even know he is?"

"He was acting all . . . I don't know, *nervous*, like he was hiding something . . ."

Yanique stops unbraiding. "So you think that means he's lying?"

"Mm-hmm."

Tati has been silent till now and when she speaks, she's earnest. "Oprah says—"

"*Oprah?* You about to quote *Oprah?*" Julie just about falls out. "You're spending too much time with your granny."

Sheree shushes her. "Oprah can be my granny. What'd she say?"

Tati's cheeks are a little flushed. Sheree always gets under her skin. "She says listen to your gut. Your body knows!"

As the last strands fall away from Yanique's face, her brown eyes are more luminous. "What does your gut tell you?"

Shani doesn't hesitate. "He's lying to me. He is."

Sheree sucks her teeth. "Then whatchu waiting for?" She slashes the air with her blades. "You're a badass. Do something about it."

Shani hates it when Sheree acts like she knows everything. "Who said I was waiting?" This grabs their interest. Julie is practically inside the camera and Yanique stops midway through winding her silk scarf on.

"What if I told you I had a plan . . ." Shani starts and their faces light up. As she explains about Ash playing mole, their rising enthusiasm fuels her.

Julie's eyes sparkle. "This is gone be fire. You have to gives us updates *every* day."

Yanique is all over it. "A player who thinks he's all that . . . *Check.* Hot girl with a secret . . . *Check.* The double agent guy is, like, extra."

Shani bristles a little—she didn't say he was a player exactly. But she keeps mum.

Tati nods, eagerly. "It'll be like watching Netflix but real."

Sheree gets a look in her eye, one Shani knows means inspiration has struck. "That's it. You always complain you need more subscribers . . . maybe you just need a new subject."

The BB5 chime in with ideas about how she should make a burn video and expose him. Or she could write in to one of the catfishing shows and get him on it. They're sirens singing for destruction and they fully expect Shani can deliver.

Maybe they're right. She doesn't need a boyfriend right this second; she has the rest of her life for that. She needs to stand up for herself—no, for *all* of them. Exposing a liar is not just fair; it's necessary. She can think of it as a public service.

EIGHT
JONAS

Jonas checks his email when he gets home from Sunrise House. Nothing. Each day it feels like the DNA results *have* to come. Each day, they don't.

Dinner is three frozen burritos in the toaster oven. The unit has a stove and he knows how to cook; Foma taught him to make all kinds of things, like *real* mac and cheese and chicken wings a hundred ways. But buying all the ingredients to stock a kitchen the way Foma did would cost more than he wants to spend, especially since mealtime kind of depresses him. Burritos, Pop-Tarts, sandwiches, ramen all have the same virtues: cheap, fast, and no leftovers to remind him he's cooking for only one.

Plate in one hand and iPad propped up on the crate/coffee table, he settles in to call @AshMeAnything. Jonas pretty much never says no to work, so he would've said yes to whatever the kid wanted, but when he heard the idea—green screen backgrounds for Marvel-themed TikToks—he got excited. He's done over a hundred anime portraits, which are what he's known for now, but it's getting kinda

boring, so this is a welcome change. And the price is amazing; he can't imagine being someone who can offer strangers money that freely.

At the last second, he decides against his usual seat. The kid obviously has money, so maybe the Hawaii scene looks cheap?

There's no place in the room that looks super professional. But he if sits at the dining table, only a white wall and a part of the window are visible. Maybe that's sort of cool and minimalist? Swiping mail out of the way, he sets up his new station.

When @AshMeAnything comes onscreen, Jonas is thrown. Sitting on an all-white sectional, the kid wears a soft-looking knit sweater vest in rainbow stripes of various widths over a mock turtleneck topped with a chunky metal necklace. It's the kind of outfit that immediately reads as expensive, yet would seem kind of ridiculous on the average person.

@AshMeAnything is not average: his dark skin glows and his thick black hair is pulled back in a ponytail, one perfect strand hanging free to frame his face. His expressive brown eyes and the long lashes that outline them are amplified by glossy oversized eyeglass frames. He radiates confidence.

Jonas runs his hand quickly through his own hair, tangled into a mat from the winter hat he's been wearing all afternoon. His pink hoodie could probably use a good wash. He can't explain it, but his heart is racing.

@AshMeAnything approves of the fit. "Salmon is good on you. Not everyone can pull it off. Most guys wouldn't try."

"Thanks?" Jonas isn't used to talking about clothes with other

guys. Or with anyone, really. He tries to keep up. "Your, um, sweater looks soft." It sounds ridiculous.

"It *is* soft. Raf Simons has a way."

Jonas nods even though he has no idea who that is. He needs a new topic. "You didn't tell me your name."

"What—you think it's not AshMeAnything?" The kid winks at him. "It's Ashok. But my *friends* call me Ash." Does that mean he's included in the privilege or that he isn't since they've just met? The confusion must be clear on his face. "Call me Ash."

"Okay. And I'm . . ." It comes out before he knows what he's doing. "Jackson." Why the hell did he do that? Yes, it's his birth name, but no one has used it in a decade. The real answer is embarrassing: it sounds richer.

Ash is amused. "Isn't your profile JonasArt?"

Duh. Jonas can't believe how awkward he feels, especially considering that they already texted half the night. "Jonas is my uh . . . business name. Like a pseudonym for . . . privacy stuff." After the way he handled things with Shani, Jonas decided he was going to be 100 percent honest with people from now on, that he wasn't going to fudge the details to be more the person he imagined other people wanting. And just like that, first new person he meets, he's done it again. Dammit.

"Look at your face. I'm just teasing, *Jackson*. So . . . what did you come up with?"

Jonas is relieved. To start, he texts Ash the rain-soaked military site where Thor finds the hammer in the first movie. It's all blacks and greys and super moody.

Ash tucks the loose strand behind his ear. He doesn't look wowed. "I suppose if I make my look really colorful, it would be like a contrast or something. But . . . It's more *emo* than gay, you know?"

Jonas *does* know. He was dubious about including anything from the first Thor movie, which is not his favorite, but they had spent an hour texting about it, and he likes to give his customers options. It's a trick. Always offer three sketches, placing the one you like best in the middle. Make sure the second option is significantly better than the first, which generates enthusiasm, and then follow it with a good—but not *as good*—third option. He read online that customers always choose the middle, which has turned out to be true 90 percent of the time. When that happens, his strategy makes them happy with their choice while he gets to do what he wanted in the first place.

The second option is a red and black hellscape of Muspelheim, realm of the Fire Demon Surtur in *Thor: Ragnarok,* Jonas's favorite Marvel movie. A few chains in the foreground suggest the restraints from which a bound Thor dangles in the film's establishing scenes. "Hmm." Ash says no more for a minute, the wheels turning. "Hmm." He looks at the sketch approvingly, but doesn't immediately bite. "Is there more?"

Disappointing! Jonas has already started figuring out how to replicate the glowing effect of lava. But he texts the final option: the gleaming palace of Sakaar, with the Grand Master lounging on his throne, his eyes rimmed with kohl and a stripe of makeup for a beard.

"Oh no, girl, I can't compete with that. I need to be the only one

in eyeliner." This makes Jonas laugh and Ash riffs. "And that pow-der blue goatee? Total focus pull."

"I guess he does kinda steal the movie."

Ash nods. "It would only be worse to go up against Hela. I mean, the *antlers!*"

Invoking Hela leads into a long discussion about all the relative hotness of the myriad supporting players in *Thor.* Jonas doesn't usu-ally talk like this, but Ash has no problem weighing in on how Cate Blanchett, who plays Hela, is "so cold she's icy hot," while Valkyrie is a "slow burn," though he adds, "if you're into women." He says he really wants to "eat dinner off Dr. Strange's cheekbones" (which is a weird metaphor, but Jonas gets what he means) and that Loki is a "natural-born lover." Ash says Hogun (a character so minor Jonas just lumped him in with two others as "Warriors Three") is the sexi-est, but he's underused because Hollywood doesn't know how to handle Asian men.

Jonas tries to keep up, mostly agreeing with or laughing at Ash's commentary. It's fun—and new—to talk so easily about men and women alike as fantasy material, like it's no big deal. Something about Ash's personality just opens him up, which is a good thing. Or it is until Ash asks, "Who does it for you?"

Jonas goes quiet. A lot of people are beautiful, but who turns him on is a different subject altogether, and not one he wants to talk about. "They're all out of my league."

"They also don't exist, so there's that," Ash jokes. When Jonas doesn't add more, he says, "I get it: closet Hulk fan. It's weird, but fine."

Jonas imitates the green monster's voice. "Hulk . . . smash." It comes out really corny and he just wants to get back on track. "So . . . we're going with idea number two then?"

"Obviously. It's perfect; I mean, that scene is built for fetish wear. The big horny devil thing–"

"Surtur?"

"*Terrible* name. But if you put him in a leather harness and make club lights in the lava, I'll bind myself like Thor and hang from a sling–"

Who is this kid? "You have a sling?"

"Of course not." That's kind of a relief somehow. "But you can get anything online." Ash pecks at his phone. "God, they even have them at Overstock."

"But–I mean, how will you hang it?"

"I'll find a way. My room is *huge*. Or I can set it up in the loft, which has these exposed steel beams. That could really work, actually." Ash's face glows with the vision.

"And your parents won't mind?"

This takes the luster off Ash's smile for a maybe half a second. "The box won't be marked, obviously. I'll tell them it's a new bookshelf." He pushes the loose lock of hair out of his eyes. "I'm *trying* to train them to respect my privacy, but they're a little tightly wound. My mom says until I move out, personal space is like a private island: something I'd like to have but don't."

Jonas looks around the studio apartment, an island he didn't choose, as Ash rolls on.

"Honestly, I let them think they're the boss of me, but we all know only children rule the home. I'm what they live for."

What is he supposed to say here? "Wow."

"What about your parents?"

Stick to the truth. "I never knew my dad."

Ash goes on. "Is your mom cool?"

"My mom's dead." Jonas has no idea why he has confessed this. The only thing more sympathy-inducing than foster kid is orphan. His eyes are dry but the words pack a punch.

"Oh . . ." Ash's voice is completely different in an instant. The sarcastic lilt is replaced with something more genuine. "I didn't know that."

"How could you?" Jonas manages a smile. "It was like seven years ago. I don't know why I told you now."

A look flashes across Ash's eyes. "So who do you live with?"

Why not say it? Ash is a clean slate. "I have my own apartment, actually." No need to explain the subsidized part.

"Wait. How old are you?"

"Seventeen." Is Ash's expression doubtful? "It's just how it is. There's no law against it."

"No, I'm impressed. I'd *kill* to have my own place."

"Yeah, it's great." Jonas can't help himself. The orphan thing has him at a disadvantage. No need to say he's lonely and cold a lot of the time. "I set my own hours, do what I want." What he wants at this moment is to talk about Marvel again. "Nobody cares what I do."

"I'll be right over!" Ash says it like a joke, but Jonas flinches. A rich kid here? Seeing the mostly bare walls, thrift store furniture, and windows without so much as blinds. He's silent until Ash says, "*Kidding.*"

Jonas feels his face heating up. "Oh, sorry, I–"

"You might be a serial killer after all."

The humor helps. "Do I look like a serial killer?"

"What serial killer ever does?"

This leads to another long digression, this time on the relative attractiveness of the Son of Sam and Jeffrey Dahmer and a half dozen others; weirdly, both can recite the list as easily as the names of the states. Ted Bundy provides a source of disagreement when Jonas says, "He got away with it because he was good-looking."

Ash hops on this. "But really? I mean, he's kinda boring. Unless that's your type."

Is Ash fishing? Again? "I don't have a–"

"–type of serial killer? Good." Jonas thinks he's off the hook, but not for long. "Do you have a boyfriend? Or girlfriend? Whatever."

People aren't usually so direct. Mostly they assume he's straight, though Flasker says he reads queer. A girl once told him he was just the right mix of cute and nonthreatening for boys *and* girls; she meant it as a compliment, but it still landed funny. A guy in his sophomore class asked him out, which came as a surprise because Jonas hardly knew him, but the date never happened because Jonas's nerves got in the way and he'd canceled.

I don't think I have a type. He can't say that, but Ash is waiting for an answer, so Jonas goes with what he does know: Shani's the only person he's ever wanted to ask out. "A girl . . . a girlfriend. Her name is Shani."

It's close enough to the truth: he did ask and when he sees her on her birthday, the facts will catch up. He reverses the question. "Do you?"

"Have a boyfriend? No. A type? *Yes.* Tall, dark, and handsome."
A loaded beat.

There is no mistaking it: Ash is flirting. And Jonas doesn't entirely
mind. The warmth that comes over him is a new feeling. He's not
sure what to make of it exactly and doesn't have a clue how to
respond. The easiest thing to do is deflect.

"Like the fire demon, you mean?"

Ash fans himself. "*Hot.*"

The joke is too easy, but they both laugh anyway. Jonas's private
island feels less empty.

NINE
SHANI

Ash texts her.

His real name is Jackson. Jonas is his 'art name' whatever that is?

Her heart kind of stops. Why would Jonas say that?

It gets worse. His mother is dead and he lives in his own apartment.

It's like a parallel universe, this Jackson world. Which means one of two things, neither good.

He lied to Ash *or* he lied to her.

Why lie to either of them? Is he embarrassed by his mom, who Shani saw onscreen with her own eyes that time? Or is the dead mother story just some weird ploy to get sympathy? Is he trying to home in on *her* grief?

When Jonas texts moments later, it makes her head hurt.

Jonas. You know that new client?

Yeah? *If you only knew,* she thinks.

I'm gonna make Marvel backdrops for his gay Avengers channel.

She keeps her reply neutral. Cool.

Yah. I'm excited.

She texts a thumbs up. Then a clock. Then a school bus. It's true she's going to be late for her bus if she doesn't get a move on, but this is too much.

She's so thrown off that her eyebrows don't match. On nursing home days, she doesn't do much with her makeup, and her braids are neatly pulled back, but eyebrows are not optional. Other kids come to her for brow advice, because hers are perfect—usually. Today, not so much. She'd love to do them over, but she doesn't have time: there's only one Minuteman bus that comes near where she lives.

She heads for the kitchen, hoping her dad isn't up yet. His last fare was after midnight, so maybe he'll be sleeping in, which would be good because she doesn't feel like a chat. She pours Frosted Mini-Wheats and milk into her dad's favorite Green Monster travel mug so she can eat on the bus.

The air is so cold outside that she holds her breath. Thank the goddesses for the North Face puffer coat she found at Buffalo Exchange last winter, the fake fur lining now a bulwark against the wind. The finger-touch gloves she bought at Target don't actually work, but there's no chance she's exposing her hand to the cold. She'll have to wait to text Ash for more details.

Milo has beaten her to the bus stop, and he isn't going to let that go uncommented. "Rough night? Hangover maybe?"

"Ha ha. Just didn't want to spend more time with *you*."

"It's gonna be a long ride, then, cause you know I can't be away from you for long." Only about three inches of his pale white skin is visible through the ski mask he wears, but his blue eyes gleam.

The bus rolls into view but seems to creep up Mass Ave. Could it go slower? The cold isn't helping her mood any, but Milo helps. Everyone likes him at Minuteman, where he goes by Giraffe, a nickname he gave himself after seeing stilt-walker giraffes in a touring production of *The Lion King*, their stately walk similar to his in the arm crutches he wears for his CP. When they first met, Shani asked him if it felt like weird leaning forward all day and he asked, "Does it feel weird dragging that butt behind you everywhere?" A white boy making a booty joke is a risky proposition, but it made her laugh so hard she had spilled the smoothie she was holding. They've been friends ever since.

When the bus finally reaches them, he waves a crutch toward the door so she'll board first. The bus is less than half-full. Most kids in Arlmont go to Memorial, but Shani never even considered it; Minuteman is just as free, but also has career tracks, which works for her since one of them is medicine, so she'll graduate with all kinds of certification and either a CNA or an EMT under her belt. There are only fifteen kids in her health program, so it feels like a private school. The small student body means she never has to share a bench on the bus, but Giraffe always sits across from her. Most days, he tries out material for his stand-up routine, sometimes reworking the same bit for months. She is pretty sure she has heard every joke he knows, but she likes the routine even so.

Today, the cold weather makes Giraffe move more slowly and stiffly, and by the time he takes his usual spot, she's already on the phone with Ash discussing the claim that Jonas's mom is dead. "What the hell?"

"I was as surprised as you are."

"Did he *look* like he was lying?"

Ash seems to ponder this. "It seemed pretty instantaneous. Like it just popped out."

"He's got *some* old Black lady living with him!"

If he can tell she's upset, he's ignoring it well. He's loving the gossip too much. "He says he lives alone."

"Say what now?"

"Oh, yeah, he's all over it like Pinocchio, *Ain't no strings on me.*"

Shani's head starts to pound.

Giraffe leans across the aisle. "You look like you're about to have a seizure."

"I'm not playin' right now!" she snaps. His eyes widen and he leans back. She hears herself, mouthing *Sorry* to Giraffe as Ash goes on about how he liked Jonas—or Jackson—otherwise and it's a shame he's such a liar.

Is anything he said true? Shani wants to hurl the travel mug at a window.

"You know how many hours of my life I've wasted talking to that boy?"

"Well, it's not wasted entirely. He does call you his girlfriend."

"Cap!"

There is a tiny part of her that is glad that, if nothing else, Jonas

has claimed her as his. Her feelings are a stew of mad and confused—he always seemed so sincere, so what is this about? Maybe he told her the truth and lied to Ash, but why do that? Either way, he can't be trusted.

"My 'boyfriend' is a straight up liar."

"Isn't that the whole point of this?"

He's not wrong: she asked Ash to find out the deal with Jonas, and he did. It wasn't supposed to be so easy, just lies floating on the surface, waiting for a net. Despite having been so sure, she really wanted to be wrong.

She stares out the window, the icy world a perfect landscape for her mood.

Ash clears his throat. "So . . . what do you want me to do now?"

She sighs. "Like I know."

"This was your idea . . ."

"Yeah, but you said leave it up to you!"

Ash nods. "Trust me, I can keep going. I just . . . you look like you're not so sure."

"Do it." Anger makes her want to dig in.

He looks pleased with that reply. "I'm going to get him to meet me at Curious Liquids."

"If he says yes to meeting you before he's even met me, I'm gone stab him in the face." How soon can she put him on blast? And how? "You got receipts?"

"Girl, what kind of spy would I be if I didn't? I did a voice memo while we were on FaceTime. You can't see him but you can hear . . ."

"And you're not deleting the texts, right?" When Shani burns, she burns hot. Boy is about to taste fire.

"Now you're just insulting."

"Just making sure. I know you're an evil genius."

Ash grins. "People say that too much. Or not enough. I can't decide."

Shani ends the call as the bus pulls into the Minuteman lot. As she steps back into the cold, Giraffe calls out. "I kinda heard that . . ."

"I kinda don't care."

"This Jonas guy sounds like a jerk." Giraffe raises one crutch in a gesture of surrender. Shani shrugs. "Which is not the end of the world from where I'm sitting."

"Yeah?"

He does an exaggerated version of a sexy smolder, and almost against her will, she laughs a little. "It improves my chances with you."

Hmm. That's a joke he hasn't told before.

. . .

Whenever she's with patients at Woodlawn, Shani is a different person. Quiet, calming. No sign of dismay crosses her face when Ms. Robertson wets herself again, her thin floral housedress darkening with liquid. When Mr. Gataki makes creepy remarks about how he'd have snatched her up if she'd been a girl in his day, she just smiles and hands him his dixie cup full of afternoon meds.

She's very polite and soft-spoken on the ward. No slang, no swearing, none of the shorthand that peppers her group texts; it's miles from how she sounds with the BB5. She learned to code switch long ago, speaking one way to BB5 and on her channel, another to her dad, and yet another to teachers. It's around Ash that she sounds

most herself, a girl raised in white Arlmont but not cut off from Black culture. She also knows that what *he* finds fierce and funny would be taken as threatening and unprofessional here. Nobody wants to see her spine; they want the smile.

One of her chores today is to make up a room which has been empty since its occupant passed away the night before. Other nurses have already stripped away the old linens, so she doesn't have the unsettling task of touching the sheets someone died in. It's a one-person job and gives her time alone to think about Jonas. Why can't he keep his stories straight?

Could it be—Shani's shoulders and jaw all tighten at the thought—a race thing? Did he say that woman wasn't his mother because he doesn't want Ash to know he's Black? Or, and this feels much worse, had he lied to Shani for the opposite reason? Maybe he wants to *look* Black for her. Once the idea is in her head, she can't shake it.

It sounds crazy, but is it? How many white kids have made sure to drop mentions of their Black friends and cousins and in-laws around Shani? It's like the ultimate way of saying *I'm down*, a senti-ment they could prove just by *being down* instead of making a speech. But Shani suspects white people need validation, like, all the time.

Her dad would say *not everything is about race*, and he means it, but he's white—all white. *Irish* white. He's gone to bat for her a mil-lion times, like when the soccer coach said she couldn't play if she kept her braids long, or when the middle school teachers singled out the Black girls for noise in the hallway when they were being provoked by white boys who went unpunished. But proximity and

experience aren't the same thing, not by a long shot. Her dad can't know what it's like.

She's tucking the corner of the bedsheet in with such furious jabs, her fingers hurt. Nuri, from her class, stops in the doorway. "You're supposed to tuck it, not torture it." Nuri's sonorous voice makes even a joke sound elegant.

Shani turns to face her. They have little in common outside school—Nuri's one of four daughters in a wealthy family from Iran—but they clicked freshman year, first bonding over biology experiments and then over their classmates' sometimes clueless behavior. She's safe to talk to because she's not deeply invested.

"Would you dump a guy if he lied to you?" Shani asks. "You would, right?"

Nuri fingers the edge of her violet silk hijab. "That's a real question, not a hypothetical?"

"Yeah."

"I'd have to *get* a boy to dump one, which would be pretty tough to arrange with my parents, but yeah, of course. A liar is a liar—why would you put up with that?"

Pretty eyes and listening ears and a goofy smile and . . . Shani can think of more reasons, but Nuri is right. "Nobody in their right mind."

A nurse who seemingly hates the high school volunteers sees the girls chatting and calls them out. "Ms. Robertson needs some help. That is, if you're not too busy chatting."

Nuri smiles a polite smile and says, "We're on it," but as soon as the nurse is gone, whispers, "What a bitch." As they enter the old

woman's room, the scent of urine in the air, Nuri nods at Shani. "Be nicer to Ms. Robertson than you were to that bed."

"Always!" Shani won't take her changed mood out on a patient. Only person in danger right now is Jonas.

. . .

When it's time for Jonas's call, she takes a deep breath. He can't know anything has changed. It's hard to keep her face neutral when he appears onscreen, though, fake Hawaii in place as always. She wants him to come clean so she can forgive him, but she also wants him to keep lying so she can bury him. There's no making sense of her feelings.

He talks excitedly about their birthday date and she says she's excited, too. "But tonight I gotta study for health vocab. It's fifty percent of my term grade, so . . ."

Jonas—Jackson?—looks surprised but hangs up. It's still early for Shani, way earlier than she ever goes to sleep, but tonight she could close her eyes and sleep for a hundred years.

TEN
ASH

Ash texts Jackson from his coffee shop office, sounding casual. Brainstorming at Curious Liquids. Here all morning if you're around. No response, which is not surprising, since most teenage boys he knows are still sleeping at 9 a.m. on a Saturday. Not Ash, who's already gone for a run, watched two episodes of the original *Gossip Girl*, and finished his first turmeric latte.

Tee sets up camp across from him. They're in civilian mode today, not working the bar but nursing a horrible-looking grass-green smoothie of some kind, which Ash would love to tell them to take to any booth but his. He resists that impulse because it's a Saturday morning. The shop will be packed, so it's bad form to hog an entire table to yourself for too long. He likes to park here and work— much easier than sitting at home, where his mom might find a task for him to do, or worse, his dad might ask about his college applications—so he shares the booth as much as he can to look like a good human.

The pair work in silence for a while, Ash reading a pirated copy of the *Thor: Ragnarok* script online to figure out which lines to parody. The bits need to be recognizable enough for people to get the jokes but it also has to be something he can twist to fit his brand, which is super gay, really funny, and a lot shameless. He knows he could be accused of overthinking a sixty-second bit, but he doesn't care. This clip could go viral and he wants to engineer the best odds.

Tee, meanwhile, is making a flyer for their band's upcoming concert by hand using a woodblock stamp. Their hair is pulled up into a tight bun at the moment to keep it out of their eyes as they dip the cut-outs of individual letters into eggplant-purple ink and then press each onto a sheet of paper already boasting a grinning Cheshire cat holding a violin plugged into an amp. It's taking forever, as Tee laboriously spells out the time and place and cost, and as pretty as it is, the whole process is a little ridiculous. "You know Adobe exists, right?"

Without raising their eyes from the page, Tee replies, "Yeah, that's super Victorian."

"Just like your music." Ashok has never understood how Underland, Tee's band, ever came to be. Like, there's more than one person whose Venn diagram includes Alice in Wonderland, punk music, and string quartets? Surprisingly, the answer is yes: a fanbase of queer kids from Taft U, Mooreville lesbians, and the UUs of Arlmont.

"You do your brand, I'll do mine." Tee pauses to admire their handiwork and finally looks up, one eyebrow raised. "Oh, yeah. Nice thong challenge, by the way."

Ouch. A few days ago, Ash had dueted the clip of a clearly drunk ginger twink on Fire Island asking people if they liked his new thong—it was the tragic intersection of thirst trap and self-esteem fail. Ash found the thong online, ordered it and two red wigs overnight express, and mimicked the boy exactly, with one wig on his head and the other stuffed into the thong, ginger curls spilling out on all sides. Okay, so it was a really cheap shot, but it got 189,000 likes and launched a bunch of imitators, so it felt like a win, until a bunch of users started commenting how mean it was. Ash didn't mind at first—there's a fine line between humor and cruelty and it's not his fault other people can't see which side the video falls on. But being called a cyberbully is no good for his brand, so he took it down. Apparently not fast enough: thong challenge was already born, and now everyone's doing it.

He raises his hands in a gesture of surrender. "You win."

Tee smiles. "Right answer." Tee's gaze drifts past Ash and fix on something behind him. "Is that guy looking for you?"

There is Jackson in the flesh, wearing a too-big parka and a knit cap pulled low. His expression says he's unsure whether or not to interrupt.

When Ash makes eye contact and waves him over, the smile that sprawls across Jackson's face chases away the doubt. His cheeks become more prominent, above dimples long enough to be canyons. His eyes—more amber than brown in person—glow in way an iPhone can't capture.

FaceTime hasn't fully prepared Ash for this possibility.

Jackson is really cute.

Ash pushes the thought away. The kid isn't a date: he's a mark in a long con. He's the guy who's been lying to Ash's best friend. But it doesn't hurt that he's easy on the eyes.

When Ash tries unsubtly to send Tee a you-can-go-now look, Tee ignores it and slides over on their bench to make room for Jonas. Ash really wants to pop up and hug Jackson (honestly, Ash wants to hug everyone), but he's working on allowing people their personal space, and he learned a long time ago that most guys flinch if he just goes in for the kill right away.

"You came!"

"Yeah. I've been meaning to check this place out; kids from my school usually go to Sunny's or Starbucks."

Jackson slips off the parka, revealing a T-shirt that pretty much screams *somebody slept in me*. Losing the hat, he passes a hand through a tangle of dark curls. He's an unmade bed, and somehow it works for him.

Ash couldn't look more different. His hair and skin both gleam, and he likes the outfit he chose: an ivory turtleneck that he thinks of as Chris Evans chic, and vintage-looking plaid wool pants cropped above the top of his boots. He could have stepped out of a GQ shoot (actually, the look *is* from a GQ shoot), and when he left the house this morning, he could just envision how cute he'd look against the red leather of his "office."

Ash feels Tee's eyes on him. He introduces them. "Jackson, this is my friend Tee. Tee, this is Jackson."

"You're the artist?"

Jackson looks surprised that Tee knows this, but also kind of

pleased. "Yeah." He eyes the flyer Tee has made. "You are, too. That's really cool."

Tee loves him already. "Thank you! Ash think it's a little much."

"I think *you're* a little much," Ash lobs back. No chance he's letting Tee home in on his target. He feigns concern, eyes on the distant register. "What does Darius want?"

Tee turns to see what Ash means. "Huh?"

"He was trying to get your attention. Maybe someone didn't come in and he needs your help."

Tee turns to face Ash, half-amused, half-scornful. "Oh . . . *well*, then . . . I should pack up my things and go." Ash sends a grateful look at Tee, who puts the cap back on the ink, slips the letters into a plastic bag, and then feigns puzzlement. "Except my poster's still wet . . . How can I can put it in my bag this way?"

Ash croons, "We'll watch it for you. Come back later when it's dry."

"Good idea." Tee is enjoying this. "Hard to say how long it'll take. Could be a while, or I might be back *any* moment."

As much as Ash wants Jackson all to himself, he's amused by Tee's cleverness. He blows them a kiss before they head toward the stools at the counter.

When they're alone, Ash feels both thrilled and under pressure to have Jackson focusing only on him. He eyes the paper cup in Jonas's hand. "You ordered to go?"

"I'm usually just grabbing coffee at Dunks before work." He looks embarrassed now.

"I can see why you wouldn't linger at Dunks." Ash doesn't add, *Though I can't see why you'd drink Dunks to begin with.*

Jackson is sincere. "I don't think there's a 'for here' option at Dunks . . ." He looks around the room, taking in the mix of faux leather booths and upholstered chairs. "But I'll remember that next time I come to this place." He sips his coffee. "Whoa. That's intense." He looks at his coffee like there's magic in the cup.

"Thrillist's 10 Best. Stick with me—I know all the cool places." Ash is in his favorite position: the expert. If Jackson is going to be so easy to impress, this will be fun. But first, he has to act like he's a customer. "So, what did you bring?"

"Uh . . ." Jackson looks confused for a moment and then his face falls. "Shit. You wanted me to bring a drawing. Of course."

Ash realizes that Jackson agreed to meet him *just because he asked*—no pretense of business. The same guy who ducked out of meeting Shani live is sitting here without a second's hesitation. Intriguing. "No, no, you're right. I said brainstorming."

He angles his laptop so Jackson can see the *Thor* script. "I'm trying to decide which scene to focus on."

Jackson leans over to look, and for a moment, their heads touch. The warmth is almost too much for Ash and then Jackson moves away ever so slightly. It's everything Ash can do to keep scrolling through the *Thor* script. Can chemistry be one-sided? Because he's feeling it.

Think of Shani. Think. Of. Shani.

"Is your girlfriend artistic, too?"

Jackson sits up straight, face alight. "Not exactly. But she has her own YouTube channel."

Ash adopts a look of interest. "Yeah?"

"It's about Black hair and stuff."

He plays it off. "Yeah, there are lot of those now." Might as well seize the day. "She's Black?" The question comes out really naked.

Jackson scrunches up his face. "Um, wouldn't really be right to make a show about Black hair if she wasn't."

"Of course. And what about you—" There is no good way to ask, but fortune favors the bold, right? "Are you—"

Jackson seems unphased. "I don't know." A shrug. "Mixed, I guess? Honestly, Mom never said and I never met my dad. I ordered one of those DNA kits, but uh . . ." He shakes his head.

"Is that weird? Not knowing?"

Jackson peers down into his cup, finds no answer there, and shrugs again. "What about you?"

"Take a guess."

Jackson gives Ash a look, searching and long. It's a lot: his irises are flecked with color like Tiger's Eye. Ash has to look away first. Remembering that this is Shani's boyfriend is going to be a lot of work.

Jackson doesn't sound confident. "Indonesian?"

That's a new one. "Really? Do you know a lot of Indonesians?"

"Nah. You just . . . You look like someone I saw in one of Foma's cookbooks."

"Foma?"

"Foster mom. Evelyn Prosper. I've lived with her since I was little."

Ash makes note of the present tense. *Doesn't Jackson live alone?* He presses ahead. "So your foster's Indonesian?"

"No—just loves cookbooks. The last one she bought—" Jackson pauses, seems to catch himself. "Was from Bali. And there's a guy in it who looks—"

"Got it. And *no*. Half Indian, half Cuban."

This seems to make Jackson happy. "That's so cool. I've never met anyone like that."

"Neither have I."

Jackson leans forward, eager to hear more. "What do you call yourself?"

"*American*." (He'd give Jackson more grief about this, but it's not like he hasn't asked himself the same question.) "Or"—he winks—"Trans Am."

Will the line land? It shouldn't matter that he's trans, but there's always that moment when he needs to make it clear to test whether the listener is safe to be around.

Jackson passes the test, his smile landing square in Ash's chest. "So you're a *race car*!"

"Baby, I'm the original Hot Wheels." Whoa. He has to stop flirting or Shani will kill him. "So, what do you expect . . . from the DNA kit?"

"I don't know." Jackson lets out a long breath. "I guess it would be nice to have somewhere to be from."

Oh, please. "Having roots is overrated. Between my ancestors, I'm stuck eating rice forty times a week." He closes the laptop. "I have an idea. My house is like five minutes away and I have my car. We can watch *Thor* in the movie room and get a good look at the backdrop we want."

"There's a movie room?"

Why does everyone have that reaction? "It's more just a second living room," he says, knowing that Jackson might disagree when he sees the wall-size screen and reclining leather love seats, and when he hears the surround sound. Ash forges on. "Are you up for it?"

"Are you kidding? I can watch Marvel all day long." Jackson has his hat and parka on before Ash has even packed his bag.

. . .

Raiding the snack pantry—Jackson claiming it was the size of his apartment, which can't be true—they bump into Raj. He has come for his morning ration of dried figs and eyes their corn chips and soda disdainfully.

Raj making small talk is painful. "So, Jackson, what schools are you applying to?"

Jackson squirms a little under a spotlight. "Uh, probably something in the UMass system."

"That's all?"

Oh my god. Ash wants to strangle his dad. "Jackson doesn't need your help finding a school."

"You know he needs nine."

Raj insists that every wise college applicant needs a Golden 9: three schools that would be a reach, three that are right in the applicant's wheelhouse, and three safeties.

"If he comes up short, we'll let you know!" Ash practically drags Jackson away.

Jackson's response to the movie room is pretty much expected. "You have enough seats to have another family over!" That's exactly why they have so many, but it's been a long time since they did a movie night together.

Once the movie is on, Ash impulsively sits next to Jackson. He can feel Jackson tense up a little but not move away. They're not any closer than if they were strangers sitting next to each other in a regular movie theater. But now he's hyperaware of their closeness.

Within a few minutes, any awkwardness evaporates. They quote lines out loud together, crack up at the same jokes, and debate whether Valkyrie is supposed to be bisexual. At some point, Jackson seems to forget the distance guys usually maintain, resting his knee heavily against Ash's. *Oh my god.* The warmth is like a fire that starts at the edge of curtains and spreads, flickering upward. Jonas keeps it there and Ash knows—he *knows*—he should move his own before the heat consumes him.

The point of contact ignites something in Ash that he can't deny. He's had boyfriends (none for very long, because who could keep up, really?) and he's chatted up a few hot guys on apps. But this is different. The spark of connection radiates throughout his whole body. He's almost holding his breath now. *Don't react. Don't move. Don't break the spell.*

Jackson doesn't seem to notice. He talks happily through the end credits, waiting for the little bonus clip at the end, as Ash watches the dwindling how-much-time-is-left bar on the screen. Once the screen is black, Jackson pops up, asking for the bathroom. Ash is both happy to be alone for a moment and keenly feeling the absence of Jackson's solid form.

With Jackson out of sight, guilt swoops in. For one thing, Ash needs to call Shani before Jackson does. She doesn't know he and Jackson (er, Jonas?) have met, much less hung out at Ash's, and if she hears it from Jackson first, she'll think Ash has fallen into one of his mad crushes and wants Jackson for himself. Maybe she'd be right.

The bigger question: Could Jackson be into him? He had agreed so easily to come over. But then he'd leaped off the couch just as fast at the movie's end. Ash scrolls through the JonasArt Insta for any sign of queerness. Not sure what—photos of a cute boy? Celebrity crushes? Anything at all rainbow? Of course Shani would have seen that herself if there had been anything to find. But it's all art, every bit. He googles Jackson's name and then tries to find him on other social media, without much success. He keeps an eye on the door to make sure he doesn't get caught stalking.

But after twenty minutes, Jackson still hasn't returned. Is he wandering around the house lost? Ash hears thumping one floor up and follows the sound to find his mom and Jackson on either end of a new credenza, a huge Pop Art thing that she probably won at auction.

"Mami! Are you kidding?"

Gloria's eyes flash. "How am I failing you now?"

"Making a guy I met, like, four hours ago move furniture?!"

Jackson's eyes widen. "It's okay. I don't mind."

"He said he was your friend. I didn't see a need to ask for a timeline."

"Yeah, a *friend*, not the help."

"He's a mover. He does this all the time."

"How do you even know that?"

"I told her." Jackson is looking back and forth at the two, willing them to stop.

"Told her before or after she asked you to lend a hand?"

"Well . . ."

"Exactly! It only came up because she asked you to move furniture and you needed something to say."

Jackson shifts from foot to foot. "I left my stuff in the movie room . . ."

Gloria fixes a disapproving look on Ash. "You're scaring off your friend." Before he can argue, she puts her hand on Jackson's arm. "Do you talk to *your* mom this way?"

"We have our moments, like everyone else." It comes out so casually, it reminds Ash that the only reason he even knows Jackson (hot as he may be) is because this guy tripped Shani's bullshit detectors. Why is it so easy for this kid to lie?

Gloria nods at Jackson. "Thank you for helping me. You made a good first impression. Come back anytime."

"*Gloria!*" Ash knows she hates this.

"*Ashok!*" She mimics his tone pretty perfectly, which he hates just as much. Heading down the hall, she calls back. "Have fun, boys."

. . .

Once Jackson's gone, Ash lies on his back on the infinity shag rug in his room.

His brain is in overdrive. How is it that the guy who can afford his own apartment can only afford a state school? If he lives alone,

where is this Foma person? And the whole two names thing—what's *that* about? No wonder Shani has Ash scoping out the truth—Jackson can't 100 percent be trusted. But still. The touch of his knee. The warmth.

Ash's plan just got a lot more complicated:

- Figure out what's real and not real.
- Find out if Jackson is interested.
- Keep Shani in the dark until he knows.
- Try not to betray either of them too much.

What is it Shani's always doing—manifesting? Ash closes his eyes and tries to picture a universe in which Jackson ends up with him and Shani's not pissed about it.

Tbh, he can't quite see it.

PART TWO | IT'S BEGINNING TO LOOK A LOT LIKE MISCHIEF

ELEVEN
JONAS

Sometimes the weather report is a straight up lie, springing a downpour on a day with 0 percent chance of rain or promising a deep freeze only to bring shorts weather. Not today. The polar vortex delivers. The low will be zero degrees. Zero.

He could use this as a reason to get out of his date with Shani. Maybe he should. But he's feeling restless, ready to make the leap. He wants to see her, to show her the effort he put into her present. And he wants to know what it's like to have a girlfriend, a real one. To be *normal*.

He feels ready after his day with Ash. It had been a rare impulse to meet at the coffee shop. For years, Jonas has perfected the art of being pleasant but not super outgoing. Other kids read his cues and leave him alone for the most part. They like him well enough but don't include him in things, which used to feel fine. Life with Foma was plenty—dependable and safe. But since his move to the apartment, he's been wishing his circle was less small. Flasker's great, but if your only buddy is also your boss, that's a problem.

Ash appeared at just the right moment. Jonas can't imagine asking a friend to meet up for coffee—it would just sound *weird* coming from him. Of course he'd misunderstood; when he got to Curious Liquids (and spent half of his tiny tip from the senior center move on a single fancy coffee), he realized that Ash had invited him to work, not just hang out. Yet, in the end, hanging out was exactly what they did.

Being asked over to Ash's place—mind-blowing. Even when Foma was healthy, Jonas had never considered bringing anyone home. Seeing how easy all this was for Ash made Jonas question himself: *Is something wrong with me?* He should have opened himself up to new friends sooner. He left Ash's mansion (what else would you call it?) walking lighter than he had for days.

And if time with Ash could do that, imagine how time with Shani would make him feel.

He rummages through a dresser looking for a shirt that isn't a T-shirt or a hoodie to wear on their date, even if he's mostly going to spend the night buried in his parka. There's a black three-button Henley that Foma got him for his birthday in October. Well, Marion did, because Foma was already at Sunrise by then and had sent her sister on the errand. He hasn't worn it since he first tried it on because the fit is a little snug and he's not some bro trying to show off his body. But Shani has to know he thought about this date, that it's not just any night. He slips it over his head and doesn't linger at the mirror.

His phone chimes. It's her.

He swipes it open to find a picture of the weather report and a grimacing smile emoji.

We still on?

Of course she thinks he's gonna bail. Why wouldn't she?

He texts a GIF of a happy Baby Yoda jumping up and down in the snow. He hits send before he can stop himself. *I'm a whole new man*, he thinks.

She rewards him with a skull emoji. And a heart.

He sends a heart. And a kiss. And then—why not?—a flame.

Forget the polar vortex. Things are heating up.

· · ·

He's late to the Square, kicking himself for not having allowed more time. The damn buses always run slow when you need them to be fast. He can only hope she's late, too.

When he gets to Lucky Star Fusion, Shani's waiting outside, bouncing to keep warm. She's way cooler-looking than he is, her braids pulled up into an almost architectural sculpture, banded by a red satin headband like that poet girl at the last inauguration. She has dressed as much for a date as for the cold: black fur earmuffs, a yellow scarf tucked into her black puffer coat, and black jeans tucked into thigh-high black suede boots. He's wearing the same rubber and fleece winter boots he wears everywhere, which makes him feel dorky next to her. In real life, she's taller than he expected, and curvier, too. Less girl and more woman, which makes him even more nervous.

Worse, he's forgotten her birthday present, the drawing he finished and framed for her. It would have been too much to bring her Christmas presents, too, but he didn't mean to come empty-handed.

But the gift lies on the Formica table back in Mooreville and there's no going back for it now. Nothing can be simple.

"Hey! Shani!" he calls out, crossing the brick plaza around which all the shops and restaurants are gathered. She turns to him, one eyebrow raised, and then adjusts her face to deliver a smile.

"Thought you dipped."

"No! I just—it took me longer than I thought—"

"S'okay. My dad drove me, so I've probably been outside less time than you. You look frozen."

She's trying to let him off the hook, which is sweet but kinda makes it worse. *I have to make the rest of the night amazing.* "You shoulda gone inside without me." He grabs the gold metal door handle to usher her in, but she's shaking her head.

"You think I wouldn't? Boy, it's *closed*."

How had he not noticed the darkened windows as he approached? A hand-lettered sign in the window reads "Xmas Eve: Closed for family party. OPEN tomorrow."

It had not occurred to him to think of the people at Lucky Star as family that would need a night off. Chinese food is something you never question, like air or sunlight. He knows exactly how much an order of scallion pancakes, General Tso's, white rice, and Coke costs with delivery and tip, and he budgets for it twice a week, saving half the chicken and rice for the next day's lunch. He had believed Lucky Star Fusion to be always open.

"Shit," he says, doom settling over him like dust. He surveys the square. Allegro, the fresh pasta place, is dark, and Hot Chili, the Thai place, too. This leaves only Curious Liquids and Il Braggadocio, which serves fancy Italian. Lights glow from inside and the windows

are steamed up, meaning it's not only open but cozy and warm. If he takes her there, he will for sure run out of money in January. But he can't remember if Curious Liquids has food or just coffees. And he's not sure it feels special enough for a first date.

Trying to not look defeated, he marches across the bricks to Il Braggadocio. "This looks nicer anyway."

She lets him open the door for her. "Thanks," she says, looking amused. "So old-school."

The host is a young white woman who appear to regret the sleeveless sheath dress she's wearing, even with a big pashmina wrapped around her shoulders. She leads them to a table and leaves them with huge leather-bound menus. Jonas feels sick to his stomach but opens his with feigned excitement. Shit. The cheapest entree is $25. And as far as he can tell, that much money buys him tomatoes on pasta.

When he recovers enough to ask Shani what looks good to her, she is laughing. "Your face!" Her eyes crinkle up. "The look on your face when you opened that."

"Oh. Uh–"

"I didn't expect some bougie dinner."

Is he allowed to look relieved? "I don't mind–"

"I planned on wings and pot stickers. I don't even know what half this is." She reads a random item. "Amatriciana?" Scrolls down. "Frutti di Mare?"

He joins in. "Tufoli? Sugo? Cacio & Pepe?"

"Only thing I know here is ravioli and I can get that outta my freezer."

"Right?"

They're both grinning now, eyes bright with the pleasure of agreement.

A busboy comes and asks if they want still or sparkling water, and they both burst out laughing. Jonas chokes out, "Still," and the boy heads away, leaving them to try and regain control.

"Wanna ditch?" Shani leans forward when she says this.

"You mean it?"

She is zipping up her coat and sliding her gloves on. Jonas wriggles into his parka, aware that there is no stealthy way to don winter gear. "Let's make a run for it."

The hostess doesn't seem surprised as they race past her for the door, just clutches her wrap tightly to prepare for the blast of cold. Once they're outside, the reality of the temperature slaps Jonas in the face, but he can't stop smiling.

. . .

Lucky for him, everything on the chalkboard menu at Curious Liquids is ten bucks or less. Shani orders a grilled cheese and a triple shot mocha, and Jonas asks for a banana-chocolate-peanut butter protein shake called The Elvis. When the order is ready, Shani scoops him, paying with a debit card before he can get cash out of his wallet.

He tries to protest but she waves him off. "You get it next time. No law says the boy has to pay."

As if in sync, they both head for the back to the booth where he sat with Ash. The friend he met with Ash—J? T?—passes by with a tray of bussed dishes and winks at Jonas. He has a brief pang: Did Ash call him Jackson in front of them? This is why lies suck.

"The grilled cheese at this place"—Shani brings her fingers to her lips—"chef's kiss!"

"You've been here before?

"You *haven't*? You a Starbucks guy or what?"

"Um . . . Dunks, I guess?"

"You and my dad. Must be a dude thing."

What's he supposed to say to that? He takes a gulp of his smoothie. It's dense and he's pleased with his choice—he won't have to supplement it with a snack later. "Whoa. This is good."

Shani shakes her head. "Better than Sunny's, too, right?"

"Way better."

"All this time and you've never been." Her eyes gleam like she's found out he's secretly a fugitive.

"Just once. My friend brought me."

"Friend?" She takes a big bite.

"That TikTokker—"

"You're friends now?"

"Kinda. I mean, we hung out at his place." She doesn't seem to love that bit of information. *Why am I talking about Ash?* He steers back to Shani. "Do you come here a lot?"

"Isn't that like a cheesy pickup line old people use?" she teases. "When I can. My friends don't. My cousin Sheree and her bestie are both way more into church than me. This place is a little gay for them."

"Huh. I never thought of that." Jonas eyes the crowd, which is queerer than the Dunks for sure, but seems pretty mixed overall. "I guess it's kinda true . . . the friend who brought me is gay." He almost says trans, too, but stops. Is it okay to out someone like that

or not? Ash doesn't seem like an especially closed book, but what does Jonas know?

"Hope it wasn't a date," she says with a smile. But her eyes are very focused.

"No!" Does it sound that way? "I mean, I even told him about you."

"Aww." Shani has dispatched her entire grilled cheese already and sits back, sipping the mocha. Jonas feels like she's expecting him to say more.

"This is . . . uh . . . the only date I've been on all year."

She sits up. "Right now. This. Me?" He nods, sucking down smoothie. "Boy, there's only a week left of the year. What've you been doing?"

He can feel his face heat up. What has he been doing this year? This life?

"I'm just playin'," she says. "I only had a couple of dates this summer. A kid who was a regular at Yaki's. I wasn't feeling it, so I started leaving him on read to give him the hint. And he ended up ordering pizza all the time so I'd *have* to talk to him. Like I'm that easy. I got myself moved from register to kitchen for a couple of weeks and that was that. He gave up."

Jonas pretends to write this down. "Note to self: if you leave me on read, I'm doomed."

"Quick learner." She toasts his smoothie glass with her mocha mug.

She's so beautiful and so confident. He feels this sudden urge to kiss her, which he so cannot do. Not yet. It would be too fast, too out

of the blue. He hasn't really even imagined it before this moment—but now, he can hardly focus on anything else.

It's all going so well. Maybe this is the moment to come clean. Tell her he didn't mean to lie; he's just made a habit of offering the truth that seems easiest. But it might spoil the evening. Should he wait till a second date?

And then he hears Foma's voice in his head. *If you wanted it, you'd have done it.*

Does he want to come clean? Truly? *Can* he?

But Shani has other things on her mind. "So how's this trolley deal work?"

It can wait. Date first; confession later.

TWELVE
SHANI

Seriously, Shani did not know that there were heated trolleys. She was expecting cable cars from a movie about San Francisco—open sides and people holding on to poles—but what pulls up looks more like a train car with sealed windows and warm air blasting from the front. If she'd known, she would've skipped the yoga pants and long sleeve tee she's added as base layers under her jeans and turtleneck.

As Jonas predicted, the cold means the ride is not sold out. They could each have their own bench if they want, but that defeats the purpose of this being a date. Jonas asks if she wants window or aisle and she claims the window seat. It'd be cooler to pretend she doesn't care, but she does care: it's her birthday (not that he's mentioned it, like, even once) and she's out in a polar vortex—she damn well better have a view of the lights.

She's off her game. She came into this night with her guard up, ready to catch him in any little slip-up, any proof she was right to

doubt him. But the boy is nothing but sweet and a little goofy; it's hard to play tough when he's flashing that lopsided grin at her.

Plus, having Jonas next to her is *nice*. He isn't holding her hand or anything yet, but from shoulder to knee, their bodies touch. Something is heating up for sure. As the tour starts, both peer out into the dark through the window on her side, and when she turns to say something to him, his face is so near, she's tempted to just plant a kiss on his lips.

But then she catalogs the contradictions between the stories he's told her and the ones he's told Ash, and that breaks the spell. She looks away.

Turns out they have the same taste in Christmas lights: the bigger, the brighter, the more over-the-top, the better. They both take selfies and tag each other on Instagram at a house where Santa's electric sleigh is pulled by eight life-size light-up hogs and a blinking sign that reads When Pigs Fly! Pity the stately old Victorian outlined in tiny white fairy lights next door: both give it two thumbs down—*boring*.

They are only divided on one house, a triple-decker that has so many colorful blinking lights they almost can't see the doors and windows. Jonas whistles. "They really went for it."

"That place?" She shakes her head. "It's like bad anime: all of the colors, none of the skills."

The trolley deposits them on a short block where every house is decorated. One has spotlights illuminating the flag of Italy. There are no reindeer, no angels, no Santas on this lawn, only a big ceramic figure of a happy chef stirring a pot of spaghetti, which

looks like it was stolen from the lobby of an Italian restaurant. Amusing.

"That's a whole mood!"

"What do you mean?"

"It's like they're trying *not* to do Christmas. Like, *eff you, neighbors—we're gonna celebrate Spaghetti instead.*"

Jonas nods and then walks across the snow to look more closely. "C'mere," he says. "If you look closely, it *is* a holiday display."

Shani crunches across the crystalline lawn and peers at the statue. It doesn't look any different. "You think?"

"Don't you see: He's not a chef, he's the Ghost of Christmas Past-a!"

It's mad corny but he's cracked himself up. Why not go with it?

"You know what he's making, right?"

"What?"

"Angel hair!"

Jonas's eyes gleam. "I got one: What's he singing?" She barely has time to mentally catalog Christmas carols before he answers.

"Away in a *mangia*!"

"Manga?"

"No, *mangia, mangia*—it's like 'eat up'!"

"How do you even know that?"

"Movies." He laughs. "Or maybe it's in my blood."

"What? You think you're Italian now?" The question starts out as a joke, but once the words are out, she can see the possibility too clearly. Suddenly, the dark curls and dusky skin look different to her. Wait. Is he not Black—not at all?

Jonas freezes, but not from the cold.

➤ **JONAS**

The look on her face tells him she's asking a real question. She knows. *She knows.* The goofiness of their puns has evaporated entirely and the air is thick.

"Um . . . about that. I . . . uh . . ."

Shani's eyes are locked doors. There might as well be a sign: Closed–Come Back Tomorrow. This isn't going to go well.

"I mean, I *might* be . . ." He cringes at how that sounds. "I might be anything."

"Like Black?"

"I–I could be."

"You sure made me think so."

"I know, I–"

"So that wasn't your mom I saw?"

"No . . . she's my foster."

"When I talk about Black shit, you're all Mr. *uh-huh* and *right* and nodding like you know. Might as well have raised your fist."

"I'm sorry. I know. I just–sometimes I think I could be–"

"Sometimes? Must be nice to pick and choose."

He feels sick in his stomach. "It's not, really. I'm not white enough to just be white and not–" He can't think of a way to end that sentence that doesn't suck.

"Black enough to be Black?" Her eyes are blazing and she has inched away from him on the bench. "There're a million ways to be Black, but wishing isn't one of them."

"I know." He swallows hard, feels tears welling up. Clearing his

throat, he looks straight ahead, not at her reproachful eyes. "I thought you'd get it. You're mixed, too."

"'Too?' So now you're mixed?" The scorn in her voice! "Mixed *what?*"

What is he supposed to say? "Valerie—my mom—"

"The real one? Or the fake one?"

"Um, don't call Foma fake. She's all I have."

"I'll call her whatever I want as long you get to make shit up."

Jonas closes his eyes. He wonders if anyone else is listening to this conversation. Pre-recorded carols drift from a speaker in the next yard. He feels sick. "My *birth* mom used to tell me a lot of stories about what I was or might be."

"Well, you have eyes. Was she white?"

"Um . . ." He feels helpless. "I don't know exactly."

"You don't know a lot."

"I want to. I took a DNA test."

"That ain't gone make you Black." Her words slap him and the blow stings. He feels like a moron. She folds her arms across her chest. "What about the rest of your family?"

"I don't have any. That's why I'm a foster." He hazards a look her way, for once in his life hoping to garner the sympathy he usually dreads.

No luck. "That doesn't make it okay to lie to me."

She's taking it too far. "I never said—"

"Did you or didn't you want me to think you're Black?"

He gives up. She's right. There's no point in arguing. He just nods, knowing the night is over.

Her voice is low. "That's some weird shit. Racist—I don't even know how."

"Hey!"

He gulps and can't think what to say to that. How long has it been since they dashed out of Il Braggadocio laughing? A hundred years? A lifetime?

The trolley chimes a bell to call the riders back. Shani stomps up the stairs and Jonas follows, heart pounding, to their old seats. The trolley rolls past a house with a *Frozen* theme and heads down a block lined with LED candy canes.

There's nothing left to do but tell the truth. There's a good reason he can't give her the answers she wants; life hasn't exactly given him those answers, either. "Listen," he says. "I shouldn't have let you think I was something I might not be. But it's not like I know. And I *want* to know. I've wanted that as long as I can remember.

"When Valerie died, the social workers couldn't find any relatives at first. If they existed, we never had them in the house. I mean, my mom seemed so free of other people that she might as well have come from space. Eventually, they figured out that she was adopted. She'd been taken by an older couple, but they were long dead at this point. There had been another daughter who was equally hard to find, and when they did locate her, news of my existence didn't tug on the old heartstrings, I guess.

"Before my mom was gone, I didn't wonder about any of this. When you're a kid, you don't think so much about 'what' you are; everything you see just *is*. I was Valerie's and we were kinda tan in the winter, brown in the summer. We weren't like the Irish people

upstairs any more than the Cambodian family down the hall. We were just *us*.

"But uh . . . after that . . . all the fosters were white. Some of them made it clear I was not. Not enough, at least. One of them told me to use more soap." He's never told anyone that story. It hurts to hear it out loud now and he has to take a breath. His voice drops. "Some watched me like I might steal from them. They never said why but I, uh, I got it.

"My case worker was the only person I knew who was darker than me, until I met Evelyn Prosper and she took me in. I wondered if maybe she was my mom's mom. I asked her straight up, *Are you my granny?* She just laughed and said she was nobody's granny, but she had been like a mom to eight kids before me. She *meant* that I was in good hands with her, but at seven, I thought it was a warning, like this lady had a revolving door and I wouldn't be there long. Except she didn't and I wasn't.

"She came up with the nickname Foma, short for foster ma. I've never called her Evelyn, not out loud. And I never call her Mom. She's my Foma and I've lived with her longer than I lived everywhere else combined."

Shani stares out the window. Has her posture softened, just a little? He's not sure.

"When you saw Foma and assumed she was my mother . . . I mean, it felt *right*. I had a flash: Why can't *how I live* be *who I am*?" God, he wishes she'd say something. "It made more sense in my head. I just . . . I liked the feeling of being found."

This is the longest speech Jonas has made all year. Maybe ever. And Shani doesn't say a word. What is she thinking?

> **SHANI**

She feels him on the identity piece. It's not the same, of course—she knows exactly which people she comes from—but she's spent a lifetime being sorted by her looks. Once or twice a year, her dad grabs his pennywhistle (which she thinks of as the whitest instrument ever) and goes to an Irish session in Mooreville at the Crag, which hosts live music jams every weekend. When she was little, she thought the sessions were fun. But the older she got, the more she noticed how often she was the only Black person, her skin and hair giving no hint of any shared history with these people. She might not have minded, except that some of them seem to notice, too. Their eyes read her like a book in a foreign language. She stopped going.

So, fine, maybe Jonas has had a taste of what it's like to be not quite white—every brown kid can tell you how eyes follow them in a store. But that isn't Black. She can't explain what it feels like in her body, in her soul, how she is connected to something and has been since she could see and hear. She can't explain it; he has to *know* it. Which he doesn't.

It's not about him being mixed. She's gone on dates with mixed and brown guys of all sorts. Mexican, Cape Verdean, Thai. Jonas's coloring isn't much lighter than most of those guys; the difference is that Jonas lied to her. What do you say to a liar once he tells the truth? How do you know when the lying is done?

He's as far away on the seat as he can be now, sagging into his parka. "I don't know what I was thinking," he says. "I really don't."

. . .

That he did it to be what he thought she wanted isn't comforting or flattering; it just makes her feel more like the target of a scam. And there are still so many questions: Where does he live? What's his real name? Is anything he said *tonight* true?

Doubt pushes into her chest, the blade deep.

She is known among her friends as tough, a girl who takes no nonsense. Her teachers see her as the good student, always on top of things. Her nursing instructors think of her as unflappable. Her subscribers get a weekly dose of confident Black girl magic. What sense does it make to let some boy rattle her like this? And what made him think he could lead her on and be forgiven just cause he's sad? That's not a free pass.

The trolley rolls along, silence heavy on their bench, until the Illuminations tour leader, a flamboyant Asian man with a purple scarf that looks like coral, comes by with a tray of hot chocolates in paper cups. Shani takes one without thinking and so does Jonas, their gloved hands touching briefly, which seems to burn him. He spills his a little on the tray and the tour leader says not to worry but looks unhappy even so.

She wishes she hadn't come. Whatever made her think snaring Jonas in his own contradictions would be satisfying? When the moment came, there was no *gotcha!* He had folded like a napkin as soon as she called him out.

Tired, not triumphant, she rings the bell to stop the trolley. She's already been taken for a ride.

THIRTEEN
ASH

Ash doesn't leave his bed, a warm cocoon of blankets. He's been lying awake trying to decide what to text Jackson.

Merry Christmas. If you're into that sort of thing.

He selects a screenshot from an old TikTok and sends it, wondering how Jackson will respond. He figures Jackson must be a little blue because, according to Shani's telling, she left him halfway through the trolley tour.

In theory, it means he and Jonas should be over, too. No need to catfish the boy, the truth being out and all. But here he is, choosing between stills of a Christmas video he filmed, desperate to send Jackson the perfect one.

And why not? It's not like Jackson lied to *him*. Ash got the real name, the truth about his foster mom, and the scoop about the apartment. Maybe what Jackson needed all along was a boy, not a girl, to be true to. If that's the case, it's better for Jackson and Shani both that their date went south. Ash has done them both a favor.

Now, maybe, he can do one for himself. He chooses a cute pic and hits send.

➤ JONAS

Um, woah.

Jonas has been in a fog all morning, but then Ash started texting and, well, it's not what he expected.

Ash dressed in a tight red onesie with a buckled black leather belt and a Santa hat. Jonas would feel ridiculous in any part of that outfit, but Ash makes it work. With the onesie unbuttoned halfway, it's even kinda sexy.

He shouldn't even be entertaining that kind of thought. He has damage to repair with Shani. He had thought their date was going well up until the trolley; there was definitely a spark, a live version of the connection they had online that yielded whole new sensations for him. But she got off the trolley three stops early and left him there, feeling ashamed.

Another message from Ash. Xmas plans?

The truth is too depressing to type. So he dodges. Eat junk. Sleep. Repeat. U?

In truth, his only plan is Sunrise. Visiting hours start at 8 a.m. Foma likes him to come early and he's already too late for that, but he should go soon so she isn't waiting too much longer.

Ash dings in. Your plan is terrible. Come over. Discover the magic of CubIndian xmas. He follows up with a gif of people throwing rice.

➤ **SHANI**

Shani wants to be texting Jonas so bad it hurts, but she texts Ash instead just to stay distracted.

Big plans for xmas?

Returning all my gifts online. U?

Presents. Church stuff. Chinese food. Movie.

CHURCH stuff?

Ash always gives her grief about the fact that, once in a blue moon, she goes to church. It's not like she's Sheree, there in a pew every week. It's an increasingly rare part of her life, just annual holiday visits that remind her of her mom, who loved church. Ash knows she doesn't go along with everything the church says; what he doesn't know is that she really does believe in heaven and hell. Boy would never let her hear the end of it.

One day a year I'm an angel. LOL. Praying hands emoji. Smiley with halo.

She's not feeling angelic or smiley. If she had a flamethrower, she'd burn shit down. It doesn't matter that Jonas's story is sympathetic. What matters is that once again, for a third time, she's let someone dishonest into her heart. What draws them to her? Why can't she see through them sooner?

Mantra time. *I'm tough. I'm smart. I deserve better.* It's not as soothing as she'd like.

Wanna come watch Scrooge? It's an impulse asking Ash over, but she's as sad as she is mad. She watches the old British musical every single year and knows all the lyrics by heart. If Ash comes, he'll sing all the songs with her and by the time she

has to deliver food baskets tonight, she'll be better able to plaster on a smile.

But he texts a distressed-looking cat with the caption OH NOESSSS!

And then: ANOTHER TIME.

Bah humbug.

➤ ASH

Over by the synthetic Christmas tree, a white faux spruce adorned with sixty precisely placed rose gold bulbs, Raj and Gloria are cleaning up the mess from opening presents, Gloria carefully smoothing and folding expensive wrapping paper, Raj making separate stacks of cardboard and plastic. Ash's clean-up was easy: he asked for and received only gift cards. It irritates Raj because it's impersonal but Ash insists anyway, because really, who trusts middle-aged people to shop?

Jackson hasn't answered his text about coming over. Maybe he thinks Ash is kidding. So he texts again.

Srsly. It'll be fun.

The thought of spending time alone with Jackson is like plugging in Christmas lights inside Ash. He feels brighter and warmer at the mere idea. Maybe Jackson is another of Ash's crushes, but he isn't like any of the guys from the dating apps. There something about him that says it could be great.

Or a disaster. Will he be cool? Ash hates having to consider this,

so he pushes the thought down and focuses on imagining what it would be like if they kissed. Which they can't do if Jackson won't answer.

➤ JONAS

Jonas considers it. Foma tires of company (even his) after an hour or so, two tops. Having Ash's to look forward to would change the contours of the day for sure. He has nothing cool to wear–for that matter, he might not have anything even clean–but so what? He types yes and is rewarded with a personalized Bitmoji of Ash doing a cartwheel.

At Sunrise House, it looks like there was a special on tinfoil garland. The doors and windows, the reception desk, even some of the walkers have been trimmed in sparkly gold and green fringe. Someone has fashioned a Christmas tree of poinsettia plants stacked in tiers, its base outlined with a white fence to keep the cats away.

Parelle sees Jonas and doffs her Santa hat. "Wear this! Evelyn will love it!"

She doesn't wait for him to agree; she's tugging it down over his dark curls, which he'd combed to look nice. He grimaces, but she seems pleased. "Perfect!"

She eyes the gift bag in his hand. "Aww, that's sweet. Some of our guests aren't getting presents today. Or even visitors. You're a good kid."

He's afraid she'll ask what he brought, not because he's

embarrassed by his homemade presents, but because he might cry if he has to explain.

. . .

A few days before his first Christmas with Foma, they picked out a tree from the pay-what-you-want corner at the back of the Boy Scout tree lot. The trees in that section weren't quite as bad as Charlie Brown's, but he could see why they weren't up front with the fifty- or even hundred-dollar trees. (The big-ticket trees were in a separate fenced section outlined with white string lights to announce their exclusivity.) Foma announced that she *always* got her tree from the back and always paid exactly ten bucks, making the tree a bigger bargain every single year. That year, she let him choose, and he picked a skinny tree whose top kind of curled over to one side, like a gnome tipping his hat. *How do you do?* the tree said, at least in Jonas's seven-year-old mind, and it made him so happy he barely noticed the celebrity firs on their way out.

When they got the tree home, he was glad they had a skinny tree, because it was no joke carrying it up to the third floor. Once it was hammered into Foma's seriously old-school tree stand, she said, "That's that." He figured they'd decorate it right then and there, but she said it would spoil Christmas Eve to get ahead of themselves. "There's a way to do things," she told him. "You'll see." And then it just stood there for two days looking kinda forlorn, which made him sad. That gnome wasn't tipping his hat—he was hanging his head.

Foma woke him on Christmas Eve morning, yanking off his

blankets and telling him they had a big day ahead, so no more lolly-gagging, a word he'd never heard before. First order of business: make ornament dough.

Valerie hadn't been crafty. Their apartment had never been home to projects like turkeys made of paper plates and handprint tail feathers. He hadn't actually had his own box of crayons till Foma sprung for the sixty-four-pack with the sharpener on the side (warning him that he had to make them last). But Foma loved to make things herself. The bathroom had a spare roll of toilet paper hidden beneath the hand-knitted skirt of a Black Barbie. The quilt on her bed matched their potholders, because Foma made both from remnants she got at the fabric store. And Christmastime was the ultimate. She'd create gift wrap from butcher paper covered with stenciled filigree outlined in metallic marker, and she always spent three or four nights making different flavors of fudge to fill tins for her friends.

That first Christmas Eve morning, she showed Jonas how nothing more than salt, water, and flour could quickly become like Play-Doh, which was the greatest invention he'd ever seen. They rolled out the dough and used cookie cutters to make snowflakes and gingerbread people and pigs. (He never did ask where the pig shapes came from.) After she showed him how to use a straw to poke a clean hole for the ribbon, they baked the ornaments-to-be until they were good and hard. Some they painted, some they covered with candies, all brushed with layer of Mod Podge to make everything shine.

It took all morning, and Jonas was so excited, he forgot to eat,

which was rare for him. But after he scarfed down three bowls of cereal for lunch, it was popcorn time. Foma used their biggest stockpot to make popcorn on the stovetop, and when it was ready, she taught him how to string the kernels on thick strands of coated thread. He'd never used a sewing needle and must have poked himself a half dozen times, though that was partly because she had *How the Grinch Stole Christmas* on TV and he kept looking up to watch. Before he had the last kernel strung, she'd gotten a second batch of corn finished. She joined him on the couch and they singed their fingertips with the fresh arrivals. As the corn cooled, they strung garland after garland, stealing kernels to eat as they went. They only paused to change the tape in Foma's VCR: *Rudolph's Shiny New Year, Polar Express*, and then back to *The Grinch*—her favorite— one more time.

It was getting dark when she finally started to wind colored lights around the branches. She shooed Jonas away while she worked, saying lights were the most important part, and that you have to be sure no branch feels unloved. It seemed to take her forever to work her way up the boughs, but it was a kind of magic when she got to the top and the last bulb on the string fit perfectly in the crook of the bent top. Even then, she didn't plug the lights in, not yet. *There's a way to do things.*

Decorating was the easy part after all that, pigs and snowflakes and popcorn garlands brightening up the green enormously. It no longer looked skinny or forlorn; it felt alive, bursting with personality.

Foma told Jonas to close his eyes while she plugged in the lights,

and he hopped up and down as he waited. It took her longer than he expected, but he didn't peek, and when she said he could look, it was amazing. Their spindly gnome had become a carnival ride. The lights cast their colors on the ornaments, while the green of the tree deepened to velvet. It took him a moment to see the top: Foma had Mod-Podged his photo onto a paper plate trimmed into the shape of a star.

He cried so hard, it almost scared her. He hugged her and hugged her while she hushed him. When he begged her to let them eat supper under the tree instead of at the table, she understood that his tears were not sad ones. She pulled out a picnic blanket and they sat cross-legged on the floor for a dinner of her best meatloaf and creamed corn. It became their ritual, unchanged all these years, even when Foma's back was bad and getting up off the floor was like paying for sins in a past life.

. . .

Last night was the first Christmas Eve Jonas had no tree. The smoothie he had with Shani was as far from meatloaf and creamed corn as possible. And though he still has Foma's VCR and the old tapes, he didn't watch *The Grinch*. He couldn't.

But he stayed up late into the night anyway, determined to keep at least some tradition. The proof is in his hands as enters Foma's room. She is propped up in bed but fast asleep. He doesn't wake her, just sets to work. From the gift bag, he pulls the popcorn strings he'd worked on in the dark early morning hours. By himself, it took a lot longer, and he hasn't made quite enough to go around the whole

room, but what he's brought adds cheer immediately. This year, he was generous with cranberries, which they started adding when he was eighth grade, and the pop of red helps the garlands stand out against the pale walls.

When he finishes hanging the popcorn, he pulls out a half dozen pig ornaments, his favorite. But now he's stuck. There's no tree and he probably shouldn't hang them on any of the equipment. He just stares at them, a decade of Christmas useless in his hands.

"The windowsill."

He turns toward the bed and Foma is watching, her face creased with pleasure to see what he has done. "Put them on the window-sill and I can see them from here."

He sits on the edge of her bed and rubs one of her hands between his. "Merry Christmas."

"Merry Christmas indeed," she says. "You probably broke some rule by smuggling in popcorn—some old bat is allergic to it, no doubt—and I *love* it."

She nods toward the water pitcher that is omnipresent on the rolling nightstand. He reaches for the pitcher to fill her cup and sees a box wrapped in reindeer paper. "Foma!" he says, swallowing hard. How can she have gotten him a present now?

"Don't get too excited." She sounds exhausted and very pleased with herself all at once. "Parelle asked if she could pick anything up for me at the store and I had a silly thought."

He doesn't have to open it to know it's Pop-Tarts.

➤ SHANI

Her dad's gift is . . . "Wow!" Shani forces a big smile. Says "Where did you get this?" with as much wonder in her voice as possible. Is she selling it?

She holds up the cartoon print scrubs and eyes the explosion of stylized figures–Chocotella, the Black girl from the donut planet, and her friends Candy Girl and Banana Anna–repeating in dozens of poses on a space backdrop alongside edible rockets and sugar constellations. She's seen them on stickers and notebooks, figurines, even handbags, but never like this.

Her dad's voice is full of pride. "I googled 'anime' and 'scrubs'– wasn't sure anything would come up and then I found this toki-doki guy. Bam! Perfect present for you."

Shani resists the urge to correct him: tokidoki's the brand. The artist is some Italian guy. And tokidoki isn't anime any more than it is Japanese. No point in explaining that and letting him have a sucky Christmas, too.

But now, he's second-guessing the present. "Is it okay?"

"Trust me, dad, no one else is going back to school next week in anime scrubs. You nailed it!"

She immediately dons the scrubs over her pjs, trying not wince at her reflection in the mirror. She isn't a girl who wears a lot of text or big prints, and these have both. Up to this point, she has always picked out her own scrubs, and she usually goes for Olives, a brand that looks more like athletic wear. She likes a fit that shows her curves and moves well. She might be emptying bedpans, but she

can still look sleek. This set is a little boxy, the only really shape being breast darts right out of the fifties. And the pattern is so noisy, it should come with a trigger warning. She'll wear it out the door on the first day of the term, making a big deal out of it, but wear her *real* scrubs underneath and peel off this nightmare before she's even off the bus.

"Let's get a pic." Snuggling in next to her dad, she snaps a selfie, knowing it will do the trick. And it does. He's relieved and starts talking about how hard it was to get the scrubs here on time, and how nervous he'd been. Might as well let him be happy, even if she's already thinking of a funny caption for this photo to send to Jonas.

Ouch.

There's a Jonas-sized void. The spontaneous texts she'd send him—who will those go to now? Who is she going to talk about *Tomo-e Girls* with? Not the BB5, not Ash. Jonas filled his own slot in her life, one she didn't know was there till six months ago, and in one night, it's an empty space again.

"Sweetheart?"

She doesn't know she's crying until her dad goes on. "I know you don't like hugs, but . . ."

He holds out his arm and she accepts it. Her dad isn't a big talker. He's tenderhearted but not an advice-giver or speechmaker. His love is in the doing, usually, and that's what he goes for now. "Want me to watch *Scrooge* with you? I can make us some brownies quick."

That's more like it. The scrubs are a miss, but he knows just what she needs otherwise. She surprises him with a kiss on the cheek. "I wish all guys were like you."

"Ahh," he says. "Boy trouble." He squeezes her close. "Tell me all about it."

And, for the first time in a long time, she does. She talks to him like she talks to Ash, trusting that once in a while, a dad can be a friend. She can use one today.

FOURTEEN
ASH

How do you dress for a date with a guy who doesn't yet know it's a date? This isn't actually the first time Ash has asked himself this question. It's not even the first time the guy in question is a friend's boyfriend. But somehow, this feels different.

Is Jackson into it? Ash takes stock of what he knows: Jackson liked Shani but has never mentioned other girls or boys. He could be bi or pan, or maybe just *open*. Openness is a good start; dating a trans guy is both like *and* unlike dating a cis guy. Jackson seems physically comfortable with Ash, so that's a positive sign. Hopefully, by the end of this afternoon, Ash will know whether or not he has a shot.

He snaps pictures of a cream-colored cashmere turtleneck and a long black sweater with leather-and-metal shoulder pads and texts them to Tee: Which is hotter?

It takes them a minute to reply. Is that all the merry xmas I get? Merry xmas! ANSWER.

Is it for that guy?

You know it.

The cream is too "rich Aunty."

Okay. Thx.

+ The black is too goth. He doesn't look goth.

??

Yellow zip-up.

OMG. Yes. (It's GOLD btw)

Why hadn't he thought of that? Ash signs off and rifles through the smaller of two closets to find a zip-up hoodie from Saks he coveted after watching the back-to-school haul of his favorite influencer. Gold with thick saffron stripes from shoulder to waist, it's a perfect complement for his coloring. He'd wear it more often, except St. Joe's has a dress code, plus it's already appeared on his social media and he doesn't like to repeat. He wriggles into soft crimson track pants and admires himself in the mirror. Tee for the win.

Gloria is reheating lechon asado for sandwiches. Most of the year, she's all about a plant-based diet, which she forces on everyone else, but Christmas Eve remains Nochebuena, with pork roasting for hours, the air redolent with garlic, sour orange, and cumin. Ash likes it even better the next day when they slice the meat for medianoche. He and his mom make their sandwiches on Cuban white bread rolls, which no one around here sells, so they have it delivered from a place on the North Shore. Raj, on the other hand, insists on making his with rustic whole wheat bread, which is a crime of some kind.

When Ash busies himself making two plates, precisely layering

lechon and ham and pickles and Swiss, Gloria pauses from making her own. "Are we having company?"

"Didn't I say?"

"No." Gloria eyes the living room, looking for hints of imperfection. "You did not."

"It's just Jackson. Your *mover*."

Gloria's green eyes glint with curiosity. "Oh? Is he . . . *special?*"

"God, you're embarrassing," Ash says, but he also wants to answer. "He might be . . . with a little help."

Before she can ask more, the doorbell chimes and they hear Raj, sounding surprised, invite Jackson in. Two parents at once is going to be more than any friend needs, so Ash quickly scoops black beans and rice onto each plate and heads for the hallway, leading Jackson up the stairs before Raj can protest.

In Ash's room, Jackson paces nervously, plate in hand. "Are you okay?" Ash asks, worried that he's made a mistake by bringing Jackson up here. He hadn't meant it to be a real seduction, just a place to be away from Raj and Gloria, but he realizes he could have brought Jackson to the movie room again or the game room or the finished basement. The color-changing LED lights ringing the room probably only ramp up Jackson's suspicion that Ash is coming on to him.

"Um. I . . ."

Following Jackson's gaze as it leaps from the white leather sofa to the fur bedspread to the glass desk topped with a MacBook Pro, Ash gets it. "Oh, god, don't worry about spilling. Our housekeeper's amazing." To prove it, Ash hops onto his bed crisscross style and takes a big bite of medianoche.

Jackson looks relieved and settles in on the sofa. His face brightens when he tries the rice and beans. "What do you call this?"

"Moros." Jackson waits for him to say more. "Short for 'Moros y Cristianos.'"

"I don't know what that means."

"Uh, Moors and Christians. The beans are the Moors . . . honestly, I think it might be racist."

"Weird." Jackson takes another bite. "But good. Really, really good. Is it easy to make?"

Like Ash cooks. "You'll have to ask my mom. But if you do, I'll never hear the end of it. 'Your friend's so nice. Why don't *you* appreciate me that way?'"

"Do you not appreciate her?"

"Of course I do, but she's such a validation queen. Says she needs to *hear* it." Mocking someone else is one of Ash's favorite bonding strategies, and he warms to it. "I'm like, Mami, you signed up for this when you and Dad had sex. No one's throwing a parade for you, because it's your *job* to do this shit for me." He rolls his eyes. "I shouldn't have to explain that I'm seventeen. At our age we get to take parents for granted. Am I right?"

Jackson doesn't answer, and it's still a full five seconds before Ash hears what he's just said. He sets his plate down and swallows. "I'm. So. Sorry. Your mom—I—"

"Nah. It's okay. My mom doesn't really factor into things . . . It's Foma." Jackson's voice is thick.

Ash goes to the couch. "What about her?"

"She's sick."

"How sick?"

"Her doctor said a healthy person in liver failure can last six months—"

"Oh, Jackson."

"—but she's *not* a healthy person." Jackson closes his eyes. Tears spill out between dark lashes anyway. Ash can't think of what to do but listen. "He said it just like that. Foma's heavy, sure, and I know she took stuff for her blood pressure, but the way he said it—like, criticizing her when she's gonna . . ." He gulps. "She's gonna die."

When Ash puts his arm around Jackson, it is purely for comfort. He is not wondering about Jackson's sexuality or trying to capitalize on the moment. Just being the best person he can be, the one you want by your side if you're crying. Jackson is taller than Ash is, and to rest his head on Ash's shoulder requires him to slouch way down on the sofa. But he settles in even so and cries.

It is rare for Ash to be grateful his dad is a new age guru, but at this moment he can hear his father's advice. *Lead by listening.* He doesn't speak for Jackson or prod with questions, just lets his friend work it out until the sobs wane. He rubs Jackson's arm and shoulder, listens to the quiet breathing, and matches it with his own.

The little flickers of guilt about betraying Shani that had been licking around his conscience all morning have disappeared. Someone needs to be here for Jackson. Usually, Ash isn't super focused on what other people need, but today he is. And it feels, well, right. He doesn't know how long they sit this way, Christmas distant as Mars.

Jackson breaks the silence. "Sorry about that . . ." He struggles

to sit up, and the awkwardness of the angle makes him fall a little. He places a hand on Ash's chest to steady himself.

Something happens then. Ash feels more than the pressure of the warm fingers. It's electric. Jackson seems to feel it, too. He looks at Ash with widening eyes and neither of them look away. He doesn't move his hand. They both lean into the touch without moving at all.

Ash has had so many crushes and boyfriends and dates, and still, he has never wanted to kiss anyone this badly in his whole life. He can feel the shift in the air, the way the distance between them might close. He can almost feel the softness of Jackson's lips, wet with tears, against his own. He could make the kiss happen if he leaned forward just a tiny bit more.

But he can't do it. If they are going to kiss, he doesn't want it to be a moment when Jackson is weak or vulnerable. It has to be a real choice.

He lifts Jackson's hand from his chest and solemnly presses his lips to Jackson's palm before placing the hand back on Jackson's own chest. If one person can simultaneously look confused, relieved, and thrilled, Jackson does.

Ash is thinking of a joke to break the spell when Jackson whispers, voice huskier than usual. "I don't know what just . . . I mean . . . did you *feel* that?"

Approximately never at a loss for words, Ash can only manage, "Yeah."

"Whoa." Jackson pulls away, slowly, shaking his head. "Thanks?"

It's a confusing sentiment, ending on a question mark like that.

And thanks for what—listening? The moment of spark? Not kissing him?

Jackson is on his feet, eyes on the door. "I'm gonna go."

"You don't have to—"

"I—Today's been a lot." He chews his lip for a minute and then looks Ash straight in the eyes. "But I'm glad I came."

Ash nods, heart racing. "Me too."

"Good," he says.

A sun breaking through rain clouds, Jackson's lopsided smile returns at last.

FIFTEEN
JONAS

The day isn't even over and it feels like it's been a week. He woke beating himself up over how he'd botched things with Shani, then just about fell apart when he saw Foma's present at Sunrise, and now he's just returned from Ash's, where he came this close to his first kiss ever. He'd felt all three things so keenly: shame, loss, hope. It was exhausting, and yet he can't pretend he isn't energized by the near-miss with Ash.

Maybe that's what I've been looking for all along?

The question of race wasn't the only thing that had kept Jonas from meeting Shani. He had worried just as much about whether they would have any chemistry. When he imagines being with someone, he's always pictured a girl, but he doesn't fantasize about them like most boys do. He doesn't really fantasize at all, which makes him worry that something inside is broken. Is he deficient? Because he's never really dated, there's been no way to tell. The longer he didn't meet up with Shani, the longer he didn't have to find out.

Ever since he first heard the term asexual, he's wondered if it applies to him. He's just never been *horny*—it's embarrassing but true. Then last night with Shani, he experienced the first hint of that thing that everyone talks about. Electricity, maybe? It felt like the beginning of an answer to the puzzle of attraction—at least until he went to Ash's and felt something different but equally potent.

What does it mean? Nobody goes from ace to bi in twenty-four hours, right? He can't tell if he's more or less confused.

What he does know is that when Ash calls him, he will answer. Aside from the way he's fudged his name, Ash is the only one he's told the rest of his truth. This means not waiting for the other shoe to drop, not keeping his stories straight. Possibility fills him.

He sits down at his iPad Pro and taps the glass. The print screen is still up with the gallery of art he made for Shani; his glow dims a little. A day ago, he felt possibility with her, and now he's already considering someone else. What is wrong with him? Maybe he's not meant to date *anyone*. Maybe he was better doing what he always did before: keeping everyone but Foma at a distance.

His stomach rumbles. He dials Lucky Star, grateful that the family celebrated last night and are back to work today. He splurges, ordering a double order of scallion pancakes to go with the General Tso's and rice. And when it arrives, he makes sure to give the guy a decent tip—he knows firsthand how much tips matter.

If Foma was home, they'd be watching a movie now. He finds her favorite, *Princess Bride*, on one of those illegal download sites to stream it. It's not the same, watching it without her, because they always said the best lines out loud together, and it feels weird to do

that alone. But there's something comforting about it even so; when he first moved in with her, he had seen Foma as being like the movie's grandfather, a not-parent taking care of a little boy. And for years, he thought Wesley and Buttercup, with their funny banter and inability to resist each other, were the model of a couple. Looking at them now, he realizes that both are equally beautiful—and a funny question pops into his head: *Am I a Wesley or a Buttercup?* No answer comes.

Right in the middle of the "Wuv, Twoo Wuv" wedding speech, the phone rings. It's Flasker.

"Merry Christmas, bud."

"Merry Christmas. You at Melory's?"

"*Actually* . . ."

"Actually what?"

"I'm at Layla's."

"Layla who?"

Flasker laughs. "I can't help it if everyone loves me."

"You are the biggest player I know!"

"Nope. I just have a wide capacity for love."

A question starts to form that might or might not be totally wrong to ask. "Can I ask you something . . . personal?"

"Shoot. You know me: open book."

"What's it like to date a trans guy?"

"I wouldn't know. I'm into women."

Jonas cringes, but Flasker is only giving him shit. "I'm kidding—I know what you meant. But there's no universal trans dude. Not in body, if that's what you're asking, and definitely not in personality.

There's no manual—you learn as you go with the person you're with. Which is *always* true for everybody, anyway."

"Yeah, I guess that's obvious. I just—"

"You've never been kissed, right?" It's that obvious. "I didn't know you were into guys."

Jonas gets up and paces while answering, the jitters shaking his legs. "I didn't either. I don't know if I really am now. I mean, I'm into one guy at least. I just felt *something* with this kid—"

"That you hadn't ever felt?"

Well, not exactly. He felt something like it on the date with Shani. But he's ruined that, so . . .

Flasker gives up waiting for confirmation. "If you have chemistry, you have chemistry. Get it."

Standing at the window, watching the silver clouds scudding across the sky, Jonas almost whispers. "I think he has more experience than me."

"Someone always does," Flasker adds. "That's actually good news for you, virgin. The worst is two people groping about in the dark cluelessly their first time."

Whoa. Jonas hasn't actually pictured his first time—not with Shani *or* Ash. He's still trying to get his head around the near-kiss this morning. Why is he so behind every other person his age?

Flasker picks up on his silence. "You there?"

"Yeah . . . I just . . ." He swallows hard. "I just don't want to be a letdown."

"Bad news: you have no say in what he'll like or not like. The only person you have control over is you. So do what feels right for

you and if it's a match, it's a match. If it isn't, someone else will give you that feeling."

"Sure, you'd say that—you make it look easy."

"I wouldn't say it's exactly easy to do Christmas at Melory's and at Layla's in the same day, but I feel ya. And I better get going—it's not too late to hit a third house."

Jonas laughs, even though he's not sure Flasker is kidding, and says goodbye.

His eyes fall on the box of Pop-Tarts on the counter, but they're too precious to eat. He opens the second bucket of scallion pancakes, which he meant to save for tomorrow, and starts in on them. *Do what feels right for you* seems like impossible advice, since all his feelings are so new. Is he into Ash because he's still hurt that Shani ditched him? If she hadn't, would they be a couple now? Does he want either of them the way they'd expect a guy to?

Impulsively, he types a question in to Google: WHAT IS WRONG WITH ME? He's not expecting a real answer, but the search engine delivers 1.3 billion. As far he can tell, none of them apply.

SIXTEEN
SHANI

There has never been a better time to deliver holiday food baskets than now. Having something to do keeps Shani's mind from spinning uselessly over things ending with Jonas.

Shani's dad is being a good sport about driving Shani, Sheree, and Yanique (the only ones who showed up) from address to address on the church's donation list. Big families get packing boxes full of canned soup and bags of rice and cake mixes. It takes two girls to carry just one of those boxes, the third acting as doorbell ringer and explainer. (That matters because no one knows the food is coming—surprise!) They have to walk sideways like crabs, one girl on each end of the box, and it's a struggle. Shani likes it better when it's a single person, especially someone old, because the load is just one large grocery bag and not so heavy.

Most of their destinations have been in Mooreville, and their last stop is no different. After this, she and her dad will eat turkey (her dad insists it's a Christmas food) and watch the *Home Alone* movies

in order until he falls asleep on the couch, which might as well be his bedroom for how often he passes the whole night there. Her dad has a routine: he falls asleep ten minutes into the *Late Show*, which is his white noise (like, white in every way). It's been six whole years since her mom's accident, but he still calls his room "their" room and kind of avoids it. Some nights, he wakes up on the sofa and realizes he never went to bed and moves into "their" room, but more often, he just stays where he is. It used to annoy Shani because she couldn't just watch TV when she had trouble sleeping, but her phone takes care of that now. She likes to joke with him that he should use the money he saves on pajamas to get her a car.

Her dad parks in a half-cleared spot on Prospect St. Like most things on Prospect, the building isn't pretty; just a *Minecraft*-square box of brick. It's affordable housing of some kind and they have to make multiple stops. Fortunately, no families this time, so at least no massive box.

They have a routine: one girl knocks, the next makes a little speech, and the third hands over the groceries. They're going to start on the top floor and work their way down. Shani is surprised when the first person to answer the door is around her age, a freckle-faced redhead in a Billie Eilish hoodie. As soon as she says thank you and takes the food into her apartment, Shani and her friends have to debrief.

"What's that about?"

"Right? Old people, people with kids—that I get. But some white girl old enough to work?" Sheree's disdain is large. She has a firm idea of what a charity case should look like and that isn't it.

"Maybe's she sick," Yanique interjects.

"She don't look sick."

Shani prods her cousin. "She also doesn't look *deaf*." She gestures at the door hoping Sheree will consider that the girl can probably hear them.

Her dad just wants to keep them on task. "Let's keep it moving, girls," he says.

The second stop is clearly a solo, based not only on the size of the bag Shani is holding, but the predominance of single-serving ramen cups. It's Sheree's turn to knock and she's not shy about it, rapping the door so that the sound echoes off the painted concrete hallway. Shani uses her free hand to check her phone as the door opens.

She hears Yanique start the speech. "Every year at this time, Grace Fellowship collects goods for the needy—" She corrects herself too late with the preferred wording. "Um, *our friends in need*, to help make the holidays brighter. From us to you," she says, pausing long enough for them all to join in on cue for the finish.

"Merry Christmas!"

Shani raises her eyes from her phone and suddenly she's staring at Jonas.

For a moment, they all just stand there. Jonas is frozen. The other girls don't seem to know who they're seeing. Sheree has no clue why Shani is suddenly a statue and grabs the bag to hand over to Jonas, who receives it numbly. Maybe Jonas means to say thank you, but what comes out is "I'm . . . I'm the *needy?*" He sounds wrecked.

Shani's dad is on it. "We can all use a lift once in a while. I've been there."

In any other situation, Shani would want to know what her dad's talking about. When was he poor enough for a food basket? But right now, all she can focus on is Jonas's face. He looks like he's been slapped and his ears are still ringing.

Forget the stories, the confusion over whether there's a mom or stepmom or anyone else behind that door. She thinks about the date, how he bravely opened the door for her at a restaurant she now knows for certain he could not possibly afford. She thinks about the trolley ride tickets and how the pair probably cost more than the groceries in this bag. Pushing past her cousin, she stands in front of Jonas. "Are you okay?"

He looks away, embarrassed.

Yanique clocks it. "No shit. Is this the guy?"

Jonas sags where he stands. Shani has to do something. "Yes. Sheree, Yanique, Dad . . . this is Jonas."

Jonas's eyes meet hers and what she sees in them isn't entirely happy, but not entirely sad, either. He takes a deep breath. "Nice to meet you guys." He tries, but fails, to smile at Shani's dad. He doesn't invite them in. "I . . . uh . . . didn't know you were coming."

Shani takes his free hand. "I didn't know you lived here . . ." Echoes of his past half-truths float on the air between them. She pushes them away. Goes big. "Aw, who am I kidding? I'm just a stalker!" They both laugh weakly at this.

"Selfie time!" Yanique has been wanting to take pictures all afternoon, but that's a no-no. The church only allows it if the

recipient asks for one; otherwise, it's a little like saying *Look at me being more fortunate with the less fortunate.*

Maybe because he's not exactly a stranger or maybe because they're all thrown off by this turn of events, they do the selfie, all crowded together behind Yanique. When Yanique calls out "Say Cheese!" and makes an upside-down peace sign at the camera, Shani does her best this-is-fine smile, but watching Jonas's reflection in the viewfinder, she can see how much work it is for him to do the same.

Her dad coughs, signaling time to go. Jonas thanks them, solemnly shaking hands, and that would be that, but she can't leave it this way.

She turns to the girls. "You guys do the last few without me. I'll meet you at the car."

Her dad uses eyebrow telepathy to say he doesn't want to leave her alone with this guy, but Sheree and Yanique are already headed down the hall. He follows reluctantly, but not before throwing Jonas a dad-on-the-porch-with-a-shotgun look.

"I really didn't know," she says when they're alone.

"Yeah . . . that's kinda my bad," he says, and opens the door.

His apartment is a room. A biggish one, but still a room. Like it's a dorm or he's an inmate somewhere not awful. Hawaii greets her from behind his sofa. There's not a lot of other decoration, aside from a framed photo of him and the woman she'd seen that first day. His foster mom's smile tells a story of a happier time; it practically leaps out of the frame.

He sees her looking and sighs. "So . . ." He sets down the groceries and the story comes out.

Foma's illness.

Maple Crest.

Sunrise House.

Moving into the apartment.

All of it had happened in the time since they met online, and it's the first Shani's heard of it.

"Why not just tell me?"

He raises his hands in a gesture of helplessness. "I hate it when people feel bad for me."

"What? Why?"

"Nah, I mean it. Like, sympathy is the worst."

Today must suck. "Oof. We brought you *food*."

"Yeah, you did." He stares at the bag for a moment. "How did they even pick me? There must be poorer people."

"Boy, you're seventeen, paying for an apartment on part-time mover money."

He shrugs and then manages a half smile. "I guess. I have some help." The smile dims again. "In middle school, saying I was a foster was the kiss of death. So I stopped telling people. In high school, I just kind of stayed vague. Who really wants to know about anyone's family anyway? I just wanted to be normal, and I kinda felt like I was . . . until this happened."

Shani wants to say something comforting, but what? She knows firsthand what it will cost him when his foster mom—the realest mother he's ever had—dies. And she can't convincingly say what her dad would: *It'll be okay, I got you.* Humor is her escape hatch. "Normal's overrated anyway. You weren't attracted to me for my dull personality."

She detects the tiniest reaction when she says the word "attracted."

His reply helps. "Your name and the word 'dull' have never appeared in the same sentence."

"*Facts.*"

And then it is quiet again, his eyes on the unopened grocery bag. Should she offer to take it away? "Will you eat that stuff, or . . ."

He nods. "Yeah . . ." he admits, voice low. "It'll help me get by till my next gig." But he doesn't touch it.

That's all she needs to hear. Shani goes to the bag and produces the six-pack of noodle cups. "Where do you keep ramen?"

One item at time, they unpack. Mac and cheese. Minute Rice. Cans of chicken noodle soup. Stovetop stuffing. Pringles and Wheat Thins. The gloom begins to lift as they discuss the relative merits of each item, discovering that one guy's trashy is another girl's treasure: he loves Dinty Moore beef stew, which she finds vile, but she is equally passionate about the fried onions in a pull-top can, and he can't imagine being excited over such a thing.

"Do you recycle?"

He takes the emptied bag from her hands, their fingertips brushing. "No. I need it to hide my shame." In a flash, he has pulled it over his head. It's a joke, but it's too close to the truth.

She lifts it away from his beautiful face, no longer caring what the duskiness of his skin means. "You don't need to be ashamed! Just be honest with me. Okay?"

They are only inches apart and he looks like he wants to close the gap. He doesn't, instead murmuring, "Okay. *Okay.*"

She can almost feel him, they're so close. The space between them almost pulses, as if they are magnetized. Ever so subtly, he moves closer. His amber-flecked eyes search hers, but he doesn't say a word. Should she take the lead? Should she kiss him? Something warns her off.

"I better get going. My dad's gone have mad questions."

"Thank you for coming." He's so earnest, it hurts.

"Didn't plan to!"

He takes her hand. "I mean for staying after . . ."

"Sometime, you can invite me for real."

"Sometime, I will."

SEVENTEEN
ASH

Ash loves that Christmas and New Year's are exactly a week apart, because it forces schools to give kids at least that entire week off. Years that both days fall on a Thursday are the best, because no one sends kids back to school on January 2, so you get a bonus day. No luck this year with both occurring on a Monday, but it's still great to wake up knowing the rest of the week is his to do with as he chooses. Today, he will do the insane thing of going to the mall, which will be full of a zillion other kids who A) are returning clothes because their parents think they have any idea what teenagers wear or B) are like Ash and have wise parents who gave them gifts cards instead.

Raj offered to drive, which Ash now sees was a ploy to trap him into a lecture. Currently, his dad is explaining how malls are the blackheads that show the toxicity beneath the pretty face of capitalism. Fortunately, Ash had asked Shani to come, so he isn't enduring this speech alone. Ten minutes into Raj's jeremiad

about the tragedy of wage inequality, Shani texts Ash from the backseat.

Isn't ur dad a millionaire?

Ash replies with a head-exploding emoji. Irony was never Raj's strong suit.

It's a relief when he deposits them by Nordstrom and says he'll be back in a few hours. Ash, per usual ritual, makes a beeline straight for Ebar, the store's café. He orders two Mexican mochas, knowing the way to Shani's heart is through caffeine and chocolate. She hates Nordstrom—the prices *and* the aesthetic—but he needs to keep her mood elevated. He has competing tasks: make her feel good about ending things with Jackson *and* prepare her for the moment he reveals his own crush. Both will involve dropping hints about Jackson liking boys, but he'll start with good best friend behavior, which means a big mocha and only a small amount of time in the Topman section of Nordstrom.

"I'll be quick," he says. "And then you can drag me to Sephora or wherever."

"Deal," she says, looking too pleased.

"That was easy."

"Wasn't planning on Sephora, though. I'm gunning for PINK."

Bra shopping? Doesn't he deserve a get-out-of-jail-free card on this one?

When his expression curdles, Shani pokes him. "You'll live." She pushes him to toward the Topman racks. "Now hurry and buy some ugly-ass thing you saw in a magazine. If we stay too long, they'll think I'm shoplifting."

He hates it when she jokes like that, partly because it's true. And because it doesn't apply to him. No one has ever followed him around a store; it's as if they just know his wallet is *stocked*. Even in ambiguity, his brown registers differently to racists than hers; his Indian features usually move him into a safe category. Not white exactly, but white-adjacent.

Trying not to linger, Ash discovers a red felt overcoat with hidden pockets secreted into the side seams. It would be perfect for Valentine's, now only six weeks away. He can already picture how cute he'll look wearing it with a black turtleneck and leather pants when he and Jackson go—hmm. When they go where? Maybe somewhere in Harvard Square. Definitely not Arlmont.

"Are you gone buy it or just feel it up?" Shani breaks his reverie and he returns to the moment. He doesn't even try the overcoat on or look at the tag. He just grabs his size, feeling the spark of satisfaction that happens whenever a shopping trip starts so well, and heads straight for the cash wrap to ring out.

When he's finished, she's smiling at her phone.

"What is it?"

She shows him a text from Jackson (well, on her phone it's Jonas, but he knows better); it's a selfie of him sniffing a bowl of Dinty Moore beef stew. YUM!!

Nasty! she texts.

Don't be TOO jealous.

This was not in his plan. "You're texting again? Didn't you storm off the trolley in flames?"

"I saw him yesterday . . . unexpectedly." She doesn't explain

further, which is very unlike her, and Ash feels a little flutter of panic. Who's playing who here?

Sound casual. Sound casual. "Oh, yeah? Where?"

"His apartment."

This is news in every way and he is not loving it. Before he can figure out how to press for more details without sounding like the supremely jealous person that he is, Shani is distracted by a white woman with two Nordstrom bags hanging from each elbow and a fifth slung over her shoulder; she hurries by, fanning herself as if it's all too much. Shani discreetly snaps a shot of the woman's grimace and texts it.

"Show me!" Ash practically whinnies.

Of course the snap is to Jackson. The caption stings. Hard to be rich.

The reply isn't much better. I'll never know. LOL

They cannot be bonding over lack of income! This is so not good.

Then Shani gasps. "Shit."

She shows Ash Jackson's text: Are you at the mall? My friend Ash is there too! I feel left out. LOL

Shani looks at Ash with wide eyes. "How does he know that?"

"We were texting about the project and I said I was going."

"Great. Now I have to say something!"

"Do you though?"

"He used your name. How many Ashs can there be in this town?" She makes a decision. "I guess it had to come out sometime, especially if he's going to be my boyfriend—"

"BOYFRIEND?"

Was it not just yesterday that Jackson was in Ash's room filling the air with lightning like Tesla?

"I got it," she says, and taps the screen.

You mean ASH PATEL?

Jackson's reply is immediate. You know him???

Her fingers fly. Laugh emoji. I'm-dead skull emoji. Exclamation marks. He's one of my best friends!

Jackson sends back a gif of a cartoon head exploding.

Shani breathes out. "That wasn't so bad." She nods as if affirming her own wisdom. "It was perfect, really—came out all natural, not weird."

Ash does not love this. He should be steering the ship here, but suddenly Shani is back in the game. He pulls out his phone to get back in the ring.

You know Shani?!!

Yes!

I'm at the mall with her right now.

That's the girl I told you about!

Ash texts a meme of a minion saying WHAAA??

Nothing suggests Jackson sees through this, but it still feels dicey. Usually, Ash loves the thrill of nearly-but-not-quite caught, the adrenaline of pulling one over. This feels different: he doesn't want to be caught at all. The game has gone from exposing a secret to keeping one. It's all he can think about as they head for lunch. Toting a PINK bag the size of a mini-fridge, Shani drags him to the food court, where everything bad for you. He always ends up getting a cupcake filled with a shot of ice cream or a bacon-covered hot dog anyway—the mall is where standards go to die.

Today, he orders an Oreo milkshake, which he's secretly very excited about, while Shani gets a large order of tangerine chicken from Walk the Wok. Sadly for them, there's nowhere to sit, and they end up crowding into the family benches that outline the indoor play area, getting dirty looks because they obviously have no kids in tow. One dad in the suburban uniform of chinos and Allbirds, looking deeply aggrieved, points to the NO FOOD ALLOWED sign, and they studiously ignore him.

"So when did you go to Jackson's—" He adjusts, to play nice. "Jonas's?"

Shani tells him about the grocery delivery. "You had to see his face."

"When he realized it was you?"

"That too, but more when he saw the food basket. Like he didn't know he was poor until that very second."

"Nobody wants to be poor. Broke, sure, because it sounds temporary. But poor? Poor is like a *condition*."

"It's nice to know the truth. That he wasn't lying about the apartment."

"Well, not to *me*. I don't remember him telling you about it." God, that came out bitchy.

"You know what I mean. Everything's in the open."

Ash sucks on the straw. "*Maybe...*"

Shani's brows knit together in irritation. "What's the matter with you? I'm telling you I've seen his life with my own eyes now. This changes things."

"I'm just saying, don't get your heart set on him ... He may not be what you think." This is going to be even trickier than he imagined.

He needs to make Jackson sound bad for her, but not universally bad, because at some point he needs to win her over to the idea that Jackson is good for him.

She sucks her teeth. "Well, you weren't there."

Right back at ya, sister.

He has to play it cool but he also can't let it go. "I think," Ash begins, "you've been burned before. Twice! Even if you didn't tell me until, like, days ago, catching him in a lie hurt you enough to plan this whole con. And suddenly you're all Lady Miss Trusting?" He shakes his head. "It's *my job* as your friend to keep it real."

"Well, it ain't your job to tell me my own mind."

Ash knows her this-is-the-time-to-shut-up voice, and wisely, he surrenders. "I wouldn't dare."

A chunk of Oreo is stuck in the straw and he focuses on it like a major task so he doesn't have to look at her. The day is going to hell. Selling Shani on not trusting the same guy he has a crush on is a recipe for disaster. If Jackson wants to be with Ash, shit really will hit the fan when Shani finds out. She's going to remember this conversation and know what he was up to and it won't be pretty. He wonders if he should have just kept his mouth shut, period.

The thing to do is to let go of these feelings entirely. But they're so new and so *delicious*. Their near-kiss was a mutual thing. Ash reminds himself that dropping Jackson for Shani's sake would actually be selfish, ignoring Jackson's *obvious* attraction. And letting Shani chase Jackson when the boy is clearly into him would be tragic. No, it can't be done.

It doesn't help to sit here talking about him. "So what else is

going on this week?" He doesn't really care about her answer—it's Arlmont, how much could there be?—but it's time to change topics.

"Have to do some stuff for my channel. And start applying for scholarships. My English teacher hooked me up with a website."

"Isn't it a little early for all that?"

"Not all of us can pay cash for school."

"Come on. It's not like I'm a *Kardashian*."

"Not with that flat ass." Touché.

But Shani is right that he feels no particular pressure. He has only dream schools; he won't need safeties. He can afford to go wherever he wants as long as they let him in. He'll apply legacy to Stanford, and his mom is on the Board of Trustees at Amherst. And he's bound to graduate summa, assuming Ms. Lim checks her damn wheelbarrow more closely. Okay, so there's a disciplinary note or two on his transcripts, but nothing, like, firestarter-level. He'll just balance that out by milking his unique heritage (really, how many of him can there be?) and writing a fantastic personal essay about TikTok fame as being definitive of the Gen Z experience. Easy.

Shani closes the Styrofoam tray and stabs her chopsticks through the lid, a weird habit of hers he's never understood. "What about you? What are you up to?"

"Probably work on the gay Avengers thing," he answers instinctively. He realizes too late it's the wrong thing to say, since it returns Jackson to the conversation, and he hurries on. "Maybe watch the Guardians movies back-to-back." He doesn't say that he's hoping Jackson will join him.

"Didn't Chris Pratt cheat on his wife?" Of course she'd have to bring that up.

"Don't believe everything you see on TikTok."

"Says the queen of TikTok."

"People's mistakes—"

"Uh-huh."

"—don't have to define them."

"You're just saying that cause you think he's hot."

"Well, it doesn't hurt."

But Shani nods as if he's said something really wise. "I hear you. What you're really saying is that I *should* give Jonas a chance. Mistakes or not, boy is cute."

How the hell did this go so wrong? Pratt rules do not apply here!

Desperate times call for desperate measures. As Shani browses the latest line at Bath & Body Works, Ash darts behind a display to text Jackson. It shouldn't matter if Shani sees him texting—it's not unusual for Ash to be on his phone. But he's feeling the need for stealth now that he's texting the same boy she is.

We need to talk. Free later?

Have a job at 4 but home by 8. Everything okay?

Jackson's concern both melts Ash and burns him. Because the phone call he's going to make is likely to blow up everything.

EIGHTEEN
JONAS

He's in his head, brooding. His mood is made worse because his back is killing him. Why did Flasker think a two-man crew was enough for today's job?

When they got to the house on the hill, some of the rooms weren't fully packed, which means they had spent two hours boxing shit up before they could even start the loading—and all that had to wait until they'd shoveled out a spot big enough for the truck. The couple's taste in furniture—elaborately carved wood and wrought iron—made for a lot of straining under heavy objects. Jonas thought it would never end, a sentiment he didn't hide from Flasker, who told him the tips were all his today. Jonas didn't argue because he figured (correctly) people too lazy to pack their own boxes would probably also be cheap.

Now he's lying on the futon, starting *10 Things I Hate About You* for the nth time. Old teen movies are a weird kind of comfort food. His school bears little resemblance to the ones he sees on film,

which are so removed from actual life they might as well be set in the Marvel universe. But still, somehow, they get some things right: the character who feels like an outsider . . . the way you can scorn kids who conform at the same time as you secretly dream of being included . . . the longing. That's it, really. The *longing*. "I burn, I pine, I perish . . ."

Ash will be calling soon and Shani after that, but he kind of just wants to go to sleep. He's had too much today. Foma looked awful when he went in this morning, gritting her teeth when spasms seized her. Miguel explained that the hospice team is likely to up her Ativan soon so she won't feel as much pain, but it also means she will start sleeping more. They're waiting on her doctor's approval, but if they make the change, Jonas needs to be ready: she will be less herself every time he visits.

He wants to close his eyes and have it be another time—either way before now, when they used to daydream about doing a road trip to Disney World, or way after, when he's lived through these next few months and is still standing.

Maybe by then, he'll have figured out the whole Shani and Ash thing. For the past two days, it's been a constant buzzing in his head: *What am I doing?* What am I *doing?* His initial feelings for Shani had caused a huge shift in him, a kind of connection he hadn't felt before. He'd leaned into the sensation and felt ready to chase it. But then the almost-kiss at Ash's upended his surety. That too was new, and he wanted to follow where it led.

He's never had a crush on a boy before. He can appreciate a guy's looks, and he's never minded when they flirt with him. But it wasn't

a *thing*. He's always been open to anyone, at least in theory, but whenever he's pictured going to prom or getting married, it's been a girl at his side.

Was the spark in the air between him and Ash simply proximity? After years of keeping his distance from people his age, perhaps all the physical closeness was too new a sensation for him to process easily.

And then he had felt something similar when Shani helped him unpack his groceries, tension hanging in the air for a few seconds, moments when he understood that any other guy would be kissing her.

What might happen if he kisses her the next time? Will his whole body light up? What if he kisses Ash instead? Will they fall all over each other like horny teens in a movie?

His greatest fear is that nothing more will happen with either of them. That possibility kills him. It feels like everyone on Earth but him is sure of their body, while his remains a mystery. He doesn't want to get intimate with someone only to disappoint them, but how will he know if he can deliver unless he goes for it? It's like some terrible trap.

He would love to be able to tell someone this. Forgetting the movie entirely, he closes his eyes and practices the speech he wishes he could make.

I'm sorry I didn't kiss you. I wanted to. I was afraid. It's just . . .

I think I'm kinda . . . slow in a way. My body isn't like everyone else's, or at least not like you see in the movies.

But with you I feel . . . something. Like I wanna be close. Really close.

And it kind of freaks me out because it's new, right? Because I don't know how to do any of this.

But I want to. You just light me up.

How is it possible that he could make the exact same speech to either of them and it would be true?

He gets up to grab an ice pack from the freezer. Like the fridge, the freezer is almost empty, and he knows he needs to fill both, but the idea of going to the store in the cold makes him even more tired. He slides the ice pack into the top of his jeans so it presses against the small of his lower back and lays down on the futon again, hoping for relief.

He reruns the speech in his head, editing out the most revealing parts.

I wanted to kiss you but I don't know how to do any of this.

You just make light me up.

Better. Simpler. Plenty of time to explain later.

But who's the speech for?

He tries to think what Foma would say. Once, they had a coupon for a three-course meal at a better-than-their-usual restaurant; at the end of the meal, he'd needed to choose between an ice cream sundae and chocolate cake with whipped cream. He wanted both so badly, his head hurt; he'd actually teared up in frustration. Foma wasn't having any of that nonsense. "I am not watching you make a crisis out of a blessing. You pick one right now and be glad you get dessert, or we're leaving without either." Ashamed, he'd picked the cake. Of course, she then ordered the sundae for herself, and when they came, he ate the majority of both.

The lessons of that night were a bit contradictory: count your blessings . . . don't be a crybaby . . . but maybe you can have it all anyway. Jonas is pretty sure only two of those apply here.

Out of fairness to Shani, who has been the highlight of his day for months and months, he needs to give that a chance. She's practically his girlfriend, even if he botched the asking. Ash is a great guy and it's fun to have someone to hang out with, but Jonas and Shani have put in the time. That's it: he needs to step up. When they talk tonight, he'll make the speech. Or, well, the shortest possible version. *I want to kiss you.*

Ash's call startles him out of his deep thoughts, even though he knew it would come. Jonas sits up on the futon and turns on a lamp.

"Hey," he says, hoping he doesn't sound nervous (which he is). "About the other night . . ."

The problem is he doesn't have an end to that sentence.

Ash takes a deep breath. "I owe you an apology . . ."

This is not what he expected. "Huh?"

"You know when I hired you? Before we got to know each other?"

"Yeah?" Wherever Ash is going with this, Jonas can't guess. But something tells him it's not about how close they came to kissing.

Ash's voice is missing its usual breezy confidence. "Well . . . I didn't exactly find you online. I mean, I did, but I knew who you were. We both did."

"What do you mean you 'both'?"

"Shani and me. It was her idea, actually. She wanted you and me to meet so she could prove that you were lying . . ."

Jonas feels dizzy.

Ash tries to sound sympathetic. "You have to understand—she was really into you and she's been hurt before, so when you lied to her—"

A flash of anger pierces Jonas's fog. "Stop saying that!" His sharp tone seems to silence Ash. "I wasn't lying about how I felt." Jonas hears his voice crack a little as his throat goes dry.

"I *know*. I only went along with her plan because I hadn't met you yet. For all I knew then, you were a bad guy and—"

Jonas interrupts. "Her plan? What plan?"

"I was supposed to get to know you and find out what was true and what wasn't."

"Why didn't she just ask?"

Ash nods, the picture of sympathy. "Right?"

The twinge in Jonas's back becomes a sword thrusting through him. "And then what? Is that the whole plan? Talk about me behind my back?"

"Um . . . she was going to, like, confront you at least."

"At least?"

"Her friends wanted her to make a YouTube video—"

He has to be joking. "A video?"

"—about how you catfished her."

Catfished her? The unfairness of the description burns. "You know I didn't!" His heart pounds.

"Of course I know that *now*. You're a good guy. A *great* guy, actually."

Ash keeps talking, but Jonas only half hears. He closes his eyes and leans back. Yes, he'd kept stuff from Shani, but it wasn't some big plot. It wasn't like he was *trying* to take advantage of her trust. It wasn't like—

He sits back up, his eyes flying open.

It wasn't like what they did to him.

"You guys were going to make a YouTube video about me being an asshole?"

Ash parts his lips in surprise and he practically chokes. "No— her friends wanted her to. She didn't go that far."

"And you were helping?"

"Well—"

"Like when we were talking, you'd be telling her whatever I said?"

"At first, but I didn't know you well enough—"

"—to know that was really shitty?" It's clear from the horrified look on his face that Ash did not expect the call to go this way.

"I'm so sorry. That's why I'm calling. To apologize."

Ash offers his most humble look but Jonas isn't buying it. "How is it okay for *you guys* to lie to me if *I'm* such a dick for not being honest with her?"

"It isn't! Okay? *That's* what I'm saying. I realize this now that we're friends."

"Friends, huh?" Ash's past questions about his life play on a loop in Jonas's head. It was never getting-to-know-you, it was reconnaissance.

"Yes!" Ash's brown eyes are pleading. "And maybe . . . maybe more than? I mean, the other day . . ."

"You mean the day I told you everything and you told me nothing?"

Ash looks stricken.

Jonas burns. He'd forged two new bonds that had felt powerful

to him—and now both have disintegrated in one conversation. Beyond Foma, has there ever been a soul on earth he could trust? There must be something that makes it easy to shit on him. But he doesn't have to make it easier. Not for Ash, not for Shani.

Jonas fixes Ash with a look he perfected as a kid, a hollow-eyed you-can't-reach-me gaze, perfect for leaving yet another house. He's done. "Pay me for the Thor sketch. You have my Venmo." And then he hangs up before Ash can reply.

The worst thing is that his first instinct is to run to Foma's bedroom to tell her what has happened. But there is no other bedroom, no Foma to ask. He turns off the lamp, plunging the room into semidarkness, light from the street his only companion.

His back . . . his head . . . his heart—everything hurts.

He starts a group text for Shani and Ash and wrestles with a million ways of expressing all the things he is feeling. He types and erases and types and erases a dozen lines before settling on just five words.

I don't like liars either.

He taps send with an angry forefinger. But the message doesn't quite feel like enough. The job isn't done.

Five more words:

Don't ever call me again.

Send.

There are only two things left to do.

Block both contacts in his phone.

And cry himself to sleep.

PART THREE | THE SPARROW, THE CARDINAL, AND THE UNICORNS

NINETEEN
SHANI

She feels like a walking cauldron. The things boiling inside
her may spill out at any moment, which wouldn't be great
while she's volunteering at Woodlawn. When she woke up this
morning, maybe three hours after finally falling asleep, she told
herself that the distraction of the job would be a good thing, but
now she's not so sure. Angry crying in the shower left her tired
before the day even started, and she can barely remember the
ride here.

"Too rough!" Mrs. Robertson slaps Shani's wrist with one of her
brittle, spotted hands. She has no choice but to let Shani help, the
freshly wet gown clinging to perpetually cold skin. Usually Shani
is more careful, strength with a velvet touch, but today her mind is
nowhere near her hands.

"I'm sorry, Mrs. Robertson. You're right. I'll do better."

Her words seem to pierce the perpetual fog that clouds the old
woman's eyes and she, too, softens. "That color is nice on you," she

murmurs. "I like any shade of blue . . ." Shani pats Mrs. Robertson's forearm, thinking, *Once upon a time, she was seventeen, too.*

At lunchtime, Shani is tasked with rolling trays to all the patients on the first floor. The cart can only hold six trays at once, and there are sixteen rooms in each wing, so there's no fast way to accomplish the task. Usually there are two aides, but it's Christmas week and they're short-staffed, which means it's just her, which also means that the people stuck waiting for the fifth and sixth round of deliveries are hungry and unhappy.

She doesn't have the emotional reserves to be yelled at today. When Jonas went dark, it was a shock. When she called Ash and discovered why, it was a stab to the gut. She still can't process that Jonas is done with her, just like that. Jonas really thinks what she did was so much worse than what he did? And then Ash—how could he have done that? Did their friendship mean nothing at all?

She approaches Mr. Diallo's room. He looks so much like her grandfather on her mom's side that it always throws her a little bit. His head is mostly shaved, but the ring of hair that remains is flecked with white that matches his goatee; a potbelly springs forward from an otherwise spindly body. If her mom's dad had been gay, he'd be Mr. Diallo. He wears silky two-piece pajama sets all day long unless his husband is coming to visit, in which case he, very slowly, and entirely under his own steam, dons a crisp shirt, knit cardigan, and dress pants. He owns two sets, both in a blue-and-gray palette. Each week, his husband, an Italian greyhound of a man, brings the previous week's ensemble, freshly dry cleaned to be ready for the next visit; before leaving, he helps Mr. Diallo back into his pajamas

and collects that day's ensemble. The pattern never changes because Mr. Diallo is precise like that. Shani has reason to fear bringing his meal late.

She knocks on the door and a woman's voice tells her to come in. A small crowd has gathered around Mr. Diallo's bed. Is it a vigil? Through the sea of shoulders, she spots a balloon and realizes it's his birthday. This sort of thing is supposed to be highlighted on his menu, and it isn't. *Not only am I late, I'm late in front of his family and with a custard cup instead of a slice of cake.* She adopts the brightest tone she can. "I didn't know it was your birthday, Mr. Diallo! You must be excited." But she keeps her focus on the cart, as if it's tricky to maneuver, instead of looking him in the eye.

The family members part like water as she approaches the bed. "I *was* excited for lunch, but that sensation seems so long ago, I hardly remember now," he says in the sonorous voice that she finds cool when he's not chastising her. She starts to apologize but he waves it away, smiling ever so slightly. "My grandson made me a cake so large, I'll need new pajamas."

Shani is grateful to be (sort of) off the hook and follows his eyes past the towering strawberry topped cake to the grandson in question. Impossibly, it's Milo from school. *But Milo's white.* It's a ridiculous attempt and she knows it—the world isn't bodied so neatly. And still: *Milo?*

What comes out is, "You bake?"

Milo's cheeks redden a little. "Why wouldn't I? My grandfather's a chef."

Mr. Diallo enjoys the look of surprise of Shani's face. "You didn't

know that, did you? I was the pastry chef at L'Atelier for twenty years. And you thought I was just a little old man on your lunch route."

A light-skinned Black woman swats at his arm. "Leave the girl alone or she'll take away that lunch you've been complaining about."

Shani is relieved to leave Mr. Diallo to his visitors, but she's not all the way to next room when Milo steps into the hall. "Hey!"

"Hey."

She's not really up for someone to ask *How are ya* today, which is fine, since he doesn't.

"Merry Christmas!"

"Boy, Christmas was two days ago."

Milo just grins. "Then Happy New Year!"

"Are you always this cheerful?" Seriously, she can't remember a day when he wasn't smiling.

He nods. "It's a myth that comedians are all sad on the inside!"

There's nothing clever to say to that and she really wants to deliver the last meal, but he's not going anywhere.

"What are you doing this week?"

"Working. Here and Yaki's both. You?"

"I've got a show at First Night!"

"Seriously?" Boy bakes cakes and has a gig at the huge Boston New Year's Eve celebration?

His eyes gleam. "Not by myself—I mean, there's twenty-six of us, but it's official First Night stuff and everything. The basement at Arlington Street is hosting Up and Comers Comedy Marathon—we all get ten-minute sets. Mine's early because I'm youngest but cool, right?"

"Yeah. It is. Really cool."

He pulls a folded piece of pink paper from his jeans and hands it to her. She unfurls it to reveal the headline Up and Comers! Over a grid of headshots, including Milo's junior yearbook photo. At the bottom, next to the details, a big stamp in all caps reads COMP.

"That's for you. If you're free that night, you can just show them this. You don't have to get a First Night button or a pass or anything."

Shani stares at it without speaking. She has no plans for First Night after all. An ache in her chest reminds her of the plans she had imagined making. Either the universe has swooped in to fill what would otherwise feel like an empty space or the gods are just reminding her how her vision has gone up in flames.

When she looks up, he is waiting so expectantly, so eagerly, she is reminded of his joke on the last day before break. She knows now for sure it wasn't a joke. Milo's into her. On this day of all days, it's a lot to take in. "Do I have to decide now? I need to like . . . ask my dad if I can go."

Milo plays it cool. "Course . . . but, um . . . do you have my number?"

No, Shani does not have his number, never considered having his number, never saw him through this lens until the other day and only then for a few seconds, but here they are now, swapping digits in the hallway of nursing home when she should be working. The delight on his face, even as he tries to play it cool, touches something wounded in her. Normally, she'd be texting BB5 about him immediately. But right this minute, she really wants him to go back to his grandfather's room and let her finish up her shift.

Exchange completed, she tries to return his smile, but nods at the (now not remotely warm) meal on her cart. "My last patient could die waiting for me to deliver this, so . . ."

His laugh is sincere. "You're pretty funny, too. Pretty *and* funny." He looks surprised that he said that out loud. "I think I hear my grandfather." And he giraffes it back to Mr. Diallo's room as fast as he can.

. . .

By the time she is home from her shift, Shani feels drained. She keeps looping around over what happened with Jonas. Fair? Unfair? Fair?

She texts the BB5 and tells them that Jonas found out what she'd done.

Sheree replies that this is too big for texting and starts a video chat. "What'd he do?"

"Blocked us both. On everything."

"But you brought him food!" Yanique sounds shocked.

"I don't think he liked that so much anyway. He was embarrassed."

"Probably not as much as when he figured out his girlfriend was playin' him." Julie's rarely gentle. "I'd block your ass, too."

"Bitch, who's side you on?" Sheree has Shani's back.

Yanique does too. "Yeah, Jules—you were all over this plan!"

Tati tries to help. "Oprah says no matter how flat you make a pancake—"

"You're a sixty-year-old woman," Sheree interrupts, unable to hear more Oprah.

Shani wants to throttle Tati. "How are we talking pancakes?"

"No matter how flat the pancake, it will always have two sides."

Yanique cocks her head. "I get the two sides, but why flat?"

Tati looks aggrieved. "It means no matter *how* it looks, right, like a perfect pancake to you, there's a whole other side. It could be burned or whatever."

"So which side am I?"

"Oh, I get it," Yanique leaps in. "Doesn't matter—burned side, perfect side, you only see yours."

As they talk, Sheree starts applying a face mask that turns her skin green. "We don't need to see any side but Shani's, burned or not."

"Maybe. But his side is that Shani and Ash were making a fool out of him when he thought she liked him." Whatever has gotten into Julie, she's on a roll.

"I *do* like him!" Shani is so frustrated she could cry. She leaves her phone on her desk and goes to her vision board. On impulse, she rips up the decent boyfriend sign and then starts tearing off everything else, crumpling the papers into balls that pile at her feet.

"Where you go, sis?" her cousin's voice floats from the phone.

Tati chides the others. "She needs support right now. It was pretty mean of him to block her instead of letting her explain. She gave *him* a chance, so it's only fair."

"SHANI," Yanique shouts. "Come back!"

Shani does, but not without a stab. "Why? So Julie can shit on me?"

Julie adopts a know-it-all tone. "You're overreacting. To *all* of it."

Tati shakes her head. "You feel what you feel, Shani."

"Is that Oprah, too?" Sheree asks, looking for all the world like the Hulk.

"Dr. Phil, I think. It's good though, right?"

Julie does her version of making amends. "He's just mad. Give him a day and he'll call."

Shani refuses to validate any idea from Julie.

"If he doesn't, there are other guys . . ." Yanique thinks this is helpful. And maybe it is. Shani doesn't tell them about Milo yet, but the flier sits in her bag, a pink reminder that she has options.

"What you gone do about Ash?" Tati asks.

For a few minutes, Shani had forgotten the betrayal piece, that this was two losses, not just one. "Before or after I kill him?"

• • •

By the time she is getting ready for bed, Ash has texted twenty-nine times. She has not replied to him since their middle of the night phone call, when he'd confessed that, feeling "overwhelmed with guilt" (uh-huh), he'd told Jonas about the plot. It hadn't taken long before the rest came out: yes, he had a crush on Jonas, too. He swore that wasn't his real motivation, that after Jonas almost kissed him— which he *resisted* (uh-huh)—he was thinking of *them*: helping Jonas be his true self and preventing Shani from being strung along by someone who could never deliver. But she could see through that. She doesn't want to hear his story any more than Jonas wants to hear hers.

She tries to remind herself that her past experiences mean it wasn't irrational to doubt him—but that's little comfort. The fact is

that, in the end, he had come clean and she had not. *She* ended up the liar. And now, in outing their plan to Jonas without telling her, Ash has evaporated something in their friendship.

As she sits at her vanity, folding her braids up into her longest silk cap, Shani senses her dad's presence in the Studio. "Thought you were asleep on the couch."

"I heard you girls talkin'..."

"So you know."

He sits on the edge of her bed. "You okay?"

That's a question none of her friends asked. It's the one that undoes her. She starts to cry and can't answer. She can feel how much he wants to hug her in this moment, knows the work it takes for him to just be present, letting her have the space.

"Your mom and I broke up, too, back in the day. I'd got a bonus at my first real job and spent the whole thing on a Vespa. Thought it was cool." A Vespa? *Her* dad? "Didn't even have a parking space for it. We were engaged by then and your mom said if I couldn't grow up, then I could wait at the altar till hell froze over. Got rid of the Vespa and kept her. Good move, right?"

This is supposed to cheer Shani up, tell her there's still hope. But it feels too removed from her situation. There's no easy object to target, no ultimatum to accept or reject. She's mad at Jonas for not letting her explain, but even more so at herself for having made this mess to begin with. But at least her dad didn't say *I told you so*, which he could have, and he's up trying to be comforting when he should be asleep. His presence, not his attempt at words of wisdom, is the gift.

Shani goes to the bed and sits next to him. Doesn't hug him—that's just never gonna be who she is—but scooches close enough that she can rest her head on his shoulder. She can't see him smiling but she knows he is. "What color?"

"What color what, sweetheart?"

"Vespa. You tellin' me a story, tell it right."

"Yellow."

Shani starts to laugh. Her dad was a fool. "Yellow!"

"It looked really cool. I swear." He's laughing, too. "If you could have seen your mom's face."

"Tell me," she says. "Tell me all about it."

So he does.

TWENTY
ASH

The Hammer dropped.

That's what Ash texts Tee while waiting for Family Council to begin. He wishes he could text Jackson or Shani, but he's kind of made that impossible.

What did you do now?

Grades.

Srsly?

Raj had opened the Hammer portal last night (the day after Christmas, which reveals a sick compulsion, if you ask Ash) to find that his son's grades in English had plummeted along with the History grade. Ash's defense—he knows for a fact that all his work is in—led Raj, naturally, to compose an investigative email to his son's teachers, which is how he and Ash learned that the two teachers had somehow discovered Ash had written the same essay for *both*, with only the most gentle tweaks to fit the respective assignments.

Ash is now in the not-entirely-unfamiliar position of waiting in

his room to be summoned to Family Council. It's corny enough that they have formal family meetings, but the pretentious branding as "council" makes it even worse. Why couldn't he have normal parents who don't have to verbalize everything? If he dies young, it'll be from *process*.

And what's the point anyway? He's seventeen. Too old to be intimidated by a stern lecture. All they're going to do is vent about what they think of as bad behavior when it really is no big deal. It's not like the grades will stay low—he could pass those classes with his eyes closed. And nobody seriously doubts he's going to college, so all this is just drama for parental self-esteem's sake. Humoring it is everything.

"Ashok!" Raj fires the *k* like a bullet, and Ash puts away his phone to follow him to the main living room.

Gloria is waiting for Raj on the black leather sofa. Ash takes his place in one of the matching club chairs, groaning when he sees the wooden rainstick his dad brought back from a trip to Chile. The rainstick is never a good sign. You can only speak if you're holding the rainstick, and when you're done, you pass it on to someone else.

Raj joins Gloria to make a united front. Naturally, he takes the rainstick first. "We are very disappointed, Ashok. You have been irresponsible before, inconsiderate, too, and certainly selfish." *Wow. Nice summary.* "But you've never been a cheater."

That's too far. Ash motions for the rainstick, but Raj hands it to Gloria, who picks up the lecture. "You are too smart and too accomplished for this." Ash likes her version of him better. For about two seconds. "It's both unnecessary and beneath you to cheat."

That word again. He reaches for the rainstick and this time gets it. "I wrote that paper. Every word of it!"

He relinquishes the rainstick to Raj, who takes on a prosecutorial tone. "Did you or did you not turn in the same essay for credit in two different courses, which each had their own requirements, in essence doing half the work of your fellow students taking both classes?"

Rainstick returned, Ash defends himself. "It's *my* work. Instead of you being mad, you should be impressed that I found a topic that fit two assignments equally well. That's not cheating—that's efficiency." Looking at his mom, he adds, "I'd think you'd be all over it!"

Gloria snaps her fingers and he hands over the rainstick. "By that logic, a plagiarist deserves props for saving so much time!"

"You can't plagiarize yourself!" Ash is nearly screeching.

Gloria looks shocked at this breach of protocol. "You don't have the rainstick!"

"Screw the rainstick! I'm not a cheater." He's gone too far, but what came out came out.

Raj grabs the rainstick. His voice is lower than ever, burring like a chainsaw revving up. "You will not speak to us like that again, Ashok. Don't mistake our indulgence for softness." He speaks sternly. "You'll write two new papers—from scratch, with no overlap— before you go back to class on Tuesday."

Whatever; if agreeing gets him out of Family Council faster, fine. He takes the rainstick. "I'll do it. But let the record show I don't feel this is a just punishment."

Gloria does a finger snap. "Punishment? No, Ash, the papers are

mere responsibility. Your *punishment* is no car until those papers are turned in and graded and the teachers have expressed satisfaction."

He pretty much snatches the rainstick back without waiting to see if she's done. "You've got to be kidding me! It's vacation week *and* New Year's—I have to have a car!" He can see this is not persuasive to either of them. "It's freezing cold outside, like, so cold it has a nickname, and you really want me to *walk* everywhere? How is *that* good parenting?"

Raj takes the rainstick. "We worry about you. We let you have space to be who you are. We encourage your independence by supporting the TikTok thing and we've never made you pursue our interests. But we're *not* enabling bad behavior . . ." He pauses a moment, perhaps reaching for words, perhaps deciding whether to say them. "Sometimes I fear you tend towards narcissism and myopia."

Ash sits back in the club chair, shook. That's a lot. And they don't even know the half of it.

Gloria takes the rainstick, and he hopes, for half a second, she will tell Raj he went too far. "What we're saying is that we're not raising an asshole, so *get it together.*"

. . .

Curious Liquids is busy even by Curious Liquids standards. Christmas vacation means all the college kids are back home, and every seat is taken. Ash's office has four people crowded together already when he arrives, so the best he can do is sit at one of the counter barstools, and even then he has to stand behind someone awkwardly until his lurking makes them uncomfortable enough to leave.

He couldn't sit in his room anymore, and he obviously wasn't going to hang with his parents. Losing his car isn't the worst thing about his day, though it certainly claims the number two spot (just above number three: having stained a pair of cute suede boots walking here). The real problem is having blown up two relationships at once: his friendship with Shani and his now dead-on-the-vine romance with Jackson.

He has spent hours running all the possible options and doesn't know how to solve either problem. He has no way to reach Jackson at all, short of stalking him; the only thing he knows for sure that Jackson lives *somewhere* on Prospect, so that's not helpful. Shani he can reach by phone or email, and if he can deal with the bus (ugh), he could even go to her house right now, but she's not taking his calls or replying to his messages and he has a feeling if he shows up, she won't let him in. How do you prove to people that you're sorry if they won't even look at you?

"So I guess you won't be coming to the show tonight?" Tee slides Ash's turmeric latte across the bar toward him. Today, Tee is wearing a full Sailor Moon outfit over wide-legged jeans, and Ash thinks it's maybe a little much for a Wednesday morning, but doesn't comment. He's already been told he's an asshole today, and he needs to prove otherwise.

"Sorry," he says. "You know I would. But with no car . . ."

"Catch me on New Year's instead."

"Um . . . that's like four days away. No chance I'll have the car back."

"Poor baby."

"*Right*? My life sucks." Ash raises his latte cup as if to say cheers.

Tee gets a funny look on their face. "I think you misheard me."

"Huh?"

"'Poor baby' was *sarcasm.* Would it have helped if I'd said it in a baby voice?"

"Whoa—"

"There is no universe in which your life sucks."

This can't be happening. "Oh, no. Not you too. Not today."

Tee folds their arms across their pinafore. "It's a bummer to lose access to the $60,000 car you got at sixteen. It's a drag that your parents actually pay attention to your grades. And it's even annoying that your office is taken. But does your life suck? I don't think so."

Tee is always giving him shit but this feels unnecessary. "Can you wait for another day to remind me that you think I'm privileged?"

"I think?"

"Fine. I have some privilege. But will you listen to me for a minute? Shani and Jackson both stopped talking to me."

Even Tee knows that takes precedence right now. "Oh my god. That does suck."

"I told you!"

"What did you *do?*"

Ash wants to cry. Everyone is so ready to pin the blame on him! Granted, it's fair, but it's not very nice.

"I . . . I told him what we were up to."

Tee is shaking their head. "And lemme guess: you didn't warn Shani first."

"I was trying to help—"

"–yourself. That's what you mean, right? I know you're not about to say it was for their own good."

He *was*, actually, about to say that, because it would have been. Why can't anyone see that? "You think I should have just kept playing double agent? How is that fair?"

"It was never fair for him. He was a lost cause the moment you guys started. But for Shani? She's your friend, Ash. You should have talked to her."

He can't argue because Tee's not wrong. At least about Shani. He should have told her about his feelings instead of setting her up. They've weathered a lot over the years, including the surprising one-off crush he had on her in ninth grade, disapproval of each other's taste in boys, and an ongoing debate about what is and isn't racist. Yes, she'd still have been mad at him, but she wouldn't feel betrayed. Ash sips miserably at his drink, not even half-finished. It's already cold.

The seat next to Ash comes open and Tee comes around the bar to sit with him. "You're not saying anything, which is creepy as hell. I don't know if that means you agree with me or you've had an aneurysm."

"Both."

"I'm half-cool with that," Tee jokes, nudging him. "So, Mope Queen, what are you going to do about it?"

"I guess going to Curious Liquids looking for sympathy is out."

"Ha!" Tee pats his arm. "If you're looking for Kleenex, I'm the wrong queer."

Ash scans the room. "I'm going to need new friends!"

Tee sizes him up. "But are you gonna deserve them?"

Oof.

The question haunts him all the way as he trudges home, cold air stinging his cheeks and crystals forming on his long lashes. Up to this point, it's been pretty easy coasting on charm and confidence, the two gifts the universe bestowed on him. It won't be that easy to make this right. He has to start with Shani; she means too much to him to let pride stop him. Being a rich kid means he's never had to beg, but that's about to change.

TWENTY-ONE
JONAS

He sits by Foma's bed, holding one of her hands in his. She is asleep now, as she has been almost all day. He's been here since he woke up this morning, seven, maybe eight hours ago. It's his longest visit by far, but he hasn't dared to leave. In the span of twenty-four hours, she has disappeared under the waves. Miguel told him this morning that Foma has a few days left at best. It wasn't what the doctor said just yesterday, but Miguel says the doctors are never there at the end. Nurses are. And nurses *know*.

Hospice is never a beginning. Jonas knew what Sunrise meant from the first: that the life he and Foma shared would end. How the end began the day she moved into Maple Crest and he moved to Prospect, their warm home full of crocheted blankets and Jonas's drawings diluted into two cold rooms across town from each other. The original prognosis—that the true end remained months away—was a shield to batter away any thoughts of what the universe would feel like with her gone. When the doctor amended it to "a couple of

weeks," shaving away some of the distance, Jonas had done the math: Foma would ring in the New Year. He could almost fool himself into thinking of losing her "next year" as something far away.

Suddenly it's "any day now" if Miguel is right, and Jonas is not ready. So he sits by her bed. When the increased morphine schedule nears the end of each cycle, Foma rises from the deep and sees him, though each time she says less. Sometimes, she starts talking with the drugs still holding her in another world. Last night, eyes closed, she told him she saw his wedding, and he looked so handsome. He had leaned in, waiting for more, but she repeated only the word handsome a few more times, the word slurring and fading away, before she was under again. The last time she woke, she nearly jackknifed with a spasm, her half-open eyes spilling tears, and when he leaped to his feet, panicked to see the evident pain, she murmured only, "I know. I know."

Honestly, it's a relief each time the next round of meds sends her back beneath the waves. But the time passes slowly. Marion came early but left to open the gift kiosk she runs downtown at Faneuil Hall, and she won't be back for hours.

One of the hospice tenders says hearing is the last thing to go, so Jonas has played Foma her favorite music, all the Motown stuff she listened to while cooking and the Dolly Parton albums that were her exception to a general no-country-music rule. He has read the headlines of the news to her and played the latest episode of *The Young & the Restless*, which he has watched with her so long that Victor and Nikki feel more real to him than Valerie at this point.

Now, he absently uses one hand to trace patterns back and forth on her palm, while he scrolls through his phone with the other hand. On Instagram, he finds a couple of new art requests, but there's not much else to see; it's a struggle not to look at Ash or Shani's walls. He doesn't dare linger on TikTok for the fear that Ash will appear in his For You page. He opens Discord to see if there's any news of the rumored *Attack on Titan* OVA, but there's not. It takes all of two minutes to inventory his whole social media presence and find it barren.

He could get up and walk around the room, but he feels so heavy, he just sits in the chair. Maybe he could look up cat videos for Foma. She won't see them but the sound might make her happy. As he searches YouTube, his eyes keep closing, and he has to shake himself awake.

With a brief tap at the doorframe to announce her presence, Dorice joins Jonas. Today she wears a lavender sweatshirt with a floral turtleneck, the fine line of not too cheery, not too grim. "I came just in time," she says. "You don't look like you'll make it."

Dorice is a volunteer "tender," sitting with Foma when Jonas or Marion cannot. She's ready to settle in, but he doesn't get up. He appreciates Dorice's kindness but can't take her up on it. Surely she understands that if he leaves this chair, this room, he might miss Foma's passing. And he's afraid to say that out loud because the universe might hear him and make it true.

He closes his eyes a moment and tries to think what to do. Leave now, be at his apartment in half an hour. Sleep a little, eat something, and still be back two hours before visiting time ends. He can

hear the quiet whirring of machinery on the table next to Foma's headboard. In the distance, a voice that sounds like Miguel's is telling a story, and laughter follows. Dorice is saying something to Jonas but he hears only his own breathing. His forehead feels so very heavy. It pulls him down.

"Jonas!" Dorice's voice, now sharp, wakes him. He has fallen asleep where he sits. He shakes his head to clear it. "Go home. Sleep. Even a little bit will help."

Foma's eyes are closed, her breathing shallow but steady. She won't miss him. But he leans in close to whisper, "Wait for me, okay?"

· · ·

Of course, today, the 23andMe results arrive. Jonas sees the headline in his email "Your reports are ready!" and it suddenly feels ridiculous. Why care about that now when his anchor is about to be lost to the sea? What will knowing what distant place his blood comes from change about life in this apartment on this street in this town this winter? Whatever he is, whoever he is, it's not in the email. He doesn't even open it.

He crawls onto the futon and lays on his side, eyes reading the darkness like a newspaper. He knows he needs to rest but his mind is whirring. How could it not be? His two favorite days of the entire last year were lies.

Watching *Thor* at Ash's—ugh, being hired to begin with—was only because Shani *told* Ash how much Jonas loved the movies. Had she also told him that Foma and Jonas always rang in New Year's with a Marvel marathon? Did Shani really take something so special and give it away to be used against him?

And their date, when they were riffing on the Italian light display—he's embarrassed to think of it now. The whole time, she was thinking: *Amateur. I'll show you how a secret works.*

He would be angrier if he couldn't hear all the little half-truths and evasions of his own, playing over and over on shuffle in his head. Can you be angry-sad? Sad-angry? Sangry is not a real word, and yet he feels it. *I'm so sangry.* He can see the letters on a blank page in his mind. He imagines turning in an essay with "Sangry" as the title. And then he is asleep.

Foma is a talk show host. No, a game show host. She wears a seventies leisure suit and holds cue cards. It's one of those old TV game shows she likes, the kind you find on nostalgia cable stations. He can't tell if it's *Newlywed Game* or *Dating Game* and he wonders why she's never told him she was the host. He is in the audience and everyone else is dressed in vintage clothes, which makes him self-conscious, until he looks down and sees that he is wearing a silky polyester shirt and plaid bell bottoms. Did Ash help him pick it out?

There's a big shiny curtain and she says that the contestants are behind it. Backlights show silhouettes and Jonas knows immediately that Shani is on the right and Ash on the left. Foma is explaining that the judges will ask each contestant the same three questions and, based on those questions, choose only one winner to take the grand prize trip to Hawaii. Jonas wonder why they must be behind curtains. How would seeing them change anything?

As Foma asks "What's the ideal first date?" Jonas doesn't really listen to the answers because he's obsessed with the middle figure, who he can't quite place. Is it Tee from the coffee shop? He thinks

so a moment, but then the shadow shifts a little and he thinks, *Flasker?* No. *Miguel.* It has to be someone from Arlmont—he's convinced. Foma is on to the next question ("What's your biggest deal-breaker?") but Jonas can only think of the middle contestant, whose edges blur and shift and solidify and blur again. Who is with Shani and Ash?

He has to know. Leaping from his front row seat, he races up the curtain to pull it away. Foma rolls with the disruption, winking to the audience and saying, "We have a live one here, folks," which earns undeservedly hearty laughs and applause. Jonas yanks hard on the gauzy fabric, but it won't come down.

"I have to see!" he says. "Let me see!" The crowd just laughs and then cutting-to-commercial music plays. Suddenly Shani is on his left and Ash on his right, the curtain in front of him hiding the audience from view.

"That's not cool," Shani says.

"You didn't have to come on the show at all," Ash chimes in.

They each take one arm and sit Jonas back down in the middle chair, where he has been all along, except he can't have been, and now he's scared, but he can't stand up, and somewhere beyond the curtain, Foma is saying it's the lightning round. There's a melody playing and he has to name it. It's on the tip of his tongue—

The dream disappears.

It is replaced only by darkness and surety.

Foma is dying right now.

Instantly awake, he scrambles into sitting position. He has never been so sure of anything in his life. He's paralyzed. Should

he call Sunrise and tell them, and how would he sound if he did? Should he just run for it, run all the way there, in hopes he'll make it in time? He is shoving his foot into a still-wet boot when the phone rings.

"Jonas." Dorice speaks with the gentleness of bad news. "Evelyn has just passed. I'm holding her hand. I wanted you to know she wasn't alone."

She was, he thinks, bitterly, tears coming hard and fast. *We all are.*

. . .

He has never been in Sunrise after visiting hours. It's only 9 p.m., but the patients are almost all asleep and the lights on Foma's hall are dim. It is not Miguel, but a night nurse who joins him for what will be his last walk down this hallway. At the door, she hands him off to Dorice, who tells Jonas that Marion is on her way and that he can sit with Foma as long as he likes. Rules no longer apply.

Foma has returned and departed all at once. With the pain ended, her face has relaxed into an expression he recognizes, the face she wears when drowsing on the couch during a movie after a too-good meal. But she's not there: the stillness of the look, the subtle absence of a rising and falling in her chest. If he kisses her cheek, it will be cold.

He takes her hand in his and traces a little heart in the palm, then gently folds her fingers to hold it close.

Jonas will be gone when Marion arrives. She's Foma's family. Not his.

I'm it, he thinks. *I'm all I got.*

TWENTY-TWO
SHANI

What am I getting myself into?

As she enters the Ivy with Milo, she knows it's too soon. It's her own fault, saying yes to a date with Milo seconds after the Jonas thing blew up in her face.

When Milo asked her through Snapchat, it seemed like a good distraction from the mess she'd made. She said yes on the spot, despite him looking like a porcelain teacup. If she hadn't met his grandfather, she'd have applied her no-white-guys rule to him, though lately, the rule seems suspect anyway. He's nice and funny— and it doesn't hurt that he's into her.

The Ivy is old, one of those dark wood and painted plaster joints from the nineteen twenties, and if it wasn't for the posters of *Jaws* and *Pulp Fiction* and *The Color Purple*, it would be kinda creepy, à la *Five Nights at Freddy's*. Tonight, Friday night of Christmas vacation, the room is as crowded as it can possibly be. The Christmas movies have been swapped out for *When Harry Met Sally, Are We There*

Yet?, and *Snowpiercer* in honor of New Year's. Shani has seen all three—*Snowpiercer* four or five times, but never on the big screen. She's glad she ordered their tickets online because all three movies are now sold out and the Ivy is turning people away, the sidewalk a mosh pit of ski jackets and parkas and knit hats.

By the time they choose their seats, they've already discovered they disagree on nearly every aspect of moviegoing. It started in the lobby.

Him: "How can you eat Butterfingers? They stick in your teeth!"

Her: "Says the boy buying Twizzlers, which ain't even food."

Him: "Who gets iced tea at the movies?"

Her: "The blue dye in that Slushie is antifreeze. You know that, right?"

Picking seats is a whole new terrain for them to disagree on.

Him: "Where do you sit?"

Her: "Row four."

Him: "I like the back."

Her: "Close enough to be in the action but not so close I have to crane."

Him: "Way back."

Her: "Aisle or middle of the row?"

Him: "Aisle, so I can get out faster."

Her: "Middle for best view!"

Their comparative lateness means they don't get to choose either. They take their far-end-against-a-wall seats about one-third of the way back in the theater, trying not to step on purses and popcorn tubs of the people who got their seats sooner. A trailer for *The Host*,

by the same director as *Snowpiercer*, is playing as they settle in, and Shani's excited.

"Have you seen that? It's killer."

"Shhh." Milo looks mortified that she's talking. Nods at the screen. "The movie."

Shani gives him side-eye. "It's called a *preview* because it's *before* the movie."

"It's still *part* of the movie and people don't talk during movies."

"Seriously?"

"Do you hear anyone talking but us?" His face is splotchy and red, and whether it's embarrassment or anger, Shani doesn't care. This isn't going anywhere and the night has just begun. She doesn't even point out that she's whispering, not really talking. She could turn up the volume if she wanted. Way up.

During the movie, they both relax. When the villain Wilford makes the speech about how she is a hat and the passengers are shoes and then hisses, "So it is," Milo break his own rule by muttering under his breath, "What a dick." Shani thinks, *That's more like it.*

Both are into the action scenes, and by the time the two little kids from the train are stepping into the snow at the finale, he is holding her hand. Maybe their rocky start was based on her mood. So when he suggests getting ice cream at Udderly, next door to the Ivy, she doesn't come up with an excuse to duck out.

Udderly is a local chain, branches scattered around Boston and nearby towns, easily recognizable for its aesthetic of black-and-white cows in hot pink tutus. The shiny resin tables are shaped liked udders, and the staff wear T-shirts with slogans like *Milk It for All It's Worth.* It's the best ice cream in Arlmont by virtue of being the

only ice cream place left open, but it kills Shani to pay five bucks for a single scoop, no matter how delicious. Today's special is her favorite of their rotating flavors: Cow Patty, dark chocolate froyo with crushed Reese's peanut butter cups and pretzels. She's so happy that she doesn't comment that nobody, *nobody*, goes to Udderly and orders French vanilla, which Milo does.

With orders in hand, they look for a table and realize too late the place is packed as full as the Ivy. Shani holds both cones as they debate whether to stand outside under the awning by the heat lamp or to linger in the crowd until a table opens up.

"I'll just try to look really pitiful on my crutches until someone feels guilty," Milo says, eyes twinkling.

"Would you do that?" Shani isn't 100 percent sure he's kidding.

"Would I? It's the only perk I get with these. Well, that and advantage in the high jump." He mimics using the arm crutches to fling himself into the air.

"Then let's aim for that lady." Shani points at a white woman in a World Wildlife Fund T-shirt. "She'll fold immediately."

Milo shakes his head, pointing past dolphin lady to the back. "Is that a friend of yours?"

Tee is there at a table for four, waving them over. Shani hesitates. She only knows Tee through Ash, who she feels weird about right now—but what's she gone do, pretend she can't see? "Friend of a friend."

"Sweet." Milo has no compunction about accepting this offer and forges through the crowd.

At the table, he's gregarious. "Thanks—you saved us! I was going to play the crip card soon."

Shani can hardly believe that's his opener with a complete stranger, but Tee is up for it. "I only invited you over cause I'm earning a merit badge in Fake Sympathy." Tee gives Shani a hug. "Hey, you. Ash'll be here any minute."

Ugh. She *wants* to forgive him. He's been begging enough for it. And not talking to him has hollowed out a safe place inside her. God, she misses him, but her pride is as bruised as her trust.

. . .

Twenty minutes later, Milo and Tee are both laughing so hard they can't breathe at some joke she didn't hear the start of. They're shaking the table, which sends his removed arm crutches sliding to the floor, and she finds herself picking them up, while they keep cracking up. "What?" she asks, irked. "What'd I miss?"

It's a TikTok edit of spliced scenes from *Big Bang Theory*, a TV show she finds almost unwatchable. The clip is all dialogue from the tall guy with the odd social skills, ending with him saying his genitals are functional and genetically pleasing. This amuses Tee and Milo to no end, and they replay it as soon as it's done.

Ash's arrival, which she dreaded seconds ago, feels like deliverance. He's apparently decided that the temperature warming up into the thirties makes it spring: he wears a thin brown leather blazer that he once swore to her was the exact one Ross wore on *Friends* after becoming a doctor. Ash looks cold, but that doesn't entirely account for his stiffness. "Can I . . ." He motions at the seat next to Shani.

"Why wouldn't you?" She sounds more combative than she means.

Ash looks relived but doesn't answer. Instead, he eyes Milo. "So, Tee, who's the cutie?"

Milo looks startled but Tee looks amused. "Why are you asking me? Ask Shani—he's *her* date."

"You didn't tell me about a date," Ash says, one eyebrow raised like an accusation.

"I also wasn't talking to you, so . . ."

"Are you the friend?" Milo asks.

"Huh?"

"Shani said Tee was a friend of a friend, so I'm doing the math—or are you a couple?"

Shani and Tee both loudly answer, "NO!" at once, which causes Tee and Ash both to look at Shani. She could kick herself: of course Milo wasn't asking her.

He teases Ash. "Whatever you're doing, man, it's not working!"

"Unless what I'm doing is trying to die single. Then I'm right on target."

Milo extends his hand across the table. "I'm Milo."

"Milo? As in Giraffe?"

Shani would have sworn that she'd never even mentioned Milo to Ash, but Ash never forgets a detail.

Milo's smile doubles in size. He scooches his chair closer to Shani, putting his arm around her, obviously pleased.

The arm feels, well, wrong. There's none of the electricity that flowed when she was standing in Jonas's apartment on Christmas Day. It's as if the idea of an arm around her on a date bears no resemblance to the fact of that arm around her now.

"So she talks about me, huh?"

"Not nearly enough," Ash coos. "Tell us everything about you."

And Milo does. For like twenty minutes straight. Tee listens with real interest and Ash puts on a good show, though Shani knows him well enough to know he's thinking, *God, this kid is vanilla.* Instead of really listening to Milo, Shani finds herself staring at Ash and noticing how pretty his expressive eyes are, how strong his features, especially next to Milo. Even sitting there just listening to the Milo monologue, there's something about Ash that feels more mature, more sophisticated. More her speed, period. What if—

Ridiculous. She catches herself. The Jonas thing must have really messed her up if she's letting her mind go there.

When Milo says he's a stand-up comedian, Tee asks where they can catch his routine. He pulls out a copy of the same flyer he gave Shani and Tee takes it, excited at first, but then darkens. "Shit. I have a gig that night."

Ash fills in the blanks. "Underland—they play music you won't understand in clothes you'd never wear."

Milo looks surprised. "I know Underland!" He says his best friend is obsessed with them and to prove it, he pulls up Insta shots of the friend at the band's last few shows. When he asks what time Tee's set happens on New Year's Eve, he discovers it's after his show—win.

"A comedian, a rocker, a YouTuber, and a TikToker walk into a bar . . ." Ash quips. It's a subtle redirect to get himself into the conversation, but it works, and for a while they're comparing notes about followers, likes, and branding, and debating whether it's possible at their age to *not* have some public thing they do.

The conversation is flowing along just fine but Shani feels tired all at once, the roller coaster of the week finally catching up. She pretends her phone is vibrating, and she gets up quickly. "Sorry. I need to take this . . ." and weaves through the throng to stand outside.

In the open air, she takes a long, deep breath. She keeps the phone up to her ear, so that if they look out the window, her lie checks out. She really just needs space. A bus rolls by and she looks up at the people in the windows, their faces made yellow by the interior lighting, and wonders what moment she has caught them in—the day one was fired, the night another will propose? Do they know they are being observed; would they care if they knew?

Maybe the universe is watching her the same way. But is it laughing or crying? One day she was plotting against Jonas, then she was on a date with him, then she was a girl with the power to be forgiving, and now suddenly she's the one who screwed it all up. In the last twenty-four hours alone, she's gone from not speaking to Ash to checking him out, even while on a date with someone else. Her emotions are confetti, scattered, impossible to collect into a whole.

TWENTY-THREE
ASH

Things aren't going his way today.

The sling comes in the mail. It isn't a great moment when it arrives, the box being enormous and his parents still nursing our-son's-a-disappointment moods. Gloria wants to know how much he spent on it and why, while Raj eyes the thing suspiciously, trying to find out if it is sexual without asking directly. The only reason they let him keep it is because Ash has the inspiration to claim it's for yoga, making the case that if he can't drive, he'll be home a lot more, and this way he won't just be lying around like a sloth.

Setting it up by himself is a bear but it's way better than asking for their help. He spends a good part of the morning watching You-Tube videos about how to put in an anchor. (Do his parents realize he is a putting a hole in the ceiling? No, they do not.) The only upside is that focusing so hard on the task at hand allows less time to stress about Shani and Jackson.

Now, he's in the fire-orange silk swing and he's more impressed with his construction skills than his vision. His phone is perched

outside the swing on a cellphone tripod, so every time he wants to retake the shot, he has to get out of his cocoon, which is not, um, *easy*. As he rolls out of it to drop to the floor, he thinks maybe, all things considered, he hung it too high. But he can't keep the phone on him, because no one will be able to see the sling—it'll look like he's just taking a selfie.

Into and out of the damn thing three times already, his mood is increasingly terrible. *Nothing* is working as he imagined. Yes, his Thor outfit is flawless: the black bodysuit is padded with ripples and bulges that are Batman-in-latex hot, the red cape satiny and vivid. But once he's ensconced in his creation, the effect is lost as he tries not to fold up like someone being eaten.

Attempt four, sitting up on his knees, aiming for Vajrasana pose meets sex kitten, he pitches over, arms flailing as he ends up face down in the sling. And then: pop. The anchor bolt releases itself from the ceiling.

Thudding to the floor shakes the house and bruises his ego. *Of course*, his dad opens the door right then, without even knocking first. Raj starts to speak and then stops at what appears to be his son, clad in fetish wear, writhing in a pile of silk. All he says is, "This does not look healthy," and closes the door.

The cell phone is still filming. For a moment, Ash just gives up, lying there in the remains of the sling. If Shani was speaking to him, he'd turn this into a funny story immediately. He'd edit the clip of the collapse and put some catchy text on it and send it to her. He might even post the disaster on @AshMeAnything with a #fail hashtag. Pure FYP bait.

But he and Shani haven't truly worked things out and he's not

in a laughing mood. If he can't solve the first problem, he's not going to be able to solve the second.

. . .

So, buses.

Living close to the Square means Ash can walk to most parts of his life if he chooses: Curious Liquids, St. Joe's, the Ivy, the salon where they understand just how opinionated he can be about his hair. Having a car means that half the time he doesn't bother walking, but at least he knows he could. Anywhere else he needs to go, his Jaguar has it covered.

Suddenly, without wheels, he *has* to walk to the Square, and the world beyond that means buses. He didn't ride buses even in elementary school: Raj dropped him off and Gloria or the au pair picked him up. He's simply never had a need and he hadn't honestly given it that much thought. It's not that public transportation is beneath him—he has no problem parking his car at Alewife and taking the train into the city—so much as it has always seemed, well, like something *other* people do.

Am I spoiled? This is a question that has never, not once, crossed his mind. But the last few days, it's been lingering around the edge of all thought. He doesn't want to be that guy.

So here he is, standing awkwardly on a melting snowbank waiting for the crosstown bus that will bring him to Shani's. When the bus pulls up, it's packed. He's already inwardly groaning about not getting a seat as he approaches the fare box. He looks for the credit card slot and can't find it. The driver has a sour look on his face and

the person behind him, trapped in the stairwell, mutters, "You gonna be all day, pal?"

Ash's stomach clenches as he waves the card at the driver. "I don't see where—"

"Are you kidding?" The driver has a look that clearly says *I'm done with these fools.* "He points at the reflective CASH OR CHARLIE CARD ONLY sign on the fare box.

Cash? Seriously, who uses paper money anymore? Ash feels the injustice of this restriction in his gut. He knows what a Charlie Card is—there's an old one in his wallet from his last trip to Boston—but he can't even add money to it, because all he has is his VISA card.

"Jeezus Christ, kid." The man behind him is pissed because the driver still hasn't closed the door of the bus. In fact, Ash is pretty sure everyone on the bus hates him right now for slowing up their commute. He has no choice but to get off.

But a stranger, a mom with her baby Björned to her chest, reaches past him to tap her preloaded fare card onto the reader to pay for him. Embarrassed, he tries to thank her as he pushes by into the throng, but she shushes him, indicating the sleeping child. She mouths the words *pay it forward* and smiles.

Sandwiched between a hipster-brewer type with a beard that could easily hide forest creatures and a high school student who appears to regret taking upright bass lessons, Ash questions his impulse to seek Shani out in person. Every time the driver brakes, the bus lurches, and everyone standing folds forward like wheat in a wind. It happens so often, Ash is getting nauseous. He nicknames

the driver Brakesy and wonders if the guy can be reviewed. Is there a Yelp for MBTA?

By the time he gets to Shani's stop, he's pretty sure he smells like the woody cologne that the bearded guy was wearing. The fresh air is a relief and he's surprised to find it's not that cold. The polar vortex has moved on, leaving mere winter.

Shani and her dad live in the top floor condo of a house with three units. The building has two front doors and a side door leading to the back staircase, which is the one rising up to their floor. The sidewalk to their entrance is shoveled, but patches of black ice are turning into puddles and Ash tries to navigate the wet carefully, having had his share of falls for the day. A woman peers at him from a window on the first floor, then quickly moves away once she realizes she can be seen. Ash, wearing a belted felt trench coat and wellingtons, is pretty sure he doesn't read as a big threat.

He hesitates before ringing the bell. Shani always has him text when he arrives; her dad naps between fares, so the bell is annoying. But she hasn't been returning his texts so much, so ... The sound of footsteps in the stairwell lifts his spirits, but it's her dad. "Ash!" He says this so happily that it means either he doesn't know about the drama or must want it to end. "Come on up!"

Shani's in the Studio when her dad calls out, "Ash is here."

He feels trapped in the kitchen in the silence that follows. Does he dare just go into her room, or should he wait? Her dad asks how Christmas was and he tries to mumble answers as naturally as possible, but his eyes stay on the door to the Studio. Is she going to come out or not?

When she appears, she doesn't look happy, but she beckons him. "What are you waiting for, fool?" she says, and heads back to her room.

Where to sit? Normally, he'd be flung across her bed like a throw, but now that feels presumptuous. He chooses the sofa, a little stiffly, like he's sitting in the waiting room about to get a tooth pulled.

Shani sits at her vanity, facing the mirror. "So? Say what you need to."

It's awkward talking to her face in a reflection, while her back forms a wall between them, but he has no choice. "I'm sorry. I'm so sorry."

"That's not news."

"But it's true. I feel terrible."

"About what exactly? Be real specific."

"I should never have tried to break you and Jackson up."

"That ain't it."

"Okay, I shouldn't have been macking on him—"

Shani sucks her teeth and turns around. "That ain't it either."

Ash feels clammy. What is it she needs to him to say? And then he knows. "It's not about Jonas at all."

Shani releases a long breath and closes her eyes. "Nope." To his horror, she squinches up her face like she might cry.

She does cry. No sound. Just tears escaping between lashes tightly pressed together. *Oh my god. I did this.*

"I'm a shitty friend," he ekes out, close to crying. She murmurs something like agreement but doesn't open her eyes yet. "I should

have been honest with you about my feelings for him . . ." He can hear the shame creeping into his voice. "And I should have talked to you before I told him."

"Yes, asshole, you should have."

Shani gets up and crosses to her bed, where Grave Bear rests on a pillow. She grabs him and holds him in her crossed arms, sitting on the end of the bed. "What makes me worth so little to you?"

"Oh, god, no–" The distance between them feels too far. Ash goes to the bed, sits next to her. She stays put but leans away.

"That's the opposite of how I see you! You're the most impressive person I know, the only one who seems to know who they are. I think about you–what you'd like, what you'd think is funny, things we can do together–more than I think about anyone else, like, all the time."

"Then why play me like that?"

"Maybe I was just fooling myself into thinking it would be okay. I started falling for Jackson–"

"*Jonas!*"

Not the time to argue. "I started falling for *Jonas* and thought I could have him and, if I handled it just right, you, too. I wanted to believe that because I can't lose you."

"It's not just you. Everyone thinks they gotta lie to me. Timmo . . . that other kid . . . Jonas . . . my dad–"

"Your dad?"

"I never told you what he did when my mom died?" She shakes her head. "I met you like six months later, I figured I must have."

Ash knows better than to interrupt.

"The night she died, he had the neighbors take me out for Chinese food. He said she had to work late and he knew Chinese would make me happy, right? So we go to my favorite place—the old Mei Fun that closed after the fire, remember—and they say I can have anything I want, but I notice they're not really eating, and the dad keeps checking his phone. My friend Anya kept looking at me with these big eyes like I was, I don't know, covered in zits, and finally I said, 'Girl, why are you making that face?' and she covered her mouth with her hands like to keep from saying something. And then the mom was trying not to cry and I said I wanted to go home, they were spooking me. But they took me back to their house and said it was a sleepover and it would be fun. Like anybody was even close to having fun.

"And in the morning, while I was waiting for him to come get me, I hear Anya and her mom in the bathroom whispering, so of course I put my ear right against the door, and Anya said she'd made it through the night without telling me. You know I tried to open that door right then to make them tell me what, but it was locked. So I pounded on it hard till they opened it and they both looked so guilty, I knew it was something big. 'Are they divorcing?' I shouted, cause it had to be about my folks, and then Anya started to cry. That girl never cried—never once, and I was like, *shit.*

"And just like that I knew. I *knew.* And I knew that *they* knew first and that made it worse—which doesn't make sense, how much worse can it be, right, but it *was* worse. And they still wouldn't tell me.

"When my dad came, I walked right up to him and punched

him in the gut! I'd never punched anything or anyone, but that's what I did. I felt so alone.

"He said he couldn't face me that first night, that he was a wreck, that he needed to get himself together and be strong for me when I heard. He couldn't be a mess when I only had one parent left. And I was like, *But* you *got to see her!* He didn't lie to watch out for *me.* He lied because it took care of *him.* Just like you—someone I trust enough to be my best and worst self with. Even Jonas—he let me think he was something he wasn't because he figured he'd look better if he did.

"What am I supposed to think you all see when you look at me?"

Ash puts his arm around her. "Someone we're afraid to fail. Someone we fail because we're weak." She doesn't say anything. "And in my case, someone I figured was so strong, she'd skate right by this."

"Do I look like I'm skating?" The question is an opening.

Ash speaks softly. "I don't know those guys from before. Some people are just assholes and that's not about you. But, for me, you're so important. I value you. So much so that none of the reasons I did what I did even matter if I lose you."

Shani lies back, staring at the ceiling. She doesn't speak for a long minute. "That's better."

Ash lays back, too, their arms touching. "Does this mean I'm forgiven?"

"You didn't get to *Forgive me* yet. You barely got past *I'm sorry.*"

He rolls on his side to face her. "I'm sorry for not being honest with you. I'm sorry for being a bad friend. You own five years of

prime real estate in my heart, and I didn't act like that was true. Will you forgive me?"

She rolls to face him. Her dark eyes are dry now, but the lashes are still wet. "I don't know," she says. "But I'll think about it."

He rests his forehead against hers. He closes his eyes, whispers. "Thank you."

They lie there for a long while, their breathing aligning. Snippets of whatever Shani's dad is watching on TV can be heard faintly, joined occasionally by the sound of passing cars or a police siren's wail. Shani seems on the verge of sleep.

Ash opens his eyes and looks at her. She's so beautiful and so herself. He remembers the first summer they met, how much he wanted to please her. How desperate he was that she be his friend. And then the fall of ninth grade, when he found himself wishing she was a girlfriend, not a friend. But then she found Timmo and he met a cute boy on the debate team and the idea seemed silly.

The old memories wash over him charged with something new. He registers this feeling with surprise. Is it just that they're both so vulnerable right now?

What it would be like to kiss Shani?

Not a stranger he met on an app. Not a boy (who might or might not even be into him). But a girl he knows by heart. Does he dare?

Instead, he reaches up to brush her cheek with his hand. Her eyes open and search his, asking questions neither can answer.

She doesn't say a word, but in a moment, her hand traces the outline of his face. He has never felt this with a girl before. He has never felt *exactly* this with anyone.

Feeling the spark of the moment is confusing. What does it mean? Is he not just gay? Is he bi and never knew? The thought unsettles him—knowing himself is a point of pride. But he leans into the closeness, hearing his body speak. *Just kiss her.*

Her dad knocks at the door and they both sit up as if burned. When he steps into the room, he can see the you-caught-us looks on their faces, and he doesn't try to hide his confusion. "I didn't mean to . . . uh . . . interrupt." They all know what he's saying. "Am I interrupting? I—"

"C'mon, Dad, as if." Shani leaps off the bed and makes a show of rolling her eyes. Ash doesn't say anything. It's the second time today a dad has walked into the room to find him a position that looks less innocent than it is. But that's not the real issue. Honestly, what just happened? Maybe it's a good thing her dad broke the spell.

"Okay, well . . ." Shani's dad looks unconvinced. "I'm going to the grocery store. What do you want?"

"Like I'm trusting you!" Shani grabs a scarf from the floor and wraps her head. "I'm coming with." She turns to Ash; he finds the look on her face unreadable. "Need a ride home?"

The ride is quiet. What is she thinking? Did she feel what he felt? Or did he make it up?

They are almost to Ash's house when Shani turns to her dad. "Don't be pissed, but we need to make a stop first."

"It's a grocery run, not an Uber trip."

As tired as her dad sounds, Shani punches an address into his GPS.

"Better make it short."

Ash hates to be in the dark. "What are we doing?"

She addresses her dad, not Ash. "You have to turn around. We're going to Prospect Street."

. . .

On the way to Prospect Street, Shani explains to Ash. "You wouldn't let me hide from you. I thought I was fine being pissed off, but it was harder to stay that way once I saw you. Jonas needs to know that we aren't going anywhere. That we're sorry. He needs to *see us*, period."

"I don't know." Ash watches streetlamps flying past. "I don't think it'll be that easy."

"I didn't say it would be *easy*."

For the rest of the ride, Ash is quiet. Shani's right—they need to fix things with Jonas. But what about what just happened? Whatever it was, it wasn't any ordinary Friday night for them. She had to have felt it, too. Are they going to talk about it? Or is this whole excursion a way to pretend nothing changed?

Shani's dad drops them off in front of the building, saying he'll shop without her. From the sidewalk, it appears half the units are dark, and though the front door opens easily, the door from the lobby to the interior is locked. The wall of buzzers doesn't help; it's alphabetical and Ash realizes they don't know his last name—the perils of social media friendships. Alongi, Botnen, Baykan, Dowd, Esposito, Frangos, Goyne, McGuinn, Vincent, Waring. No Prospers. Nothing screams Jonas.

Both inner and outer doors are glass, making the lobby a little

translucent box, so Ash feels exposed. It feels dicey to be two brown folks hanging out in the lobby of a building where they don't live. They need to get someone to let them in, but who?

The first candidate is a handyman who so doggedly avoids eye contact as he enters that neither of them dare speak at first. He's already slipping through the inner door, which he has opened just enough for himself, when Shani hazards an "Excuse me, sir—"

"Nope," is all he says before very deliberating pulling the door shut behind him.

Hope arrives in the form of a girl their age, her face a galaxy of freckles. She and Shani recognize each other instantly. "Hey," she says. "That was nice of you—the food. I didn't expect it."

Shani is thrilled at this development. "Glad you liked it." She seizes her moment. "Hey, do you know Jonas . . ."

"Vincent? He's two doors down from me, but . . ." Immediately, the galaxies rearrange into constellations of sympathy. "I think he's still at the wake."

Oh, shit. Foma died? *Now*? Ash clutches Shani's arm and knows she's feeling it, too.

"Did you go? How does he seem?"

"Oh, no, we're not that close. I mean, he's kinda shy. I've tried but he's usually so closed off, right? Then he was in the elevator looking like a mess, so I just pressed a little, you know, like, to be a Good Samaritan or whatever . . . and it all came out. Heard the whole thing—his foster mom's fall and the liver stuff. She was like a real mom, or, well, like a *better* real mom. Like, I was crying, too, but I think he was kinda embarrassed that he said so much, cause you know how boys are."

Ash hates that this girl knows more about what has happened than he does, but he has no choice but to ask for more. "What about the funeral?"

"I offered to go, which he was kinda surprised by, honestly. And I *would*, but, um . . . it's in *Dorchester*." She gathers a tangle of red hair in her fingers and twines strands together while she contemplates that. "I mean, like I said, I don't know him so well, and I don't think I'd fit in." She reads Ash's expression—he has deciphered her code correctly and judged her for it—and blushes. "I *want* to. But I don't really like funerals, you know, so . . ."

Shani stops her. "I feel you. I'm not sure I'll go either." Ash knows by her tone she doesn't mean it.

The girl seems to know, too. She tells them the name of the church and the time, then cocks her head. "If you do go, tell him Shelby says she's sorry for him. I think he knows my name. I'm not sure. Maybe just say the girl down the hall." And she heads inside to the rest of her night, unaware of the bomb she's dropped on them.

Alone again, Ash can't help wonder if it's almost selfish of them to go; even asking such a question is new for him. "What if we show up and it makes him feel worse?"

Shani considers this, nodding gravely. "We'll have to be discreet. I just . . . I feel like we *have* to be there for him."

"*Both* of us."

"Boy, you know you're not going alone. Can't be trusted."

It's almost funny. So why does he feel like crying?

TWENTY-FOUR
JONAS

"Winter rain is the worst. It just goes right through you." Marion is shaking a black umbrella in the pastor's study at the church. She is making small talk in a voice that Jonas finds painfully like Foma's, and yet not quite right. The rain started last night and hasn't yet stopped, coming down like a magic eraser, dissolving weeks' worth of snow into thick, slushy creeks. She picked Jonas up for the ride to Waymark SDA and neither of them have been outside longer than it takes to get from car to door, yet he knows what she means: he feels wet and raw in the thin polyester suit he got at Goodwill. Marion had offered to buy him something nicer, but he'd refused; for one thing, he wants no keepsake from this day, and for another, he wants to owe her nothing.

It's better not to love, he thinks. *Better to have no ties at all.* He hasn't said more than *Thanks for the ride* all morning and he isn't feeling inclined to now. In the past two days, during which she arranged a wake and funeral and repast with marvelous speed and focus,

Marion has also, in her way, suggested that Jonas will remain family, even with her sister gone. She's never been the cuddly Auntie, it's not her way; there were always presents on Christmas and birthdays, but she was not the "fun" sister, someone whose visits excited Jonas. Perhaps now, in the face of this loss, something has softened, or maybe it's the guilt of having rented his home out from under him. She's trying harder now, reminding him that he still has a place to go for Thanksgiving and Christmas, like that's not almost a year away.

The pastor's chamber fills with Foma's nieces and nephews, all older than Jonas, some he has never seen, and others he remembers from summer barbecues back before most of their own parents passed. Foma was the youngest sister; she should have been the last to go, but instead, Marion is left to shepherd the clan with efficiency if not actual warmth. Her only child, Judit, who always calls him Cuz, envelops him in a hug and he hugs her back, his eyes brimming from the forgotten power of being held.

"I heard you got your own place," she says when they finally part.

Jonas chuckles ruefully. "Nothing great."

"I'm sorry Mom is . . . Mom." He knows that Judit thinks Marion should have offered to take him in. "Though I don't think you'd really have enjoyed living with her so much. Why do you think I went to college all the way in Georgia?"

"Ha." It's hard but he squeezes out a smile.

Judit envelops his hands in hers, plum-colored nail tips reaching near to his wrists. She holds his eyes with her own. "You have anyone looking out for you?"

The question hurts. What would he say? The girl down the hall? "I'll be okay."

She shakes her head. "That's a no, then." She keeps his hands locked in hers but steps back. "I got you. You call me for whatever. No Prosper goes it alone."

"How about a Vincent?"

"Prosper by proxy. It counts." She squeezes his hands one last time. "It does."

Across the room, he sees two of Foma's older fosters. Both are twice his age and he's heard of them but never met them. Today, he's not up for it. He wonders if the fosters who aren't here even know she's gone.

A very round Black woman in a berry-colored suit steps into the middle of the crowd. "For those of you who do not know me, I am Pastor Jonquil Carnegie, and Evelyn and I went to church school, high school, and college together. I'm grateful that Pastor Hall is lending me his pulpit for my friend's homegoing. The church is more than full now, with folk standing along the sides, so it's time for y'all to go in." She scans the room. "Where's the son?"

Judit steps aside so he can be seen and the pastor beams. "Evelyn sent me your school photo every single year. Did you know that?" He shakes his head, numbly. "Apple of her eye. *Apple* of her eye. Amen?"

He's not sure if he's meant to respond but some of the others answer back for him. "Amen!"

Opening the door, the pastor gives orders. "Follow me, Marion and Jonas first, then the older kids, the nieces and nephews and their partners, and everybody else. All right? Let's go."

An organist is playing "Abide with Me" as they process up the center aisle, the pastor setting a slow, deliberate pace. Marion has hooked her arm through Jonas's and is leaning on him heavily. Her commander-in-chief demeanor is gone and she cries all the way up the aisle. At one point, she rests her head on his shoulder, and it's so unexpected, he almost recoils. The realness of the day just keeps getting realer.

➤ SHANI

Watching Jonas go by, eyes down, a weeping woman on his arm, Shani feels like an imposter. She hasn't been invited here and doesn't know the grieving woman or any of these people packed together tightly into pews.

She has done what she could to fit in; she took her favorite black party dress and layered a black wool sweater over it to hide its sleevelessness. She doesn't have hose and can't imagine owning any, but sees that many of the woman here today do. Thankfully, she has tall suede boots, so her legs are less bare than usual. The farmed pearls her mother wore on her wedding day, a treasure that Shani keeps in a ceramic box on her vanity, gleam white against her dark skin. Before this morning, she has never even tried the pearls on; they're sacred to her.

Though she may look the part, she knows this is not truly her place. The organ music, the candles flickering, just being in a church surrounded by melanated folk—she is transported back to her mom's funeral. Shani spent that day angry at her dad, at her relatives, at

the pastor who didn't even say her mom's name right, at cousins who were playing games on their phones, even at her mom, though she couldn't explain why. And oh, the anger she felt toward people who didn't belong.

A flash of memory: Allison, a girl in Shani's class, was there with her moms, who Shani had ever seen only at afterschool pickup. This outrage was too much. Allison didn't know Shani's mother, not at all, and for that matter, the two girls weren't close. She didn't deserve to be there, to witness the most awful day. And bringing *two* moms, when Shani no longer had even one, seemed evil. Shani had given Allison the most awful look she could from all the way across the church. The girl withered, which disappointingly made Shani feel no better at all.

"Should we go?" she whispers now to Ash, who is quieter than she's ever seen him.

"What? *No.* It'll make a scene if we get up."

Shani's not convinced this is true. The family is all seated many rows away, facing the dais, where a woman in pink-red wool commands attention amid a trio of portly men in black suits. She and Ash could slip out the back and none would be the wiser. But one of the men is rising to speak and the room is hushed, so she stays put.

"I invite to you kneel as we all seek the Lord's blessing on our beloved Evelyn."

People still kneel? Shani's mom's church, to which Sheree still drags Shani to sometimes, isn't like that—you stand or stay in your pew for prayer. And that's all the church she knows, since her dad,

Catholic by nature more than by practice, hasn't been to a mass in years. Crouching on the carpet feels foreign, just one more reminder that this isn't her place. As the prayer winds on—whoever the man is, he is milking his time in the spotlight—she grows increasingly aware of Ash's body, how the narrow space has crowded them together side by side. His presence feels different today.

She can't stop thinking about the moment in her room, when the air changed. In any other context, it would have been chemistry. But he's gay, which should have dulled that edge for both of them. Maybe what happened was like his version of her saying yes to a date with Milo: Ash just put his feelings about Jonas into the wrong basket? Except she knows that bodies are not built for predictability—there's a reason why people have started using the word "fluid" to talk about sexuality. She just doesn't know where on a continuum this would fall.

If Ash was a stranger, someone she met in passing, it would be easier to ignore. But he is not. Ash means more to her than anyone but her dad and Sheree. What happens when you mix that with attraction? She isn't sure she wants to know. They haven't talked about it because she's left no space at all for them to. Whatever the pastor is praying about is as far from her mind as can be.

When she finally hears the words, *In Jesus's name, amen,* she returns the amen by instinct, like the church girl she didn't grow up to be.

➤ ASH

He is happy to unfold himself upward and back into the pew. He didn't mind the prayer—can't be raised by Raj without learning how to roll with some meditation, after all—but he hadn't factored kneeling into the equation when he chose his outfit: an oversized double-breasted sharkskin suit from Gucci he was saving for graduation. He hopes kneeling on a carpet wet from boots won't mar the pants.

It's a release from being pressed so tight to Shani's side. He'd figured in light of day that maybe the spell of last night would be entirely broken. No such luck. The air still hums with questions.

What am I doing here? It makes no sense to be sitting in a church with a girl he almost kissed trying not to be seen by a boy he almost kissed who has since rejected them both.

He tells himself to focus on the funeral. A young woman in a dress that is all about the curves is approaching the podium. If you can rock body-con and funeral-ready all at once, she is. Clad in black head to toe, she is properly somber, and yet nothing about her says demure or humble: shoulders bare and gleaming, guns to rival Michelle Obama's, and heels so sharp they could be weapons. Ash hadn't known church could look like this.

And when she opens her mouth—wow.

The voice that comes out is round and rich, with only the faintest hint of huskiness at the edge.

Why should I feel discouraged,
  why should the shadows come,

Why should my heart be lonely,
    and long for heaven and home?

The singer pulls on some of the words, elongating them and suspending a vowel a moment before going on. The accompanist is keeping pace, eyeing her for cues, letting her lead the way.

When Jesus is my portion? My constant friend is He:
    His eye is on the sparrow, and I know He watches me;
His eye is on the sparrow, and I know He watches me.

What must it be like to believe in something like that? Ash tries to imagine who or what he trusts the way this woman trusts. His folks, maybe? But someday he'll outgrow them and they'll be done with playing safety net. And they'll die before he does anyway, so what happens then? Will he fall in love with someone who will still be there when they are old? Is that even the same? He can't see himself ever believing in God, but in this room, at this moment, he has a hint of why he'd want to.

I sing because I'm happy,
    I sing because I'm free,
For His eye is on the sparrow,
    And I know He watches me.

It's a funny sentiment for a funeral—*I sing because I'm happy?*—but the delivery makes all the difference. He can hear the yearning,

the fight to say *This is all part of the plan.* The singer's eyes are closed and her hands have come alive, fingers spread like she might rise into the air. He's getting chills.

If for nothing but this, he's glad they came.

➤ JONAS

Yesterday, when Marion asked Jonas if he had any thoughts about the service, he'd said no at first but changed his mind at the last minute. How many times had he heard Foma sing "His Eye Is on the Sparrow"? When Foma sang it, there was a little bounce to it, a cheerful working song while cleaning the house. Once, he even found her humming it when he arrived for a visit at Maple Crest. She had looked at him that afternoon and smiled a smile it breaks his heart to remember. "You too, Jonas! His eye is on you, too!"

The song is something else entirely in the hands of his cousin Judit. There are tears dripping down her cheeks but her composure is everything. She is grieving her auntie but nothing can break her faith. She dares you to question this. Think she doesn't mean it? Just try her.

> Let not your heart be troubled, His tender word I hear,
>   And resting on His goodness, I lose my doubts and fears;
> Though by the path He leadeth, but one step I may see;
>   His eye is on the sparrow, and I know He watches me.

Jonas sees Judit maybe twice a year for family stuff, so he knows they're not really *that* close, but as her voice enwraps him the way her hug did, he's already starting to miss her.

➤ SHANI

What is it about this song? Someone sang the very same thing at Shani's mom's funeral. She remembers how her relatives nodded and murmured, how some quietly sang along. Even her dad seemed soothed. But her anger that day had not been stilled by the promises in the lyrics.

> *Whenever I am tempted, whenever clouds arise,*
> *When songs give place to sighing, when hope within me dies,*
> *I draw the closer to Him, from care He sets me free;*
> *His eye is on the sparrow, and I know He watches me.*

Shani has never felt hopeless, not truly. It's not in her nature. She's never doubted that she has a future. But days when songs give way to sighs? She's known plenty of those, and this just reminds her of the worst of them.

How can Jesus's eye be on her when it wasn't on her mother? Was He really watching out for Shani if he let that happen? Where is the verse about Him not just watching, but *doing*? It doesn't matter how beautiful the song sounds, how much this singer is giving

her whole body to the cry of it—her heart bars entry. *No way*, she thinks. *No chance I'm letting that in.*

➤ ASH

"His eye is on the sparrow . . ." The singer's voice drops to the floor, the "-row" rumbling on the lowest note of the song. He can hardly breathe.

"And I know . . . he watches . . . me . . ."

The last syllable doesn't resolve. Instead, the singer lands it a few notes away from where Ash expects and then lets it climb. As the notes rise, one of her hands does, too, elegant fingers tracing a pattern in the air for her to follow. Up, up, up, into another octave, and even into the next, the *eeee* floating into the ether, finally, to resolve.

He wants to applaud, but instead, he joins the amens that roll like thunder.

➤ JONAS

Sitting in the front row of a funeral means being closest to the casket, which he finds excruciating. Polished wood, not too expensive but not cheap, reposes on a rolling cart draped in gossamer fabric. How can Foma be so near and completely lost to him even so?

Pastor Carnegie takes the podium and introduces herself,

greeted with welcomes and sounds of recognition. She begins her eulogy with an explanation. "Some of you sisters and brothers may ask why I'm dressed so bright on a day so sad. I have two reasons and I suspect y'all know one of them." Murmurs from the crowd urge her on. "I wear this color because today is a sad day, but not a dark day; a day of grief, but not of loss, not truly; it is a day of victory!" Amens rise. "A day of triumph! A day of glory! The day our Evvie goes home!"

Applause joins the amens and exhortations for her to preach, to speak on it. But Jonas winces. *Evvie?* Marion called her Evelyn, the kids all say Auntie, and Maple Crest called her Ms. Prosper. When was she Evvie and to who? Why didn't he know?

"The second reason is because raspberry was Evvie's favorite color when we were girls. It couldn't just be pink or plain red, it had to be that *raspberry* color. Now, I will tell you, finding a raspberry suit on two days' notice is not the easiest thing on earth, but earth is not the limit, and the One whose eye is on the sparrow also kept His eye on the internet and dropped this in my shopping cart." This generates a laugh. "Kindly stay away from me at the repast, cause I intend to return it." An even bigger laugh. "I'm just playing. I'm keeping this suit, wearing it whenever I need to feel Evvie near. And I will need that feeling for a good long while. Until *that* day." Amens. "Until that *great* day." More amens. "When I'm wearing the same robes as Evvie."

Jonas puts his head in his hands. He believes in heaven. But he can't picture it, really. And certainly not with robes. When you get there, do you immediately find those you've lost? Or are they so far

ahead of you that you never catch up? The vastness of it feels over-whelming to contemplate. He would be okay not seeing Valerie, but if he isn't reunited with Foma there's no point to going at all.

➤ SHANI

Maybe all pastors should be women, she thinks. This lady is so much better than the old dude who spoke at her mom's funeral.

"The shortest verse in the Bible is just two words: *Jesus wept*. The brevity of that line grabs your attention, says *Look at me*. And that's no mistake. The apostle wants you to know: Jesus gets it. Jesus cried when his friend was dead; Jesus, who held the power to resurrect the man, still acknowledges the human feeling of grief. So Jesus wept. He understands that you will, too. He feels it when you do. Jesus *wept!*"

A voice calls out, "That's right!"

"But that's not all he did!" Pastor Carnegie glows with purpose. "He got to work. He healed. He raised the dead. He kept preaching and making miracles until they killed Him for it. And you know what He did then."

"He rose up!"

"He rose up. He rose from the tomb and he walked."

The pianist rings a chord.

"I'm not expecting all y'all to raise the dead or heal the sick or turn water into wine. But I expect you to get to work. Do the ordi-nary miracles: Love your neighbor. Be kind. Get up and walk the

path Evvie did while she was here. The right path. The good path. The one that leads to home and a happier day."

From above and behind her, the words *Oh happy day!* ring out. The entire congregation turns to look as a choir in the balcony starts to sing. The song is call-and-response, the faithful echoing the choir's lyrics. This far back, the balcony overhangs the rows, so Shani cannot see the singers, but there is no escaping how the song fills the space, a joyous clap-along, and the congregation leans into it, swaying. It's hard to resist the spell, even for her.

➤ ASH

When "Oh Happy Day" kicks in, Ash feels like he is in a movie. His only previous exposure to a Black choir was a House of Blues Gospel Brunch once when his family was traveling. Now, as the voices boom out from the balcony above him and Shani, he's getting chills.

When he looks back to the dais, he discovers that this song is the exit music and the coffin has been repositioned. Four pallbearers on each side stand ready to roll it down the aisle atop its cart. Jonas is in the front on one side. And he is looking straight at Ash and Shani.

➤ JONAS

They came.

Jonas was already beyond knowing how to manage his feelings

today and this may be too much. It makes no sense. How did they hear about Foma? How did they find the funeral? Why would they come now, after everything?

A tap on his shoulder from Judit tells him they have to move. Rolling the cart is easy enough, physically, far easier than it will be when they must carry the coffin by hand. But one of the wheels catches every time it goes round, making the cart shake, and it's upsetting. He wants the ride to be as smooth for Foma as possible. The Bible says *The dead know not anything*, but who's to say it's true?

He tries to focus on his task but he can't stop looking at the last row. Shani and Ash both try to apologize with their eyes. He looks away, trains his eyes on the doors at the back of the sanctuary, which have parted now to reveal wan sunlight. Water drips from the frame of the entryway where the funeral director and his assistant wait.

Jonas slows his pace. The moment they go out the door, the funeral is over. There is still the repast and the graveside service ahead, but then those rituals too will be done. The end really will have come.

He can't help it: he looks again at Shani and Ash. If he had known they were thinking of this, he would have told them not to come. And yet they're the only people in the whole place who are there for *him*, the only ones who are—were?—his alone. Why do they have to be people who hurt him?

He's only ten or fifteen feet from the sanctuary door. Only five or six from the last row. He has to keep walking. He knows this. But he wants to stop in his tracks. To hold time here, where Foma, Shani, and Ash are all in the same space, even if he's lost all three.

As he nears their row, Ash leans forward, mouthing *I'm so sorry.* Shani reaches a hand into the aisle, her eyes making a speech Jonas isn't ready to hear.

He doesn't take her hand.

He keeps walking.

But when he is almost at the door, he turns to look over his shoulder and whispers to them both. "Thank you for coming."

It's all he can say without bawling.

TWENTY-FIVE
JONAS

Unmoored. That's how Jonas feels at the repast. He learned the word in English class as they practiced syllogisms. Unmoored is to boat as untethered is to balloon. He's definitely unmoored and not untethered. Adrift, not ascending.

After the receiving line, where people he'd never met hugged him and told him they would pray for him, he fills a plate only because Marion insists. Mac and cheese, potato salad, pasta salad—a banquet of starches he supplements with sticky ribs. He hasn't had food like this in months—not takeout, not something he pulls from the freezer to pop in the microwave. And yet he can barely stand the thought of eating. He consciously rejects the gumbo Marion brought; it is her signature dish, though she has never lived south of Rhode Island. Foma hated it, so ignoring it feels like solidarity.

Judit calls him over to her table and he plods her way. Attendees keep coming up to her, and every time, it leads to some story about Foma. Jonas is grateful to do nothing but sit quietly, not the

focus of anything, but what he really wants to do is leave. *Foma's not here. Not really*, he thinks. *She won't care if I stay or go.*

Marion approaches the table and it's clear she's looking for him. He knows she has just lost her sister, that it's no easy day for her, but he still bristles at her approach; he can't make himself feel bad for her. She who lives, who still has family, who has her home. Out of nowhere, he imagines picking the ribs up off his plate and flinging them at her, sticky sauce smeared across the lace top. But he just sits, the uneaten food cooling on a plate on his lap.

"Your friends are here," she says. "And they don't know what to do with themselves."

Jonas doesn't look up. It's wild enough that Shani and Ash found the funeral at all, but weirder that they'd come to the repast. They literally don't know a soul but Jonas, and he's not on speaking terms with them.

"They're not sure they're welcome . . ." she begins, and Jonas is thinking, *me either*. ". . . because they missed the service."

Huh? He looks toward the doorway. It's not Shani and Ash; it's Flasker and Sandy. Though part of him is disappointed, a larger part of him feels a surge of gratitude: *that's* who's looking out for him. He leaps up, dropping his untouched plate on the table. "Thank you, Auntie," he says, the first time he has used that term for her since Foma went into rehab. Marion looks so touched, he feels a little guilty as he leaves the family behind.

Jonas is taller than Flasker by a couple of inches and it's physically awkward but emotionally rewarding to hug him. Flasker squeezes the life out of—no, *into*—him. When Jonas turns to Sandy

next, she wards him off with an exaggerated show of disdain. "God, you guys. If I want to get all emotional, I'll watch *The Notebook*."

Flasker pokes her. "Dude, we're at a funeral."

She just grins. "No, we missed a funeral. This is . . . what is this called again?"

"Repast," says Jonas. "And you can eat all you want."

Flasker eyes the buffet but stays put. "Aren't you gonna ask why we missed the funeral?"

"I didn't actually expect you to come . . . I mean, you didn't even know her."

Sandy tugs his sleeve. "We know *you*. That's enough."

Once they have plates of food, Sandy piling ribs to the sky because she doesn't eat carbs anymore, and Flasker reluctantly skipping the gumbo at Jonas's insistence, they find an empty table. They are at the very edge of the hall, lit by the glowing red EXIT sign that mars the prettiness of the room. Flasker asks how Jonas is doing, really, and Jonas confesses that he hasn't slept more than fifteen minutes at a time the past two nights. He's been living on microwave burritos and staring at YouTube clips of people playing *Minecraft* and the only time he's left the house were the wake and the funeral.

"What about your girl?" Sandy asks. "Is she helping?"

Jonas thinks about how to answer. Flasker knew about Jonas's Christmas Eve date, but Jonas hadn't told him how it went. Or about Christmas and everything after. It would be so much easier to just say, *Nah, it didn't work out*, but he finds himself badly wanting to spill it. He tells the whole story.

When he's finished, Flasker is immediately sympathetic. "Dude, that sucks. They punked you."

But before Jonas can enjoy the validation, Sandy bursts his bubble. "Boo hoo."

It's like having ice water dumped on his head. "What???"

"They hid stuff from you, which is not cool, but only because they thought you were hiding stuff from them—which they thought because you *were*, so they felt, like, justified, right? And when they discovered you weren't an asshole, they had, what, like, two options: come clean or keep lying. So they came clean, which you have to admit is nicer, and you freaked out. I got that right?"

"For one thing, I didn't mean to hide stuff . . . it just happened . . . but they *meant* to play me."

"Um, I'm pretty sure if someone lies to me, I don't care if it 'just happened'—still a lie."

"And Shani didn't come clean! Ash outed her."

Flasker cuts in. "Did you let her explain after?"

"Why are you guys ganging up on me?" Jonas turns to Flasker. "Just a second ago, you were on my side!"

Sandy rubs his back. "No one's ganging up on you. Just saying it doesn't seem like the worst crime ever, especially when you obviously still dig her."

"And him," adds Flasker. "Sounds like you're into this Ash kid, too."

Sandy raises her eyebrows. "Yeah. What's that about? Which is it—her or him?"

He wishes he had kept his plate of food so he could pretend to

be eating it now. How has this migrated from his tale of being wronged to him being interrogated?

There's no good answer to Sandy's question. But she's waiting for a reply and so he says the truth. "I don't know."

"Got it." Flasker sits back, nodding like a sage who has discovered a great wisdom.

"Ahhhh. There's the *real* problem." Sandy nods. "It's easier to stay mad, because if you're not speaking to them, you don't have to figure this shit out."

Jonas groans, not because she has it wrong, but because she has it so right.

Judit comes by to let them know that the repast is wrapping up. Jonas introduces her first to Sandy and then to Flasker, who turns on the charm, because he can't ever not flirt. Jonas tries to imagine what the rest of this churchgoing family would think if they knew that one of these tables hosted a trans man and a cis lesbian. Some of his family would pray for the Lord to chase away the demons, some would pray for the Lord to soften all their hearts. A few, like Judit, would adjust on the spot and just be like: *Huh, that doesn't happen every day.* And one or two might even pull up a chair.

Apologetically, Judit reminds Jonas that the graveside service will be family only. The look on Sandy's face suggests that she is more than okay with skipping this part of events, but Flasker offers to drive Jonas over to the cemetery, and Jonas accepts.

The drive to Arbor Hills Memorial Park reveals a different Arlmont than they have seen in weeks. Sunlight on the snow makes everything feel impossibly bright; the rise in temperature melts ice and makes the droplets gleam. Little rivers run down the edges of

roadway and Jonas has a flash of memory—him racing a Popsicle stick as a boat in a rivulet along the street where he lived with Valerie. It was a poor kid's toy, genius and perfect, and he can still feel the pleasure of watching his pale canoe speed along. A disapproving neighbor yelled at Valerie, told her to get him out of the road, but instead, she joined him, sending her own Popsicle stick craft into the tiny stream.

Flasker's Jeep is the first vehicle to arrive at the park. They can see acres of headstones, mostly simple polished granite, a few more elaborate and showy. Nobody asked for his input, but Jonas suddenly hopes Foma's is pink marble. She'd like that.

Sandy has played the part of Dr. Phil the whole way to the park and she doesn't let up, asking more questions about the "love triangle," which she keeps calling Jonas's situation, a term which doesn't seem quite right. He wants her to stop; it's making noise in his brain and crowding out the space he needs to mourn Foma. But Sandy's on a mission. "If I made you choose one of them on the spot—"

"Why do we have to keep talking about this?"

"Because you're alone now!" Sandy retorts. She gasps then, literally covering her mouth like she could retroactively prevent the already-escaped sentiment from getting out. "Oh, no, Jonas, that came out wrong—"

"Did it?" he says, flinging open the door of the Jeep and striding across slushy snow. "Sounds right to me."

Flasker catches up with him first. "Pretty sure she just means she's worried about you."

Jonas stops by a black marble obelisk, sunlight mirroring off its glossy surface. "I KNOW THAT."

He turns away, gulping cool air. "I *know* that."

Sandy catches up. "You're *not* alone. You have me and Flasker—"

"Which you may be regretting right now," Flasker jokes.

"But he's got Melory and I have Anchee and I just want you to have someone, too. That's all I meant. A little love wouldn't hurt you."

Jonas shrugs but doesn't argue. A cardinal, its red heightened against the white, hops along the ground seeking berries. Foma loved cardinals, said *When a cardinal appears, an angel is near.* For all he knows, the cardinal *is* Foma. That even though her body is just now arriving in a long, black hearse, her spirit has taken new form and come to see him. He'd like to believe it.

What would Foma say about Shani and Ash? Where would he even begin to explain?

He asks Flasker and Sandy a question he can't now ask Foma. "What if I like them both? Like, really? But I don't know which one . . ." He hesitates. He can't say *I want*, because he can't explain to them the complicated universe of how romance and desire work for him. So he chooses easier language. "Which one I like better."

"Play them off each other. It'll be catnip. They'll both want you way more, I guarantee it."

Sandy punches Flasker in the arm. "You're such a douche sometimes."

"I'm just saying. It's true."

Sandy shakes her head. "Look, Jonas, you're mad they weren't honest with you, so you pretty much only have one way forward: be honest with them. Assuming you forgive them, that is." She hesitates. "Do you?"

He thinks about it a moment. "I guess. I mean, yes." Having seen them in that church, he knows it's true.

"Okay, then. Say you have feelings for both and don't know how to choose."

"I don't want to eff up our friendship." Hours ago, he thought it was over, and now he wants to protect it.

"Then say that, too. Let them work it out. Maybe they'll both be like, *Step off, bro,* or maybe they'll understand. You won't know unless you talk to them. Both of them."

Flasker chimes in. "Pro-tip: If they're talking, they're comparing notes, so whatever you say to one, you have to say to the other. You don't want to worry about keeping your stories straight."

"It shouldn't be stories at all!" Sandy lets out an exasperated sigh. "Just tell the truth."

Jonas's phone vibrates with a text alert. It's Marion.

Where are you?

He looks across the park toward Foma's plot and sees that everyone else is assembled. He gives Flasker and Sandy an I'm-sorry shoulder shrug. "They're waiting on me."

For a moment, he'd been so caught up in talking about his romantic mess that he'd forgotten why there were at a graveyard. Reality returns and he finds himself shaking as he hurries up the slushy lanes toward the Prospers. The cardinal leads the way.

TWENTY-SIX
JONAS

It is late and dark when he texts Shani and Ash. He hasn't just taken off the funeral suit; he has binned it, never wanting to see it again. After Judit dropped him off at the apartment building, he'd cried for a couple of hours and then fell into a dead sleep on the futon. When he awoke, the pillow was wet, as if he'd broken a sweat. All the lights were off, the streetlamp casting a parallelogram of its glow onto the end of the sofa.

He has showered and donned the color-block birthday hoodie. He tries to make notes of what he wants to say—but ends up drawing a picture instead. His face, floating bodiless, in the air, Shani in the pupil of one eye and Ash in the other. *I see you both,* he thinks, *and I can't look away from either.*

On the futon, still lit only by the streetlamp glow, he starts a group text. Hey. Thanks for coming today. I didn't expect it.

Ash answers right away, as if lying by the phone. We had to be there for you.

Jonas waits but Shani doesn't immediately reply. Now it's awkward: he needs to talk to both of them *at once*, and if he can't, he's not sure he can keep going. No more secondhand reporting: they both need to hear his feelings directly from him.

He's about to text and ask when they could all chat, when Shani replies. Wouldn't have missed it. It's all the opening he needs.

I need to tell you something.

Ellipses appear, which means Shani is starting to reply. He waits. No reply comes. The ellipses disappear.

Ash fills the gap. So spill.

I think I have to say it, not text it. Can we FaceTime—all three of us?

They have never done this all together. A minute passes without an answer and he's surprised (and grateful) when Shani is the one who starts the call. Seeing them both at once on his iPad is disconcerting but also makes his heart swell a little. Shani wears her night wrap and the SZA sweatshirt that is her favorite pajama top, which makes it feel normal, but she's on the sofa she uses for videos, instead of on her bed, which means she's keeping her guard up. Ash is on his bed, propped on a half dozen pillows, and wearing a plush white bathrobe, like someone waiting for a massage at a spa in a movie.

Ash breaks the spell. "Well, aren't you the Man of Mystery. Mood lighting and all."

Jonas sees himself on the screen: his face glowing from secondhand lamplight, surrounded by darkness. The light comes in slant, so half his features are in shadow canyons.

He can't start right in. "What are you guys up to?" God, that's a pointless thing to say.

"Just vibin'." Shani's answer is as pointless as his question. She must feel as nervous as he does.

Ash tries to make a joke. "I'm repenting for my sins. I do that a lot lately." But it's too close to the truth, so he goes on. "Jackson, I'm so sorry for all of it."

"I am too, Jonas," Shani says. "I never meant to hurt you."

Jonas swallows hard. "Me too. I understand." It feels surprisingly good to say that. "And, um, while we're clearing the air . . . I know you think I'm kind of a liar, but those are both real names. Jackson is my first name but Valerie called me Jonas and Foma followed her example. I mean, you can call me either, but–"

"Which one feels more like *you*?" Ash asks, with Shani speaking at almost the same time.

"Who do you think of yourself as?"

"That may be the only identity question I can answer easily. I'm Jonas. I always have been."

Ash looks a little crestfallen, but if he is, he doesn't admit it. "Jonas you were, Jonas you shall be again."

Shani smiles. "Good. I hate being wrong." They all laugh and then silence settles over the call for a moment. They want to know what he has to say.

"I . . . um, so I was talking to my friend about what happened, and she thinks I shut you guys out so I wouldn't have to deal with my own shit. And I guess that's true."

The words linger somewhere in cyberspace, an invitation for them to ask him a question. Nobody does.

Jonas closes his eyes before going on, as if saying what he has to say will be less scary if he can't see their faces. "I don't know what I want."

"*Who* you want," Shani clarifies. "That's what you mean, right?"

He opens his eyes. She doesn't look angry, only determined. Ash is biting his lip, waiting to see what Jonas says.

Time to get the whole truth on the table. "Who and what are all mixed up in the same thing. I . . . don't know if I *want* the same way other people want. I'm like this weird unicorn."

"What does *that* mean?" Ash leans toward the camera.

"It means I . . . felt something with Shani that made my heart, I don't know, bigger. Like, an excitement at the mere sight of her, and it happened on the screen as much as at the Plaza."

Shani says, "I felt it, too."

"I thought, *Okay, this must be falling in love.* But then there was this moment with you, Ash, that felt, like, electrical."

"You mean the chemistry we had?" Ash looks relieved to hear Jonas say it.

"And it made me wonder—is *that* falling in love? I keep turning it over in my head. Why does my heart beat so fast with Shani and my body feel so charged with Ash? If I spent more time with Shani, would I feel that charge? If I spent more time with Ash, would my heart race for him? Is it weird that I'm telling you both this?"

Ash looks like he's about to say yes, but Shani cuts in.

"Doesn't this just make you gay? Ash is the one that turns you on and I'm . . ." She shrugs unhappily. "Who knows what?"

Jonas's face heats with frustration. "No. You don't get it."

"I guess not." Shani has her arms folded and she's very still.

"Everybody makes a big deal of who you're physically attracted to, like that somehow defines you. But what I feel, what attraction means for me . . . the *spark* . . . is as much in my head as my body. Maybe even more."

Ash looks confused. "So you did or didn't feel a spark with me?"

"I did. And I felt one with Shani, too—just different kinds. And I liked the way they both felt."

"We *both* turn you on?"

"I mean, I hear how other kids talk about sex, being horny and needing to get laid, and it doesn't sound like me at all. I never cared when I was younger, but the older I get, it's like, *Why isn't that me?* I started to think I wasn't attracted to anyone at all, really. But you both messed with that."

"So we disturbed your isolation tank." Before anyone can respond to Ash's remark, he follows up, "That sounded really snarky."

"That *was* really snarky," Shani says, "but we've met you, so . . ." She turns her focus back to Jonas. "Go on."

"There are all these labels on the internet: asexual and aromantic, bisexual and pan, everything and nothing—" He's spent so many hours looking for the right language. He sighs. "Maybe I'm just Jonasexual."

He sees Shani trying to puzzle this out, chewing her lip. Ash has his head cocked to one side, lips slightly parted in wonder, as if he has, in fact, seen a unicorn after all. Jonas hurries on.

"None of those things are exactly me. It's like all the stories my mom told about who she was: one day she was claiming we were

Sicilian and the next we were from the Caribbean. I mean, I could have been any of those people, or none of them. My whole life is the space between."

How can he possibly explain to them? They know who they are: Shani, the confident straight girl; Ash, the super-out gay guy. They have a clarity he doesn't.

"What I felt with you," he says to Shani, "is every bit as much part of my body as what I felt with you," he says to Ash, trying to look him in the eye through the screen.

For a few moments, it is quiet. No one speaks. Shani's eyes are narrowed to slits, suggesting either she is mad or working out a complex equation.

Ash breaks the spell. "Well . . . Shani and I know more about surprising connections than you think."

"You do?"

A light dawns on Shani's face and she nods. "We've had our moments."

It takes a moment for Jonas to catch her meaning. Wait–what? "*You* two?"

Ash looks almost shy as Shani confirms. "It's not the same, exactly. But yeah."

Jonas sits up. This makes everything different. If they had a spark but managed to put it aside to be as tight as they are, anything is possible. Which means he can do this, too. The idea begins to expand in his chest: let the romance go and, with it, all the confusion. Wait till he knows himself better before involving anyone else. "So maybe we try to forget that I'm so weird and just be friends like you guys?"

"Really? You think you could do that?" Shani's question pops the balloon. "You just told us all this stuff is going on inside you—what you feel when we're together. Think that'll go away like nothing?" He tries to come up with an answer and fails, but she wasn't done anyway. "It won't for me. It'll be in the air, right? Knowing how you feel. How I feel."

"You're not the only one with feelings," Ash reminds.

Jonas groans, thinking of Sandy calling it a love triangle. This is different than that—stranger and more intricate.

For a few moments, nobody says anything. They're a portrait gallery: unmoving faces hung on an iPad wall.

At last, Shani squares her shoulders. "When Mom died, Dad made me see a therapist for a while about why I was so mad at him all the time. She said I had to state my needs and wants clearly, no cap. She called it face value. If you have a question, ask it directly: no halfway, no hiding—that's face value. If I have something I need to say, same deal: say it face value. Whatever I say, I have to mean. And if that's my rule, I can ask my dad, or anyone—including *you*—the same. I didn't exactly live by that rule with you. And I should've." She pauses to let that land a little. She takes a deep breath. "I'm telling you this—both of you—because what I'm finna say next is face value."

Jonas had thought this call was about needing to explain himself, but now he feels like the tables have been turned. "Okay."

"I didn't know what you'd say to us, like, thank us for coming to the service, or tell us to leave you alone? And then I had this crazy flash—no, he's gone admit he likes one of us, right in front of the

other. I mean, it would kinda serve us right. But part of me was still pissed, like, who says *he* gets to choose?"

Jonas can hardly believe she imagined such a thing, but she's not done.

"And I'm like, *What if he does like me? Do I even* want *him?*" She lets that float a moment or two.

Jonas sinks in his seat a little. *Why would she?*

"And I realized, yes."

Jonas feels the sensation in his heart again. "You do?"

Ash is quiet as Shani goes on. "My instinct was to not admit it because, you know, it'll hurt my pride if what you really want is Ash, so I'm safer if I keep that shit to myself. But then I for sure don't get what I want. How does that help? If I know I still want a chance, then I need to give myself that shot. Why not face value it–"

Ash is nodding now. "–And demand the same in return? I get it. If he's into it, he's into it, and if he's not, he has to say so at face value . . ."

"Mm-hmm."

". . . And you did it in front of me, so we *all* have to do it."

She grins. "You know me so well."

"Okay," Ash says, firmly. "I'm in. Not just to face value. I'm still in, Jonas. I'm still into you, too."

He kind of can't believe it. What the hell? Is their openness a stroke of amazing fortune or the worst luck ever? "Um . . . thanks? But . . . didn't all this 'face value' just get us back to where we started?"

"You think?" Shani asks. "Now we all know exactly where each other stands; we *all* know what's going on. You were talking about

just being friends, like, minutes ago, but *we're* saying we don't want to close the door on being more."

"I don't get it . . ." He really doesn't and he's tired.

But Ash is following her. "You mean like, now that there are no secrets, we all keep going for it and see what shakes out?"

She's nodding. "Why not? He and I've only been on one real date, and your little movie session was like, what, half a date?"

"Hey!"

"I'm just saying: it's *all* new, what he and I have *and* what you have with him. It wouldn't kill anyone to get in a few more dates before we make any big decisions. And this way no one gets blindsided."

"I think I like it," Ash murmurs.

How is this real? Jonas clears his throat. "Do I get a say in this? You guys are talking like I'm not even here."

"But you are here. So step up."

He rubs his eyes. "Well . . . if it's face value, then . . . I do want more time. With both of you. I want to know what's possible. So . . . I guess, let's do it." He laughs softly. "Am I supposed to ask you out now?"

Ash raises a hand to stop him. "Not just you."

"Huh?"

"You heard me. We have sparks of our own."

Was that present tense? Whatever happened between Shani and Ash isn't over? Jonas had assumed it was something fleeting and long ago, not live. How could it be?

This must be written all over his face. "Yeah," says Shani. "Ash and I had a little moment this week."

"Which," Ash jabs, "we *so* did not 'face value' until this very second."

"*This week?*"

Ash fixes a look into the screen he knows will hit Jonas. "What? Because I'm gay, I couldn't possibly feel something with a girl?" Jonas thinks, *Exactly*. Ash's eyeroll is epic. "That's pretty binary for a guy with crushes on both of us."

Jonas can't help himself. "Have you ever been with a girl?" The question just pops out.

Ash doesn't blink. "Have *you?*"

Good point.

"Look, I get it," Ash continues. "This messes with my whole brand. I mean, I'm pretty gay even by gay standards. But I felt it. Why should I pretend otherwise? Since when have the rules ever applied to me?"

Shani cuts in. "Can't we be any way we want? Like, that's our generation's whole thing, right?"

Jonas ponders this suddenly expanded universe. What they are agreeing to, it's like a brand-new galaxy appeared all at once in the night sky: a little scary but impressive. "I didn't know people talked this way to each other."

Ash laughs. "I'd bet good money that very few do."

Jonas can't quite map the contours of this new plan. "Um, what would this look like?"

"First off, no more secrets. Everything stays out in the open." Shani is firm.

Ash chimes in. "Agreed."

"Second, we don't forget the friendships."

Jonas likes this part and nods enthusiastically.

"Last: no second-guessing your own feelings. Feel them and own them."

Ash expands on the idea. "And stop comparing them to everyone else. We're way past 'normal' here."

Jonas feels a little stuck. "I love all that, but . . . um, *literally* how would it work?"

Shani seems confident. "Like with anyone you're interested in. Start with a date." She smiles. "What are you doing New Year's?"

Ash raises a hand toward the screen. "Hold up—I'm all about being open to whatever happens, but *that* is not a fair fight! New Year's is like romance central."

"Okay, so *no one* gets New Year's."

A gleam comes into Ash's eyes. "Who says? No law says our dates have to be separate!"

Shani seems to get it before Jonas does. "For real?"

"If we're making our own rules anyway . . ." Ash's smile is gleeful. "Let's all go out and see what happens."

The proposal is a little thrilling and a lot risky. Is this a double date? A triple? There's no language for it, but he finds himself leaning toward the idea of it even as doubts creep in. "Who *does* this? Outside of, like, reality TV."

"Us. We don't have to be like anyone else. We can be romance unicorns!"

"You were born one, Ash!" Shani says. "We just playin' catch-up."

"Is that a yes or a no?" His eyes sparkle.

Shani doesn't hesitate. "Yes."

It's all on Jonas now. "Yes," he gulps. "I'm in, too."

Ash looks pleased. "That's it, then. Tomorrow, we're unicorns."

Jonas looks at the clock on his phone. "Not tomorrow," he says, "*today*. It's been the thirty-first for an hour."

When they have hung up, the room is just as dark as it was before but fuller, as if he can still hear them and see their faces even after the iPad powers down.

He lies on the futon, staring out into the night, and wonders what Foma would make of what he just agreed to. Just thinking of her brings the tears back to his eyes, but the hollow in his chest isn't as deep as it was a few hours ago. Wherever she is, he hopes she takes comfort in seeing how the evening has changed things for him: Jonas hasn't lost everything after all.

PART FOUR | THE SHAPE OF US

TWENTY-SEVEN
SHANI

How'm I supposed to dress for an escape room, a parade, and *fireworks?* She'd had the perfect outfit picked when she was still thinking New Year's Eve would be Milo's comedy show: a vintage patchwork leather trench coat from Buffalo Exchange over an ivory crop-top and ultrawide palomino-colored Jaded London jeans she found on Depop. But what if the escape room has her crawling around on the floor or whatever? She's not ruining these jeans, even if she didn't pay full price for them.

She swaps out for a whole other look: head-to-toe black, a sleek turtleneck topped with a vinyl corset her dad hates, and distressed jeans that disappear into thigh boots. She checks out her reflection in the mirror: it's a hot look. It will probably be a lot for Jonas, but she's dressing for herself, not for him or any boy. Well, except maybe Ash, because he has *opinions.*

She finds him talking with her dad in the kitchen. Ash stops to admire her outfit. "Holy millennial Pussycat Doll," he whistles.

"I kind of want to swap clothes." (Her dad, less enthusiastic, tries to focus his eyes anywhere but the corset.)

When she adds the trench coat (even secondhand, it's the most expensive item of clothing she's ever bought herself), she looks even more amazing and knows it. They can't get into Ash's newly returned Jaguar until she's taken a dozen photos on the sidewalk. And not just of herself—he has this indescribable bomber-tux jacket thing that only he would dare wear in Arlmont that makes him look incredibly cutting edge, even if she's not sure she likes it.

She eyes the car. "Your parents don't hold a grudge long."

"They can be reasonable . . . *sometimes*."

He opens her door for her and she has to restrain herself from slapping his hand away. If he's suddenly going to be all corny, she's out. "You never opened a door for anyone in your life, Ash. You don't need to now."

As if to defy her, Ash does the same thing when they stop to pick up Jonas, who is dressed pretty much like he is every time she has seen him, in parka and boots. But it's unusually warm for New Year's Eve, so he has ditched the wool hat, revealing dark hair clearly still damp from a shower, and the parka is unzipped to show he's wearing the hoodie Ash helped Shani pick out for his birthday.

On the drive into the city, Shani ignores a BB5 group chat. She's been ducking them all day because she hates to lie to them and doesn't want to describe her night. How will she explain that she has a date with both boys? The girls can be judgy—which is fair, so can she—and she doesn't want their voices in her head taking away from the night.

They're fueling at The Melt, a fondue place which Ash picked but she's never heard of. Ash steers them to his favorite booth (seriously, he has a favorite seat everywhere) and tells them they don't need to look at the menu, and not just because he's paying. "Our choices are pretty much cheese, chocolate, or both. It's like a health crime. And I am so here for it."

Shani shakes her head. "Yeah, that's cause you're one of those people who could eat peanut butter from the jar all day and wash it down with ice cream and never gain a pound."

"I didn't make my metabolism—I just treat it right. If it needs to burn calories, who am I to judge?" The waiter appears and Ash orders both options for the table. But when they're alone again, he sounds almost shy. "I wouldn't mind bulking up, right?"

That's news to Shani and apparently Jonas, too. "Really?" he says.

Ash shrugs. "I'm not always down with this Peter Pan look I'm rocking. But it's how I'm built. God gave me parents made of twigs."

"Huh." Shani folds and unfolds the mustard yellow napkin at her setting. "I can't imagine wanting to be bigger. I mean. I could stand to lose a few."

"But you're perfect!" This comes out so forcefully, with no arch tone, it's like it's not even Ash speaking.

Jonas nods. "He's right!"

Shani eyes them both, brows arched. "Come on." She's not fishing; she's really not. It's just that they don't usually talk to each other this way.

"I'm serious," Ash says. "Your body is like the perfect extension of you: it matches your power."

"Boy, stop." Shani's embarrassed but honestly, she doesn't want him to stop at all. She's never thought of her body, which is as solid as it is curvy, as a signal of her strength, or that anyone would read her this way.

"You don't know it," Ash goes on, "but people pay attention when they see you. You carry yourself like . . . somebody they should watch. Somebody they should know."

Jonas is nodding. "On Christmas Eve, I noticed it everywhere. I was kind of just riding along on your drift. I was like: *I'm with her.*" He stops, as if realizing he's said a lot.

This is truly news to her. She's a little choked up. "You guys . . . Nobody's ever said anything like that to me."

It's almost a relief when their cheese fondue arrives. Their waiter makes a serious prepared speech about how The Melt is the first place in New England to serve its cheese fondue not in a pot but a fountain, because it requires precision equipment heated to exactly so many degrees. It is hard to keep a straight face because this soliloquy comes from the mouth of a pimply kid about their age wearing an apron that says *Dip it. Dip it good.*

But he's not wrong about it being something to behold: it is three tiers high, with cheese cascading level to level, which will look great on Insta and TikTok. The waiter snaps a pic of all three leaning toward the molten stream and then leaves them alone.

Like so much of life, the look of the thing is better than the fact of it. The cheese is actually really salty and with every passing moment its stream slows.

"Is it me," Ash asks, "or is the cheese sort of congealing?"

"Gross! Don't say 'congeal' about something we're gonna eat."

Jonas laughs. "How 'bout 'coagulate'?"

"That's worse! Just eat faster." They're trying to dip bread and vegetables as quickly as they can before the fondue becomes a solid.

"I swear this never happened when I've been here!"

The cheese is still sort of flowing but it's thicker and more viscous than just five minutes ago, and she's about to tell them to eat even faster when the top of the fountain stops bubbling entirely. She's not sure if the cheese has run out—they have eaten *a lot* of cheese—or just clogged up. Ash leans forward to inspect the fountain more carefully. Just as he does, it sputters—no, it *burps*, the pent-up pressure of the clog finally reaching a point where it blows a thick, yellow glob right in the middle of his forehead.

He sits back in shock, looking like someone has paintballed him. Before the waiter and manager both can arrive at their table, Shani uses her napkin to wipe Ash's face. Any day before this one, she'd have let him do it, but instead she's holding his chin in one hand and gently cleaning with the other, which feels surprisingly intimate.

Have they always had the potential of being this tender with each other? She lets her hand linger on his smooth chin, and if Jonas wasn't sitting right there, she'd be tempted to caress Ash's face. He meets her eyes and something passes between them. She is surprised to see him blushing, or at least what passes for blushing for Ash.

He jokes his way out of it. "You didn't have to sabotage the cheese if you wanted to touch me."

"Ha!" She says, "You have no idea what I'm capable of."

Jonas looks a little jealous. "Maybe *I* should spill something on me!"

"Get your own move, mister." Ash laughs.

She laughs, too, but she can't help but think how strange it is to be flirting like this, all of them together, out in the open. This isn't like any New Year's she's ever had—or ever imagined. Out with the old, in with the *very* new.

TWENTY-EIGHT
ASH

They're still laughing about this when they head up the street to Slot Borg, the newest escape room in Boston. This was Shani's idea. She knows he isn't Sporty Spice and that he hates heights of any kind, but she also knows he loves to solve a riddle; he watches *Survivor* not just for the shirtless boys but the challenges. Jonas had said yes because Jonas is agreeable by nature.

Ash had paid for everyone's dinner (after Slot Borg shockingly refused to comp them), so Shani insists on buying their game tickets, and they soon discover that they're a decent team. Navigating a pirate ship in their first game, "Avast Ye Zombies," is almost too easy. And they dominate the Princess Bride–themed "As You Swish." They each bring something to the table: Ash is sneaky and clever, able to imagine how the game maker might be trying to mislead them; she's practical and concrete, thinking about how pieces work together; and Jonas sees at a glance how to handle every physical challenge best. In their first two games, they beat the time limit by

several minutes, a huge margin for an escape room, and they're feel-ing invincible.

Their final game is "Flightmare," which is set up like the inside of an airplane cabin strewn with mannequins of passed-out flight attendants. "All women," Ash notes drily. "Like the sixties." The air-line logo—an angry hawk in flight atop the words Talon Air—appears in the seat fabric, the attendant's scarves and badges, and on bro-chures in the seatback, where it is accompanied by the slogan *Talon Air: The Key to Your Getaway!*

His family goes to Maui every February. They've offered to let him bring a friend before but he never has—he hates to compromise the little routines he's built up over the years. But maybe this year he'll surprise his parents by saying yes. He looks at his companions and wonders. Who would surprise them more?

➤ SHANI

It's silly, but Shani feels a surge of excitement when the Slot Borg staffer buckles her into the seat next to Ash. Her family went to Disneyland when she was in third grade; they still had two incomes then, and all things were possible. That was the only time she had ever flown, and she loved everything about it—watching the earth recede from view then return, and even the snacks, which her dad thought were too skimpy, but she thought of as free junk food. The plane ride was as big a part of her memory as Rock 'n' Roller Coaster. It didn't occur to her that they wouldn't do it again. She doesn't say

any of this out loud but admits, "I've only ever been on a real plane once!"

"That's one more than me," says Jonas. "Is it always this cheesy?"

"Based on the uniforms alone, I think it's supposed to be a knockoff Spirit Air," jokes Ash. "That explains the sense of doom." They are buckled into their seats, waiting for instructions, when a prerecorded voice tells them the flight attendants have succumbed to a poison gas.

"From where?" Shani asks. "Planted by who?"

Jonas cocks his head. "And why isn't it killing us?"

Ash grins. "We're magic!"

The pre-recorded details are skimpy. The pilot is unconscious but not yet dead and it's up to the players to find a way to open the cockpit door, get in, and save him to land the plane. A digital clock illuminates the remaining time in red: 18:44. Less than twenty minutes.

"I guess there's no need for us to stay buckled in," Ash says, and they start exploring the cabin. The overhead bins are mostly empty but one of them has a suitcase with a four-digit lock, which means they need to find four numbers elsewhere that correspond. First, they try row numbers in every combination, but that doesn't work. The flight number is no better and neither is the day's date.

Shani starts looking for things that aren't obviously numbers and is staring at one of the packets of peanuts liberally scattered on the empty seats when Ash gets inspired. "Look for an expiration date!" They find one: 10/22. It works like a charm.

Getting the case open feels itself like a victory, but they don't

have time to linger, as the contents of the case are not in themselves useful: oxygen masks ... but no tank. Great.

➤ JONAS

There's no obvious place in the cabin to hide an oxygen tank, so he's on his knees looking under the seats. (Ash refused, not willing to risk stains.) Jonas thinks about the logic of escape rooms: how you have to re-see what is right in front of you. He scans the walls, the windows, the illuminated NO SMOKING sign on the fake restroom door.

That's it. "You can't have flame where there's oxygen!"

Ash looks up from the floor by the last row, baffled. "Did you read that on a fortune, or are you working for the fire department now?"

"I got you!" Shani marches to the panel with the bathroom sign and presses on it. It's not mere decoration at all, but a door that folds inward revealing the airplane lavatory. Under the sink is the oxygen tank, topped by a metal valve in the shape of the Talon Air logo.

He feels absurdly happy at his contribution to their success ... for about five seconds.

Then she asks, "Now what? Do we break down the door with them?" She points out a problem: the pilots are still on the wrong side of a locked hatch.

Ash points at the clock. "Four minutes left."

They go back to their seats, trying to start from the beginning,

and she is frustrated. "We've literally seen every damn thing in this cabin now. It's something they want us to see that we're not."

Jonas flips through the safety manual, which is full of graphics of crashes, but no text at all, except the slogan on the cover—*Talon Air: The Key to Your Getaway.*

He finally gets it. Immediately, he unscrews the logo-shaped metal valves, revealing a key. He sprints for the cockpit the door and has it open in seconds. Shani eclipses Ash in the race to follow.

> ASH

Inside, the dummy captain shares space with a dummy copilot. They have two things in common: both are slumped over the controls and both are men. "Jeez, the whole plan is like a diorama of sexism!"

"Don't forget racism," Shani cuts in. Every one of the mannequins inside and outside the cockpit is white.

The captain dummy is blue-eyed blond that wouldn't be out of place on an Aryan Youth recruitment flyer. "I can't believe we have to save this guy!" Shani laughs.

Inspiration washes over Ash. "Maybe we don't. I mean it." They could just defy the purpose of the whole puzzle. "Let's find out what happens if we let the plane crash!"

Jonas's eyes are wide. But Shani is smiling. "I feel you."

With both his friends in agreement, Jonas shrugs. "Why not? We're all about breaking the rules."

Ash pulls the pilot mannequin from its seat and motions for Shani to claim it. Jonas takes the copilot's seat and Ash crouches in the space between them as cockpit alarms go off. A voice repeats, over and over: "You have less than sixty seconds remaining."

Quietly sharing the small space, they can hear each other's breathing. Ash steals a glance at Shani and then Jonas, and both meet his eyes. The air is thick now and he can't quite name what fills the space: Affection? Desire? Potential?

The voice of the gamekeeper slices the air. "Ten-nine-eight-seven-six-five-four-three-two—"

"ONE!" they say at once, then giggle, enjoying the power of the choice they've made. A patently cheesy crash scene unfolds on the monitor in front of the cockpit and loud explosion noises fill the air, but Ash feels like a winner.

TWENTY-NINE
JONAS

Ash drops him and Shani off at the Boston Common while he parks the car. "No need for you to deal with the hell of driving up Boylston Street on New Year's," he says. "Go frolic or something and I'll text when I'm done."

It's the first time he and Shani have been alone since the night she came with the food basket. It makes him a little nervous. What if he has the urge to kiss her again? Would that be okay tonight or not? This date needs an instruction manual.

With only a few hours till midnight, the garden is swollen with revelers. Jonas is surrounded by students wearing Emerson College purple and gold; they have unofficially hijacked the little bridge for a performance of some kind and they look like they're having the time of their lives. College students always make Jonas wistful. College for him will mean Charlestown Community and one class at a time while he works, assuming he can find a full-time job after graduation. He's heard good things about the courses, but it's not

like the movies, with kids living in dorms and running around together between classes. These students have that life. He can tell.

Shani looks completely at home striding through Emersonians, who part as if she has cast a spell, which she kind of does with that coat and boots. He will never ever be as cool as her. If they end up dating, will that be a problem? She can do better than him; though some part of him knew this, now it seems so obvious. What made him think he was her speed?

He's stuck in his head until she breaks the silence with a question he doesn't expect. "Hey—did you ever get your results?"

The question is innocent but he's still surprised. "Didn't you say it wouldn't matter?"

"I said a DNA test won't make you Black. But I didn't say it wasn't interesting."

His first instinct is to lie and say he hasn't. But why? To protect himself from admitting that he now feels ignorant for caring so much? Hiding from something awkward is *old* Jonas, pre-Shani-and-Ash Jonas. "Face value?" he asks.

"Face value."

"I guess I just realized that who I am *is* who I've been. Knowing my DNA won't change any of it. Wherever Valerie and I 'came from' or whatever didn't mean that much to her. She just made it up as she went."

"Huh, I wonder who else did that . . ." Shani's jibe startles him. In all the time he has regretted lying to her, it never occurred to him that he was, in a way, just being Valerie: making a truth fit the whim of a moment.

"Ouch."

As the flow of the crowd sweeps them into the Public Garden, Shani takes his arm. "Sorry. That was—" She bites her lip and he can see the apology in her eyes. "Sorry."

"No, you're right," he says. "I just hadn't thought of it that way." The sidewalk traffic slows for a moment to allow a group of tourists in New Year's hats and glasses to take a group photo. While they wait, he turns to Shani. "I like that about you."

"That I blurt out stuff I should keep to myself?"

"No ... that you've got people's numbers. I mean, okay, I didn't like you setting me up, but you were right to doubt me. You saw through my bullshit." He pauses, figuring out how to explain. "It's like you know what people are thinking and you don't look away. I think I ... I just try not to know. I wish I was more like you."

Shani doesn't say much for a moment and when she speaks, her voice is soft. "Thank you." She is quiet as they follow the contours of the swan pond to the span that crosses it. On the bridge, she stops and faces him. "We don't live in a world where I get praised for telling it like it is. Nobody's saying to me: *Pop off, Shani.*" She shakes her head. "And I can't believe after I treated you like I did, that it's *you* saying it."

A warmth fills his chest. This feels like the right time to show her her birthday and Christmas presents. "I never got to give you these ..."

He opens up an album on his phone and hands it to her. She taps on the first image and her eyes get huge. She swipes the screen: Bakugo ... Killua ... Eren ... Levi ... Kaneki ... Kageyama ... He

has made portraits of all the characters she calls her anime boy-friends. The final image is Kurai Kage, her favorite Tomo-e Girl.

She is stock still.

"Do you . . . like them?"

"I *love* them," she says, and it's clear she is trying not to cry. Instead of saying more, she pulls him in for a deep hug that over-whelms and thrills him all at once. Can she feel how fast his heart is beating?

When she pulls away, she whispers "Thank you" and rests her head on his shoulder. What to say now? What happens next?

Shani breaks the spell. "Do you deliver?"

They both start laughing. "I'll bring the actual drawings to your house whenever. I mean . . . if I'm still invited." *If.* It's a reminder the night is more full of potential than clarity. But why go there now? "*When* I'm invited."

"Good. Cause I am not lugging all that on a bus."

Ash texts. MEET ME AT PUPPET STATION.

They head for the Arlington Street corner of the Garden, where a team of First Night volunteers will be leading puppet-making. When they hit an icy patch, Shani slides her arm through his and leans in to brace herself against him.

She's still gushing about the drawings. "You need a studio!" Shani says. "You're a true artist."

"Not really." He thinks of his drawings, all of them inspired by other artists. "I'm not there yet, ya know?"

"Are you serious? I'm jealous of you. Those pictures got me think-ing, *What's my thing?*"

"You're gonna be a doctor. That's something."

"I'm not talkin' about someday. Or about *work*. Who can I be that no one else could be?"

Wow. It's a heavy question. "I couldn't answer that if I tried," he replies and nudges her. "We're *seventeen*." In reply, she leans against him and nods.

As if from thin air, Ash appears on the sidewalk. "Did you miss me?"

Shani pulls away to hug Ash, taking her warmth from Jonas. They look so naturally at ease together, he feels a little pang. Is it jealousy? Or is it just worry that the spell of this date, which has been so good, will break as soon as it's over?

THIRTY
ASH

He has, like, sixty texts from Raj and Gloria. He doesn't even read them. Can't they possibly focus on their *own* New Year's?

The sky is clear and the air is warm by Boston-in-January standards, scraping fifty degrees even this late. It was even warmer during the day, which means the annual ice sculptures are melting already, some of the carvers flecking them with sawdust to extend their solidity. It also means it's okay that he wore a jacket that's more cute than cold-fighting. It's a tuxedo-bomber mash-up: zip up front says bomber, but from behind it boasts tails straight out of *Bridgerton*. He can't think of anyone he knows who would even try to pull it off.

With Shani in all black and that Palomino stunner, they could be on their way to an art opening or concert. But his outfit looks pretty wild next to Jonas, who wears what he always wears. If they do end up dating, Ash could help counter all the cis het socialization that has led Jonas to believe those jeans fit. It doesn't matter

anyway: Jonas is so handsome, especially when he smiles, that Ash would rather look at his face than his clothes.

At the edge of the park, they find tables covered with puppet-making material being swarmed by revelers preparing for the Night Parade. Ash starts rummaging through piles of craft paper animals real and imagined, fringed with vivid-colored crepe streamers. They're a little late to the game, most of those assembled already finishing up the giant craft creations they will carry up Boylston Street in the People's Parade.

Jonas doesn't hesitate before choosing a monkey. He's already painting it orange, orangutan style, by the time Shani settles on a cheetah. Ash hasn't even narrowed the list down to finalists. "Do I want to be a dolphin, which is sleek? Or something with more bite—a tiger?" He eyes the orange paint in Jonas's hand and takes tiger off the list. Too matchy matchy. He scans the next table. A phoenix? Too serious.

And then he sees it: a narwhal. They did say they'd be unicorns, so why not unicorns of the sea? He paints it white, pink, and blue, and finds a foam tube to run through the narwhal's midsection vertically so he can make it swim.

The procession is late getting started. The trio stand in the throngs now gathered in the middle of Boylston Street, ready to roll, with Ash beginning to feel like the clock is ticking for their date; he is more than ready when steel drummers at the back of the throng finally start a carnival-inspired rhythm.

The crowd roars and comes to life, dancing forward, their puppets a sea of bobbing beasts. Ash loves to dance, is born for it, and

the rhythm of the music finds its place inside his body easily. Shani has always been pretty smooth and glides along. Jonas's hips have some learning to do but he's into it even so, bopping to the beat so that his brown hair bounces.

As they approach the Public Gardens, Jonas starts making loops around Ash and Shani. "Tag!" he bellows just to be heard, his puppet tapping Ash's.

Ash immediately taps Shani's and hurries ahead. Instantly, it becomes a game, the three of them ignoring everything but each other as they weave through the crowd, their creatures leading the way.

Jonas is first to Copley Square and Ash gets there next, breathless. "I caught you," he gasps.

"I let you." Jonas replies with a loaded smile. "I got just what I wanted."

Ash feels the urge to kiss him. Is Jonas feeling the same thing?

Shani catches up with them, complaining that she'd have beaten them both if she'd been in sneakers. But she looks pretty happy even so.

The tolling of bells at nine o'clock seems to ring right into Ash's chest. Where does this date leave him? He's feeling something with Jonas right now, but he also felt something with Shani at The Melt. He's not 100 percent sure he himself could say which feeling is "better." When it comes right down to it, what does that even mean? He needs to shake off the doubting and just stay present.

He swims his narwhal's face close to Jonas's monkey. It takes only a second for Jonas to understand and he tilts his puppet

forward for a paper kiss. Then Ash turns to Shani and their puppets kiss, too.

It's so sweet and so corny, he *has* to break the spell. "God, we're gross." And they all start laughing again.

After they return their puppets to the First Night volunteers, they head for the private valet parking garage where Ash left the Jaguar. They've agreed to watch the fireworks from Oakes Farm Park, the highest point in Arlmont, which has a gorgeous view of the city. Locals gather on the hillside every New Year's Eve, but the real reason they're not staying in Boston is that Ash doesn't want to risk driving his car through throngs of drunk people at the end of the night. The last thing he dares do is bring it home with a scratch or dent or a missing fender.

They are within sight of the garage when he sees he won't be bringing the car home at all; it is being pulled from the garage by a tow truck, which is followed closely by his parents' Lexus, a furious Gloria at the wheel. Ash grabs both Jonas and Shani by a hand and drags them into the alley next to the parking structure. The setting is so off-brand for him that Shani knows something major is up.

She immediately demands answers. "Boy, what are you playin' at?"

"Shhh," he says, blinking rapidly. "We can't be seen."

Jonas blinks. "By who?"

"My mom," Ash groans.

Shani's eyes widen. "Ash—"

"I might . . . um . . . I *kind of* stole the car."

THIRTY-ONE
SHANI

Boy is a fool.

No, his parents had not "gotten over it" yet. And he was not allowed to take the Jaguar anywhere, much less to Boston on New Year's. But since when has Ash ever really thought the word no applied to him?

Now Gloria has come all the way into the city to get it and she isn't sticking around to see how he likes losing his wheels *again*.

"How did they know where it was?" Jonas's brow is an unhappy slash.

"GPS tracker. I didn't think to take it off because I assumed they'd be too busy to notice."

"Not notice a missing car? Really?" Shani can't believe him.

"Well, we do have three." That's his answer? She can't even with this kid. But he hurries on. "And they never miss their New Year's Eve with the professors who live next to us—that tradition is sacred.

New Year's is for booze and old queens who make every night a showtune sing-along. Perfect distraction."

"That's it? That was your whole plan?" Shani could just about wring his neck.

Ash shrinks. "I don't know what I was thinking. I should've told them, okay? I should've said the truth, that this night is too important for me to miss."

"Yeah? Then why didn't you?" Shani crosses her arms across her chest. "Oh, right—because you KNEW they'd trip." Shaking her head, she throws up her hands and starts to turn away from him.

"Don't go. Please." Ash sounds like he might cry, which Shani has never once seen him do. "Stay, okay? I don't want this night to end. Not yet."

➤ ASH

Ash really doesn't know what will come of this night, which was pretty amazing before it went south (thanks Raj, thanks Gloria). And he's on the verge of tears at the thought of them splitting up.

He has spent so much of his life acting like he doesn't care about anything. Honestly, he'd kind of convinced himself that was true. His parents *have* to love him and Shani always has, so everything else is gravy. If he pisses off a teacher, so what? School is a blip next to his future. If a classmate finds him too much, who cares? He hasn't met one yet who has any impact on his self-esteem. Confidence has carried him through high school like a current.

Until this week. When he realized he *could* push Shani too far and had to face the prospect of not being forgiven. Trying to picture the rest of high school without her was awful.

And then Jackson. *Jonas.* Ash has lusted over many a handsome guy before, but he's never felt protective of one, never felt such caring in the mix. He doesn't want to give that up, either.

It's weird feeling so vulnerable. A dawning: *I need other people. I need them.*

Right now, what he needs is to snap out of it and to say so. "*Whatever* my parents do to me when I get home, I want to ring in the new year with you first. Can we still do that?"

> ➤ **JONAS**

Jonas thinks about this. He's mad that Ash has screwed up such a great night, but what is he going to do about it? Stomp off? Ring out the year alone? He already spends enough time alone as it is. There's no point in saying no to something he wants.

"I'm in," he says, finding his voice a little unsteady at first. "I've never felt like this before. When the fireworks go off, I want you both there." Flashing lights spill into the alley as the tow truck pulls the Jaguar away up Boylston. Jonas is happy for the distraction. "Um, but no more of *that* kind of fireworks."

Ash chuckles but Shani is still quiet.

Jonas would kill to know what she's thinking.

➤ SHANI

Shani can feel two pairs of eyes on her and Ash's look is especially pleading. But he can wait. She's not ready to go home yet, either, but she doesn't answer because she's thinking. Not about the trouble he's in—that's not her problem—but about what comes next.

What's a date for? Why go on *any* date? Because you think someone is cute or nice or funny, right? Because you're attracted to them. Because the prospect makes you feel a way. Because you want *more*.

Does she want more? Jonas is nice and Ash is funny and both are cute. She felt sparks fly with each of them and she can't imagine letting each other go right this moment. But which one can she see herself with longer?

What is wrong with me? she thinks, clarity seizing control. She realizes that she has been spooling out this one night, this single date, into a future, like anyone seventeen and still in high school needs to commit to *anything*. Other kids date casually and carelessly all the time; it's part of growing up. Her feelings about Ash and Jonas are neither casual nor careless, but she's definitely growing.

She finally speaks. "Look at you two waiting on me like I'm the queen." Both boys' faces relax. "Where do we go from here?"

➤ ASH

Ash's heart leaps. The night isn't ruined!

But Jonas points out the obvious: before they can finish this date,

they should probably figure out what to do about Ash's parents. "What if Gloria is driving around looking for you—us—right now?"

Ash taps his phone screen. "I guess I should read their—what is it—forty-eight messages." The sheer volume of texts reveals their unreasonableness.

"Forty-eight? And you haven't read them?" Shani can't believe him. "What if one of them had a stroke or something?"

"Then they'd call. Who texts 'dad had a stroke, love mom'—I mean, really?"

Jonas shakes his head like this is the saddest thing he's ever head. "Um, maybe just read them."

"Fine!" This is not how Ash wants to use his New Year's Eve, but whatever. As he expected, the progress is surprise, hurt, hurt/anger, just anger, raging hurricane of anger, icy anger, strategic anger (okay, so they *did* warn him that if he didn't return with the car, Gloria was coming), followed by pleading (tell us you're not dead) with a dose of still angry, and back to anger anger, all of it under a sheen of Grand Disappointment.

The most recent text takes an unexpected turn:

If you're not heading home right now, a lot is going to change tomorrow.

There's nothing else, no explanation of what "a lot" means. And they stopped texting after that. The vagueness is what makes this message dangerous. Vague is not Gloria's mode, nor is it Raj's. This can't be good.

Only now does Ash really understand how much trouble he's in. Like, having the car towed should have made that crystal clear,

but he'd told himself that they would consider *that* his punishment—his embarrassment or shock at losing his wheels would be enough. But now that seems wishful.

"I think I better call home," he says.

➤ JONAS

He has never seen Ash's face the way it looks when he finishes talking to his parents; his expression is no longer cocky, a half second away from a wink.

"Gloria is still on her way back but Raj said taking the car tonight was the worst thing I've ever done because it wasn't just a silly impulse, but my way of announcing that I don't respect them at all, that I don't think they have any authority over me, that they're too weak to stop me from doing whatever I like. He said they knew I was independent, but they didn't believe I was this full of myself." He looks shell-shocked.

"Shit." Jonas squeezes Ash's shoulder.

"What did you say? Tell me you sweet-talked them." Shani looks worried.

"I tried—I admitted I thought they'd be mad but not *this* mad and that when I came home I'd explain how important tonight was to me, but now I get it and I *so* regret it. I said I was sorry and I love them. Raj said it's not enough to love your parents; if you don't respect them, too, they've failed you.

"And they have no intention of failing as parents."

Jonas almost hates to ask. "So . . . what does that mean?"

"If I'm not home in an hour, they're . . ." He blinks like someone trying to wake. "I mean, they wouldn't—they can't—"

"WHAT?" Jonas and Shani shout at the same time.

Ash looks numb. "Apparently, Gloria has been trying for months to talk Raj into sending me to Putney, this crunchy boarding school in Vermont, where my cousins went. It's all values and tree-huggers and the kids have *work duty*—like, one of them is called, no joke, 'barn.' A friend of the family is the dean and . . ." He can't even say it out loud. Would they really transfer him in the middle of junior year?

Shani groans. "Oh, Ash."

"That's . . . They wouldn't." But Jonas isn't convinced this is true.

"They've given me one hour to get home, enough time to take the train and a bus and walk the rest—I can't even call a cab because my credit cards are frozen." He's shaking. "I should get going if I'm gonna be there by 12:20." He's already walking in the direction of the subway stop. "I guess the joke's on me."

Jonas starts to follow Ash. The best of the night is over.

➤ **SHANI**

"Not so fast." Shani finds her voice, stops him with it. "I have an idea." She pulls out her phone and stares at an app without speaking for a moment. "Perfect!"

Jonas and Ash look equally confused.

Shani makes a call. "Dad. We need a ride home. It's kind of an emergency."

While they wait for him to arrive, she explains that she'd tracked her dad's location to see that he was in the city. The timing was perfect; he was just dropping off a fare. He could bring the kids back to Arlmont and still have enough time to get back to the city for the crowd needing rides home from the fireworks.

Her plan is simple: he'll drive them to Oakes Farm Park. The view of Boston's skyline is so gorgeous that people gather every year on Fourth of July for a concert and chance to see Boston's fireworks from afar. Fewer come out for New Year's because top of hill + winter in New England = freezing your ass off, but the combination of cold and darkness make the colors of the rockets stand out even better than they do in the summer. If Shani's dad is quick, they can get to Oakes with time to spare before the fireworks start. Granted, it'll be tight to get Ash home in time after the show ends, but the night—this endless dance mix of a date—has an hour left.

Having first been the vote that decided the night was not over and now coming up with the plan to keep it alive, Shani feels like she has found her footing again, deciding what she wants and how to get it. She's the girl people believed her to be all along.

In her dad's Uber, all three happily squish into the back seat.

"You sure none of you want to ride up front?"

"It's okay, Dad," Shani says. "We're all about togetherness tonight."

"Yeah, when I was a kid, my ride-or-dies were Smitty and Dean. It's good to have a crew. Though I guess you guys call it a squad now." He sounds pretty pleased with himself for his lingo, so Shani just makes sure he sees her in the mirror nodding like that's right.

Ash sits in the middle, Jonas's arm reaching across the back behind him, a hand resting on Shani's shoulder. Their arms and legs are all pressed close so they form one contiguous line of human warmth, paper dolls made flesh. They don't speak much on the drive, as if tacitly agreeing to soak in the city together. When they cross the Zakim Bridge, its white cables illuminated purple from beneath, like epic black light string art, she leans her cheek against the window, gazing up at the spans. She's seen this bridge a million times, but it's different to see it with the boys; it's not just any bridge now, but theirs, if only for a moment until it recedes into the dark behind them.

➤ ASH

He nestles into Jonas's shoulder and Shani pulls away from the window to lean against Ash. He rests one hand on her knee and one on Jonas's. Streetlights and neon signs flicker by, casting light inside the car, dappling their faces. He feels cocooned in the intimacy; he could stay in this ride forever.

"You kids poopin' out? Buncha teenagers can't be falling asleep before New Year's." Shani's dad blasts the music, misreading the

scene. It's Journey (it's always Journey) and he starts singing about the singer in a smoky room.

One by one, the kids join in, even Ash. "This don't seem like your kinda song," Shani's dad teases him.

"Every American alive knows this song. It's like the air at a certain point—you just breathe it in, whether you want to or not," Ash replies. Tonight, he doesn't mind. In fact, he's getting into it. They all are.

As the city lights lessen and winding roads lead them to quieter Arlmont, their singing does not abate. All four of them are belting it, while Jonas does air guitar and Shani plays an invisible synthesizer. They have better voices than Ash and he's okay with that; the sounds filling the car are so amazing that he is almost sad for everyone outside who can see only an unremarkable Uber silently hugging the turns along the Mystic River.

When they reach Oakes Farm Park, they have only fifteen minutes till fireworks, a little more than a half hour till his folks expect him home. They pile out of the car—all three being sure to offer profuse thanks for the ride—and find themselves sharing the moonlit hilltop with a handful of others. Most who have claimed a viewing spot are on the front of the hill, but Jonas has a better idea. "The Whaler!" he calls out, pointing toward the huge ship-themed play structure with its swings, monkey bars, slides, and wooden suspension bridge. There are no kids here at this time of night, so they can have privacy and, if they climb to its lookout platform, the highest vantage point.

Ash insists on walking up the slide, slipping a few times but

making it. Shani takes the stairs "like a normal person," she announces. Jonas climbs the kid-sized rock wall in two moves. And soon they are crowded together into the crow's nest of the Whaler.

The city they just left is now their sparkling horizon, and it's gorgeous. But Ash feels sadness stealing into his chest. Is this the perfect finale to their night? Or the beginning of the end to everything else? The blinking stars don't answer.

THIRTY-TWO
ASH

"What now?" asks Jonas.

"I don't know." Shani looks at Ash as if he might magically have some wisdom to offer.

He does not. There is no doubt that Jonas turns him on and makes his heart flutter. But he can't ignore the connection with Shani, the new one, deeper and more specific than friendship. It's amazing that he can feel this way about her when he has liked boys—and only boys—for so long. Having a fixed identity has been a comfort when navigating the world and this thing with Shani messes with it badly.

But isn't that what love is supposed to be? Not the average person, not the one who makes you feel like others, but the one who shakes things up? The one who makes you feel things you haven't felt? Isn't exceptional the whole point?

➤ JONAS

He looks at Ash and Shani, knowing that any choice is the wrong one as much as it is the right. The night didn't make things clearer—it only told him that desire is all at once specific and unlimited. Maybe he doesn't feel it often, but when he does, it is rooted in the way one person lights him up. Except that there are two. How could he ever pretend otherwise? Does this make him bi? Or pan? Does it matter?

If he ever chooses one over the other, what he will he lose? Can he do without Shani's ability to put him in his place and lift him up all at once? Or Ash's hilarity? He tries to picture his days with one of them absent, erasing the cheery morning messages from Ash or the nightly cam talk with Shani. Either way, his day looks emptier.

➤ SHANI

Shani wrestles with the truth: Neither of these boys is enough for her in himself. Jonas's romanticism and tenderness fill an empty spot she wouldn't have admitted that she had. Ash's understanding of her and certainty that she will be somebody someday make her feel truly seen. Together, they are all the things she deserves, but neither alone comes close. Not yet.

Who says they need to? The question springs into her mind, others crowding after. Why does everyone have to pair off like leads in a romantic comedy? Why does everything have to follow the same

pattern? Would it be so terrible to just let them *both* be what they are to her?

As if he can read her mind, Jonas breaks the silence, sounding wistful. "I can't choose. I'm sorry. I don't know what's wrong with me."

"Nothing!" Shani says more loudly than she intended. "*Nothing* is wrong with you. What's wrong is being made to feel like we have to choose. All. The. Time."

She voices the questions that hound them. "Where are you going to college? What's your major? What do you want to be when you grow up? Decide! *Decide now!*"

"God, yes!" Ash picks up the thread, mimicking the old-school questions he's so tired of. "Do you like *girls* or *boys?*" He takes on a goading tone. "Are you *sure?* Or is it a phase?"

Jonas is nodding. "I never know what to say!"

"To which question?"

"*All* of it! When people ask where I'm going, it's like they assume I can even afford college. Sure, I want to go, but it's not like I know how, right?" He pretends to be speaking to the universe: "Stop asking about my future! I can barely get through the now."

Shani hears the fear in his words, the questions unanswered. It never occurred to her that he might be afraid even college is beyond reach. She takes his hands as he keeps going.

"And the *rest* of it—I mean, I didn't know how I felt about anyone until you guys, and now I feel so many things, I can't keep up. When I see the rest of my life, there's not some complete picture. I don't know who I'll be."

Shani squeezes his hand, and Ash is nodding.

"All I know," Jonas finishes, "is how I feel right now, in this moment. Why can't that be enough?"

Ash puts his arm around Shani's shoulder. "It's enough for me."

"Me too." She looks at the beautiful boys and feels something hopeful inside. There will be no division tonight, no choosing to cut off some part of the joy they each bring.

"I think . . ." She hesitates before saying the truest thing, three words she hasn't dared say, words waiting to for her to set them off like fireworks. "I love you."

And then she adds one word more. "Both."

➤ JONAS, SHANI, AND ASH

It is Jonas who draws the others in, his long arms forming a mantle around Shani's and Ash's shoulders. Now they are a unit, Ash snaking one arm around Shani's waist and another around Jonas's. Shani cups Jonas's jawline with one hand; the other hand trails across Ash's smooth cheek.

Ash kisses her first and she feels the electricity as she kisses him back, leaning into a moment when kiss and touch are extensions of a single thought.

When she pulls away, Ash turns his face to Jonas, who kisses him, too, one hand stroking Ash's dark hair; the tenderness makes Ash feel so at home, he could cry.

Jonas turns to Shani and her lips are warm and soft, parting to

welcome his, and he feels something expanding inside him. Like shooting stars, the kisses–his first–are so brief, just bright pulses of hope. Grateful for the window into all he might be, he folds both of them into the deepest hug of his life, holding them tight as if to keep them from spinning free and floating away into space. Shani marvels at the warmth of the embrace.

When the fireworks start and the crowd cheers, they all jump. They had forgotten they were not alone.

Shani laughs. "Damn."

Ash joins in. "Right?"

Jonas feels sheepish. "Whatever that was . . . I liked it."

The crowd cheers again and Jonas, Shani, and Ash break the huddle, lining up side by side at the front rail of the crow's nest, watching the crowd watch the city. Jonas rests a hand on one of Shani's, and she covers one of Ash's with the other.

"When I was little, my mom used to bring me here." Shani's voice is soft. "I'd make her pretend the Whaler was an ice cream shop. She'd sit up here pretending to be a customer and I'd climb up with leaves or sand or whatever I could find and call it chocolate or pistachio. She'd wear out after a while, right, like it'd be ninety out and I'm still playing. How many times can you say, 'Oh, yes, I'd love sprinkles'? But she never said no; she just wanted me to be happy.

"I wish she could see me now, cause I am."

Ash and Jonas, as if synchronized, lean in from either side so that their heads touch hers. Ash pulls out his phone. "You know how I feel about these things. Pics or it didn't happen."

Ash takes so many photos that Jonas gets antsy. His eyes fall on the big-kid swing set.

Shani follows his gaze. "What?"

"Valerie brought me here once when I was little. We lived in Mooreville then and it was a big deal to come to the 'nice' playground. She and I swung on that swing set for *hours*; I'm not kidding. Some of the parents were pissed because she was a grown woman who wouldn't give up her spot—she just kept swinging and I kept swinging and I was a little embarrassed, maybe, but it was nice, and she was so beautiful . . ."

He trails off.

"No one's waiting for the swings right now. You wanna . . ."

Shani understands immediately. "Bet."

They clamber down the Whaler, Ash almost falling off the slide, and race to the swings.

Side by side, they start rocking, their bodies recalling the kinetics of a younger age. Building up speed and swing span, they stretch their legs and point their toes. There's no way to keep pace with each other, so their trajectories remain parallel, their rhythm distinct. A human pendulum with arcs that increase instead of diminish, they are joy in motion, their smiles brighter than the moon.

They can worry tomorrow. Jonas might scrape through January or might run out of cash; Ash's parents may or may not come around; Shani will or won't be able to explain any of this easily to BB5 or her dad. But tonight, it's about being young. In love. Alive.

When the fireworks finally kick in, they can't top the ones the

kids are making right there on the hill. The sky is a symphony of explosions; inside them, things feel no less spectacular.

. . .

The finale has faded to dust in the heavens, leaving only the moon and stars to hold court. They all know the moments are dwindling.

Ash twirls Shani's swing. She lets herself spin and tries to stave off the end of the night with a question. "Where do the fireworks go? After?"

"Huh." Ash digs his heels in the path beneath his swing, not worrying about his cute shoes. "I guess I figured they just sort of evaporated."

"Of course you did!" Teasing Ash makes her feel a little better, despite the fact that she doesn't know the answer to her own question. "*Evaporated*!"

Jonas shakes his head. "It's all like pressed paper, I think. Layer and layers, right? And the idea is, the fire consumes most of it until the ashes scatter on the wind."

Ash sounds concerned. "What if it's still burning when it lands?"

He shrugs, grinning. "I dunno. Ask a firefighter?"

Shani imagines the embers drifting to earth, settling like fireflies, bright for a moment. Maybe she's seen the charred bits of paper on the ground before and never given them a thought, never dreamed they once lit up the sky.

Jonas breaks the spell. "It's time."

Ash reluctantly stands. "See you tomorrow . . . if they don't ship me off first." He laughs hollowly.

Shani nudges him. "You think we're not walking you home, fool?"

"You don't have to—"

"Screw walking!" Jonas interrupts. They both look surprised, and he grins. "Let's *run* for it. Way more fun!"

He grabs their hands and, despite their protests, starts running downhill. Shani slaps his hand away. "I'll never keep up!" But she does. And Ash, gasping with laughter, finds his inner competitor and starts racing ahead.

The lamp-studded streets of Arlmont all seem eerily empty, save for Shani, Ash, and Jonas. They are noisy as they run, not caring who they might disturb. They fling their arms wide and weave circles around each other as they pass through the Square. It is the first night of *something*, and they are high on possibility.

They can hear their footsteps slapping the pavement, but it still feels like they're flying.

Because they are.

AUTHOR'S NOTE

The first line I wrote for *Brighter Than the Moon* was "He wasn't sure if he was mixed or just mixed up." I wrote the line for the character Jonas, but I could have been talking about myself.

When I was a kid, I spent my life shuttling between worlds. As the son of divorced parents—a farm girl from Maine and a Cuban exile in Miami—one summer could include picking corn in a rural town of 3,000 *and* spying on quinceañera practice in Little Havana.

My ethnic identity was the most prominent way in which I was "mixed" but sometimes it felt like that term applied to all parts of my identity. I knew I was gay at age six (thanks, neighbor boy, for that first kiss!), but I hid it because I was also a devout fundamentalist Christian.

I didn't yet know the term code-switching, but it came as naturally to me as breathing (right down to how I pronounced my own name). This was a blessing—seriously, drop me into almost any group, and I'd make friends—but also a challenge. I often found

myself morphing into the person other people needed or wanted. I could be one Dave for you and a different Dave for someone else. How can you be true to *anyone* when you're still trying to figure out who you are?

It took years for me to stop trying so hard to be the "right" version of anything and to just accept that I am the Dave I am. And what do you know? That guy's had a pretty happy life as a result.

This book is a valentine to not knowing all the answers right away, to embracing the possibility that comes with complexity. Jonas, Shani, and Ash all want the same thing: to be loved as they are. They put their hearts on the line, stumbling and making it up as they go, to make that happen.

As they discover, finding yourself is messy work, but good work. This book is for everyone who's ever tried and all the kids still trying now.

ACKNOWLEDGMENTS

Writing this book has been, like so much in the COVID era, an unpredictable journey. From its original conception as a pandemic book to its final form as a love(s) story, it has shape-shifted nearly as much as its characters.

Because I believe that my books and plays should be as diverse as my world, you will find characters who are unlike me in significant regards. Though I do populate my stories with people who resemble those I know, I'm aware that observing one's experience is not the same as living it; that's why I seek input from members of communities outside my own. Thanks to three generous, thoughtful readers: Rulas A. Muñoz for their deep read on Ash and keen eye on the way binaries creep into language; Dru Berrian for safeguarding Shani's portrayal and making sure that the voices of Shani and the BB5 stayed true; and Sarah Kate Sligh for her eyes on Milo, in practical matters and personality. The book was also bettered by Sloka Krishnan's wisdom on trans representation and

the input of Lily Valdes Greenwood (the book's first reader) on Shani in specific but all the other teens as well.

I have been incredibly lucky to have talented editors steering *Brighter Than the Moon*'s path. Allison Moore led the charge, with keen insight and good humor, and Sarah Shumway brought her enthusiasm and sharp eye to the novel's final arrival. I wouldn't know either of them had it had not been for the wonderful Annie Bomke, my agent, matchmaking me with Bloomsbury on *Spin Me Right Round*. (You have read that, right?) The whole team at Bloomsbury has been terrific—everything an author could want.

Some of this book was written during a really painful time for me, but I was lucky enough to be continually lifted up by the amazing Ashley Waring, Stacey Frangos, Jennifer McGuinn, Michelle Dowd, Amy Esposito, LeeAnna Goyne, and Kristin Botnen. (And Scot Mente, because he cooks all the meals for *Survivor* night.)

Lastly, a shout-out to my students, who show me new world after new world—and lead the way forward.